I0679196

RING OF FIRE

Edited by Dana Bell

WolfSinger Publications ⌇ Security, Colorado

Acknowledgements

Mineral Rights – © 2023 by Wayland Smith
Scorched Earth – © 2023 by DJ Tyrer
Light of the Kilns – © 2023 by Danielle Airola
The Technique – © 2023 by John A. McColley
Smoke Eaters – © 2023 by Kevin Hopson
The Hazamesam Séance – © 2023 by Robert Bagnall
A Peach for a King – © 2023 by Cheryl Toner
Kate – © 2023 by R. Joseph Maas
The Year of the Dying Fish – © 2023 by J.B. Polk
Bubble Gum – © 2023 by Moira Richardson
My Birth God is Anubis – © 2023 by Zary Fekete
Dragon Bloodlines – © 2023 by Bruce H. Markuson
Brave – © 2023 by Todd Woodman
The Moon's Tale – © 2023 by Sean Jones
Fire Breather – © 2023 by Thomas Canfield
Gravewatcher – © 2023 by Thomas Nicholson
By Fire She Was Crowned – © 2023 by Frank Sawielijew
A Story of Inyodu – © 2011 by Carol Hightshoe
"A Story of Inyodo or How the Kappa stole the Tidal Jewels from the Dragon King"
was originally published in Healing Waves from SkyWarrior Books
Dragon's Fire – © 2023 by Bronwyn Dauth
Heart Proof – © 2016 by Holly Schofield
"Heart Proof" was originally published in WolfSinger's Lightships & Sabers anthology
in 2016, has been reprinted in Luna Station Quarterly in 2018, and
won Remastered Words audio contest in 2019
Fire Wall – © 2010 by Kat Heckenbach
"Fire Wall" was originally published in *The Absent Willow Review*

Cover Art copyright 2023 by Carol Hightshoe

ISBN 978-1-944637-31-6

Printed and bound in the United States of America

DEDICATION

To God for inspiring the idea.

To all those who live along Earth's Ring of Fire
and other seismic active areas.

To my many friends
who always report themselves safe after an event.

TABLE OF CONTENTS

INTRODUCTION

I've always had a fascination with the Ring of Fire that encompasses the Pacific Ocean along several continents. They're subject to earthquakes, tsunamis, volcanic eruption, and tectonic movements. My first thought was to have apocalyptic or post-apocalyptic tales.

However, the more I thought about it, the more the idea of other angles on this intriguing idea appealed to me. So I tossed it open to the authors to see what they came up with.

They presented some fascinating ideas. Trapped in a forest fire. Dragons. Volcanoes not just on Earth, but off planet as well. Ancient Gods demanding tribute. Even a high school reunion.

The mix of writers of these unusual tales come from all over the world, each with a different flavor.

So dear readers, sit back in your chair before the blazing flames, open the book, and enjoy the *Ring of Fire*.

Mineral Rights

Wayland Smith

"Astari B643 shows a great deal of potential for resource acquisition. There are readings indicating high levels of assorted minerals and ores, possibly due to the planet's ongoing volcanic activity. While there is native life, surveys indicate they are pre-space flight and should prove no threat to VulcanCorp Personnel. The only thing worthy of note is some anomalous energy readings our technicians have not been able to identify."

From the VulcanCorp initial survey of Astari B643.

The *Shrike*, a standard mining and processing ship, settled down on the clear rocky area scans had indicated were the best landing spot. "Nice job, Hal," Isaac Richards said to the helmsman, laying an approving hand on the man's shoulder.

"Thanks, Captain," Hal Greene answered, smiling. He was new to the ship, having recently gotten his pilot certification from Vulcan Central. Hal hoped he'd be able to see more of the galaxy and earn his share of bonuses as a member of one of the mining ships. Not as exciting as the Exploration Corps, but they spent a lot of time seeking and not necessarily as much time producing and being rewarded for it.

"Start the setup process," Captain Richards directed Helen Grayson, his first officer.

"Already sent the order," she answered. Helen was bent over one of the readouts from the survey probes. "It looks like there's a lot of heavy metals here. This should be a good score for us."

Rhalocite, a key material for FTL drive cores, was relatively rare, and the scans showed several large deposits. That alone would have been worth the landing, but they were seeing several other valuable minerals as well.

"No leaks on this one," Captain Richards reminded everyone. "The last thing we need is competition swooping down on us. We'll send a full report when we're ready to leave atmosphere." Technically, by company regulation, new finds were supposed to be sent to the central catalog for further analysis. In reality, thanks to competing companies and even rival crews from their own corporation, most crews stayed quiet until they were done mining. VulcanCorp bonuses were generous, and no one wanted to lose out.

The mostly automated process of setting up extractors was underway, and the ship's mechanisms hummed with power as they assembled the machines that would do the harvesting. Efficiently and swiftly, new constructs were put together from the stored parts and programmed to begin their work as soon as they were complete.

"Send out the scouts," Richards ordered, after taking a moment or two to make sure the assemblers were working. Nothing was foolproof, and damage happened in the transit between worlds. Everyone had been at least minimally trained as a mechanic, just in case, but once all displays were shown green, they could afford to dispatch crew to use different scanners. Ship-based units were more powerful, but, as discovered early on, various planets had strange ores or magnetic fields or inherent energy disruptions that could scramble readings. The devices mounted on ground transports operated at closer range, and so with less distortion.

Mona Chen keyed the engine on her scoutbike and smiled at the rumble. She loved the sound, the feel of the powerful engine, and the sense of control it gave her. Her dark eyes contrasted with her shockingly red hair, giving her an exotic look, which was, she often complained, utterly wasted under the thick helmet and protective gear she had to wear. Then again, it didn't matter how great her hair looked if she drove through a patch of acidic fog or any of the other strange things the company had found as they explored any world they could get to. "Engine, check. Scans, check. Life support, check. Scout-One is out," she said into her coms and then shot out of the hangar. She was intended to keep her number one spot, and to do that, she needed to be the best and the fastest.

"Scout-Two, out," she heard a moment later as Juan Sedona, her most persistent rival, followed her.

A private com channel opened, and Juan said, "Today's the day I get your slot."

"You've been working on the engines without a filter again. Those fumes rot your brain," she answered. The two split off in opposite directions, and Mona directed her attention to navigating, checking for new and unique (or old and still problematic) threats, and the all-important scan results. If she could luck out and find something the ship had missed, especially Radissite, the major component of ship's fuel systems, she'd leave Sedona in the dust, where he belonged.

~ * ~

Shaorrell wasn't sure why the strange visitors ignored the tall ridge near their ship, but she was happy to take advantage of the lapse. It was a perfect spot to observe the ship and its activities, and Shaorrell peered down at the strange visitors. Old Habicon had said they would come, and he had been right. He always was. That's why he served as Speaker. Shaorrell watched, taking in as much as she could of what the strangers were doing. Their big ship was making smaller ships and they were starting to dig into the ground. Did they know they had to be careful? Did they know the Rites to ease the Rock Lords? Shaorrell didn't think so. She eased away from the spot she'd been using to watch the newcomers, and slid back down the other side of the rocky pile. Her thick, grey hide protected her from the sharp stones that made up so much of her world, and helped her blend in with a lot of the landscape.

Once she was sure she was far enough away, she ran. Her people were durable, and tough, and didn't tire easily, although they were not made for stealth. She knew enough to wait for enough distance from the strangers before letting her heavy feet pound on the ground. Before the sun was at its highest, she made it back to the Grotto of her people.

She rushed past the youngsters, dodged around some of the old ones who tended the many kinds of moss her people needed. Finally, she reached Old Habicon's cave. "They came! Just as you said!" Shaorrell boomed from the entrance. Even with important news like this, she wouldn't dream of entering an elder's cave uninvited. After a few moments, Habicon shuffled out to see her. He was old, his hide cracked, the blue glow of his eyes dimmed with time. His shoulders were low and bent, and Shaorrell had always thought this was from the weight of his knowledge and the duty of guiding the people.

"And what have you seen?" he rumbled. His voice was low and rasped in his throat.

Shaorrell took in a breath and focused her mind, trying to make things orderly, to relay her observations in a way that would help the old one, and show she was more than just a youngster. She told about the ship from the sky, the strange things it made, the way it tore into the ground without blessings or ritual, and the fast ones that had zipped away like the eels in the deep water. He nodded a few times, and asked a few questions. "What should we do?" she asked when she had finished and he had fallen silent.

"We must send someone to speak with them, to find out why they are here, what they want." Habicon let out a rumbling sigh. "We must select an envoy. It can't be me, nor you."

"But I found them," she protested, feeling slighted.

"And you are furthest along in your studies. I told you when you began, you took on the burdens of the people's needs above your own. That means preserving the teachings, and not running off to do what you want, instead of what is needed."

She slumped her shoulders. She was still a youngster after all, in spite of trying so hard not to be.

Habicon chuckled, a sound like gravel falling. "You have much to learn, but you are trying. I see that, and thank you for your efforts." He patted her on her shoulder, and both of them wondered for a moment when she had gotten taller than he was. "I will select someone. Now," he said in a different tone, "I believe your mother is looking for you."

Shaorrell sighed, almost asked if there was anything, anything at all, he might need, remembered what he'd just said about her own wants set against what was needed, and shuffled off to her home cave, albeit a lot slower than she'd gotten to Habicon's home.

~ * ~

Mona stopped her scout, triple checked the atmospheric readings, and pulled her helmet off. In one of the vids, her red hair would have cascaded down, possibly ruffled by a convenient breeze. As it was, her hair was a sweaty mass from being jammed up in the helmet, and bits of it escaped her braid. She laughed at herself for the image, and took a long drink from her water bottle, then placed it back in the skimmer. A useful little device, the skimmer collected air particles as she rode, tested and purified them, and combined hydrogen and oxygen into more water. There was a complicated scientific theory behind it that Mona didn't even pretend to understand, she was just glad it worked.

She tapped the side of the scanner with a frown. Garcia in the tech bay told her it didn't help and wasn't good for the instrument, but she swore it gave better readings after the occasional manual realignment. Mona squinted at the readings, which stubbornly refused to show her something that would make her rich, and pulled out a protein bar. They tasted like nothing in particular, and kept her body going when she was away from the mess hall. She choked on her bite when a huge form came out from between the small stone formations to her right.

First contact training tended towards, "Don't piss off the native and don't get yourself killed," but she found her fingers curling around the butt of her pistol without remembering moving her hand. It was tall, maybe eight feet. Roughly humanoid, it had broad shoulders, mottled grey skin, and three fingers and a thumb on each hand. She knew that because those hands were up at what was about its waist height, fingers splayed wide. It was always dangerous attributing your own culture norms on a species that hadn't been approached by any of the Corporations or the notional Planetary Alliance government, but it looked a lot like an "I come in peace" gesture to Mona. The head seemed to sprout from the shoulders with no neck, or none that she could see, and the eyes burned a brilliant sapphire blue. It had some kind of belt around its waist with many pouches hanging from it. At a guess, Mona thought it looked like some kind of leather.

"Um...hi?" she tried.

It tilted its head at her, which was a weird sight with no neck involved. It made a low rumbling sound that she almost felt more than heard. It sounded like a question to her.

"I'm going to try and see if this thing will work," she said, reaching into a storage bin and pulling out the translation matrix. This, too, was something Mona couldn't begin to explain, although she was happy enough to make use of as needed. This was the first time she'd been the one to start the dialogue, which left her battling a case of nerves.

The stranger said (at least she was pretty sure it was talking to her) something else, and Mona held the translator out towards him. She probably didn't need to get it closer to him, but she was at a loss for what else to do. The creature lowered its hands, but didn't seem to be reaching for a weapon or anything. Then again, it was probably twice as tall as she was, and looked massive. It could probably kill her just by falling on her.

Finally, the displays glowed, and the speakers crackled. "I can understand you now," she said, slowly and clearly, realizing she sounded like an idiot but unable to stop herself.

"My words are clear now?"

Mona nodded, and then realized that might mean something different to these people, and said, "Yes, I can."

"We need to talk," it said.

~ * ~

"So, the natives made contact with you and want to talk to us?" Captain Richards drank some more coffee and gestured for Mona to continue.

"Yes, sir. They're really big. Like, I don't think the conference room will work. I'm not sure they could come in any of the hatches. Maybe the assembly bay?" Mona had served under Richards for some time now, and had gotten used to his informal command style. Mostly.

"Well, I guess we're going to have to hear what they want to say." He went over the scans Mona's scout had taken during the exchange. "They'd make a hell of an addition to the Security Teams if we could recruit any of them."

"We'd have to refit the ships," Mona said. "Even the exos aren't that big." Some of Corporate Security used massive exo-suits in combat, and their transports had been modified to handle the suits' dimensions, but Mona was pretty sure that wouldn't work for these aliens.

Richards nodded. "Be a hell of a thing to see, though."

Mona eyed her wrist unit. "Is there anything else you need from me, sir?"

"No, I think I've got everything." He glanced at a screen and looked over some figures. "Trying to get back out there and outdo Sedona?"

"If that's all right, sir. He hasn't beaten me yet, and I'm not going to let him start today."

Richards nodded. "Go find us some good deposits. I'll make

sure your time reporting to me is taken into account when we tally up bonuses."

Mona left with a salute and a smile, and Richards keyed some orders into his command console. Armorer Wilson was going to need the heavy weapons if things went south. These things weren't actually made out of rock, no matter what they looked like, but if the scans were right, they'd be tough as hell.

~ * ~

At noon the next day, Richards was in the vehicle bay. The assemblers had been shut down so they'd be able to hear each other. They were just about done, anyway. Atmospheric scans showed the air was breathable, and no toxins or pathogens had registered. The translators had been updated with data from Chen's encounter, and now, all he had to do was wait. Chen had thought the meeting was set for mid-day, however, concepts like time could be very different from one culture to another, and they didn't have a large enough sample of the aliens' language to be any more confident. He could wait. Richards could do his reports and review the scans from down here as well as he could on the bridge. Lundquist was a capable first officer, and would let him know if something came up.

Finally, he saw what Chen had described earlier. Her recordings and the report hadn't done the figure justice. It was roughly double the height of a human, and incredibly thick-bodied. The glow in its eyes, or what seemed like they should be eyes, was a piercing blue that just hadn't read in the video. Maybe it had some kind of biochemical quality that didn't show up on recordings. Dr. Ramsey's voice sounded in his ear. "That's amazing. I'd love any kind of samples to study."

Very quietly, Richards said, "I'll see what I can do, but I wouldn't count on it. And stay off this channel."

The creature came to the entrance and stopped. Richards couldn't tell if it was staring, waiting, or sizing him up for a fight. "Please, come in," Richards said after a few moments. It nodded, which was just as disconcerting as Chen had said with no visible neck, and stepped in. The creature's large feet boomed hollowly on the deck plating, and it looked down. It raised a foot, looked at it, set it down again, and nodded at the sound this time. "My scouting officer said you wished to speak with me?"

"I am Dizrell, appointed as envoy to you of the unknown clans."

"I am Captain Richards. We are from VulcanCorp." Normally, he'd make some sort of gesture to indicate the ship and all the crew, but the guides suggested minimizing such things until better communication was achieved. No sense risking offending the natives, or declaring war by accident.

"Why are you here, Captain Richards?" The voice was low and rumbled, and the translator was giving him a strange accent that Richards was finding distracting.

"My company harvests resources for our people," he said, trying to keep his answers as short and literal as he could.

"You come to our lands to take things for your people, without talking to us, without making the proper rituals." It was more a statement than a question.

Richards shifted uneasily. He hated being the point of contact with new people. It never went well. "We mean no harm, and we can offer payment."

The creature stood taller and leaned forward. "What is that word?"

"Payment? We give you something in exchange for what we take."

It appeared to ponder this. "We do not need anything from a people so…" it looked around the bay and regarded Richards for a few moments. "…small." It finished.

"We have medicines, foods, tools," Richards said. "As you can see, we have technology you don't."

It leaned back for another few moments. "You have things that move in the air, and things that dig. You have things that move quickly on the ground. We do not need any of these things."

Richards pursed his lips. "I'm sorry to hear that. Your healers are always successful? There's no task you do that could not be made easier?"

Another long pause slowly ticked by. Richards wondered if the translator was performing as well as it was supposed to. The indicator lights on it were moving crazily, indicating it was learning a lot. "We have healers. Nothing and no one is infallible. The best of healers, hunters, foragers, make mistakes. Leaders can not see the future, and made decisions that later seem wrong. Do you claim your healers save every person who ages, is wounded, becomes ill?"

Richards flicked off the com channel when Ramsey started protesting something loudly. "Nothing is perfect," he agreed, "and many things can be made better."

"You are not our people. You are not from our lands. You are taking things that do not belong to you. I am to say this to you: you are here, and this valley is not a home to any people. Take what you feel you must, and be on your way. Do not go beyond the valley with your fast-moving things and your digging things. Do not bring your things to our homes."

Richards felt his pulse speed up and gripped the control surface on his chair more tightly. "We will do what we need to do. We mean you no harm, but we will not be dictated to." His voice was tight and strained now.

The creature leaned back. "I have said what I was asked to say. We did not invite you here, you came. You did not ask our permission, you simply began taking. This is not your land, it is ours."

"We have claimed this land, it's on file with the Alliance government."

"I do not know what this Alliance is, but they did not speak to us. They may not give you something that is not theirs." It turned and began to walk out, the heavy booming noise louder this time.

"This doesn't have to be a problem," Richards called after Dizrell.

"It does not. If you do as we have said, it will not be," Dizrell said and kept walking. For something so large, it moved fast, and was out of the bay and away from the landing area swiftly.

"That could have gone better," Richards said to himself.

~ * ~

The next few days passed peacefully and uneventfully. The mining machines gathered a decent amount of ore, nothing broke down, and although there were a few sightings of the aliens at a distance, they didn't come in close or interfere with any of the teams' operations. Until they did.

Late in the afternoon, Laramo, the coms specialist, startled Richards out of his contemplation of the bonuses they'd be getting for this expedition. "Sir, I'm getting a distress alarm from Scout-Two."

"Details," Richards snapped, leaning forward in his chair. He knew things had been going too well.

"I'm reading massive damage to the scoutbike, a distress alarm from Sedona, and a request for immediate extraction."

"Tell Hawkins to get his team together and take the skimmer." Richards brought up the data he could on his console. There wasn't much. It looked like Scout-Two has been destroyed. "If that damn Sedona wrecked his bike…" Richards muttered under his breath.

~ * ~

Kim Hawkins checked her power-armor again. The security team was used to sudden callouts, so they kept their gear in ready condition as much as they could. Every crew member had secondary duties, since the *Shrike* wasn't a huge ship and needed redundancies, but theirs were always low priority, so they could be dropped at a moment's notice.

"Status?" she asked.

"We're coming up on the beacon for Sedona," Hanes answered. A tall man with long silver hair, he was a quietly competent pilot who was difficult to faze. Hawkins did her best to use him for the skimmer pilot on all their missions. "Weapons and sensors all read green."

Hawkins watched the various screens, and marked a clear spot among the jumble of rocks, pillars, and chasms. "Put down there."

Hanes moved the skimmer to the indicated spot, hovered, rescanned the ground for surprises, and set down. There was usually a noticeable jolt when a skimmer landed anywhere besides a smooth hangar bay, but Hanes, as usual, put them on the ground without even a bump.

Hawkins nodded her approval. "Hanes, stay at the controls, be ready for emergency lift or weapons backup. Everyone else, grab your gear and let's go find our scout."

Hawkins led the four-man team out, and checked the display on her wrist. Sedona's beacon was not far away, and getting closer. She keyed up the amplifier built into her helmet. "Scout Sedona, report!" Her voice echoed off the rocks, sounds muddied and less clear with each passing moment.

She heard running feet, and then Sedona came into view. He was sprinting flat out, panting. His helmet was gone, and his short dark hair was sweat soaked, standing up in every direction. "Are they coming?" he yelled, then skidded to a stop, breathless, bending over, hands on his knees.

"Is who coming?" Hawkins asked. Three of the team took up cover positions, rifles ready. The fourth pulled a bio-scanner out of his equipment bag and ran it over the gasping man.

"Crazy natives…destroyed my scout…thought they were after me…" he panted. Finally straightening up, he looked back the way he had come.

Hawkins frowned. She checked her scanners. There was nothing showing, although the creatures here were so far from most of the life forms, they'd encountered, she wasn't sure they'd register. "Everyone, back to the skimmer," she ordered. Following company protocol, she noted the loss of the scout, then paused. "Where's your helmet?"

"Threw it…when they were chasing me."

She nodded, then logged the admission of his loss of company property. It damn sure wasn't coming out of *her* pay.

~ * ~

After a conference, Captain Hawkins led a team to where Sedona's sensor trail ended. They landed the skimmer about a half kilometer away and approached on foot. Hawkins and her team were ranged around him, Hawkins frequently throwing disapproving looks at her captain. She was sure this wasn't a good idea, and if anything happened to him, it would look bad for her. But, aside from noting her recommendations, and the names of everyone who had witnessed them, there wasn't anything she could do.

They walked through the labyrinth of stone formations. No one had reported seeing anything approaching trees, grass, or the kind of plant growth they'd come to expect on inhabited worlds. Just the occasional patch of lichen or moss, in an impressive array of colors.

The slight slope they'd been coming down flattened out, and the area ahead of them was mostly clear. Hawkins saw a few irregularities on the ground, and wondered what they were. Finally, as they moved on, she realized they were probably what was left of some of the pillars, which had been taken down for some reason or other.

Ahead, the cleared area ended in a rock face. Several caves were visible along the rock wall. They found the scoutbike, mangled and bent at an impressive angle along the main frame of the vehicle. Dizrell strode toward them out of one of the caves.

"There seems to have been a misunderstanding with one of our scouts," Captain Richards called.

Dizrell moved a lot closer than Hawkins was comfortable with and stopped. "There was no misunderstanding. We told you to not come to our homes. We told you to stay in the valley you landed in."

"I'm sure he didn't realize what he was doing," Richard said. Hawkins admired how calm he was, and wondered at the same time if it was a sign of mental illness.

"He was warned. He came on."

"Our property has been damaged," Richards pointed out, indicating the scout.

"By right, that is ours now. We do not want it. Take it. Stay where you landed, finish your collecting, and go back where you came from. Soon."

Richards managed, with effort, to not show his annoyance. "We'll be gone when we finish. It is our custom," that seemed to be the best word, "for someone who damages another's property to in some way pay for the damage."

Dizrell rumbled, and Richards thought his eyes shifted to a slightly brighter shade of blue. "It is our custom to punish those who disobey the word of the elders. We allowed your scout to leave. That was a warning from our people. There will not be another."

"All right," Richards held up his hand in a placating gesture. "We'll take the scoutbike and return to our ship."

"We watch your people. They go much farther than we have said. There will be no more warnings. Leave soon." Dizrell didn't fold his arms across his chest or perform any other body language Richards recognized; even so, the implied threat was unmistakable.

Richards pointed to two of the security team, and gestured to the scout. They slung their rifles over their shoulders, pulled out the grav-lifters, and attached one to each side of the scout. When the lights glowed green, they lifted the machine easily and retreated, pushing it along easily.

When the team was back in the skimmer, Hawkins turned to Richards. "They let us take our bike. *Let* us. And you're all right with this?"

"No, I'm not. I'm also not interested in a fight unless it becomes necessary. Make sure we have guards posted. When we get back, have one of the techs see if they can find the recorders in that mess," he pointed towards the small cargo hold where the mangled scout was stored.

~ * ~

Chen bent low over her scout, and kept the throttle at maximum. It wasn't the safest thing to do, shooting between towering pillars and random rock formations. She thought the whole planet looked like it had been a normal inhabited one once, and it had somehow been turned to stone. She was pretty sure she'd read something in the old stories about a woman who could petrify things with her eyes. She'd have to look that up later. For now, she focused on not slamming into a rock of one kind or another.

She didn't slow down until she passed the first marker buoy for the area they had judged to be "safe." There had been a few more incidents with the natives, but nothing in the valley they'd landed in. Chen cut down to half-speed, and then slower as she got the ship. She zipped up the ramp, spun the scout in a tight turn, and coasted perfectly into the charging dock. It looked like showing off, and it had been the first few times she'd done it, but she'd practiced the trick so many times, she didn't even think about it now.

With a flick of her fingers, she pulled the data-stick, and plugged it into her wrist unit as she jogged across the hangar. She typed in the command to send the information to the analyzing computer.

"You're still coming in too fast," Max Hugo, the head mechanic, groused as she trotted by.

"Argue later, big news now," she said, smiling as she passed him. She was in such a good mood that even grouchy old Max couldn't bother her.

In more civilized areas, she'd have gone to her bunk, showered, and changed. Out here, she figured it was more important to relay the news. She jogged to the captain's office, hit the com button, and waited, bouncing on the balls of her feet.

The door slid open. "Yes, Chen? More problems with the natives?" Richards asked.

"Didn't see any today. Not a problem, something really good and really big," she said. "Check the analysis."

He raised an eyebrow and bent over his console for a few moments. She could tell when he read it, because he straightened up suddenly. "Are you sure about this?" he asked.

"Saw it myself, triple checked the scans, and marked the spot."

He sat back. "I've never seen a Radissite deposit this concentrated."

She shrugged. "I thought they mostly found it in asteroids. Maybe one crashed here?"

"If that's what happened, we need to try and figure out where it came from," Richards said absently, staring at the screen. Finally, he stood and walked to the cabinet next to his desk. Opening it with the thumb reader, he pulled out a fine crystal bottle and two glasses. "If this is what it looks like, you just made us all very rich."

"If this is what it looks like, I can take my finder's fee and buy my own ship," she said, taking the glass he'd filled. They both drank deeply. This was so much better than what she could get in the crew's mess.

"Captain Chen, hmm? It has a ring to it." He smiled again. "Let's get people working on this." They both drank again and thought about what they'd do with the fortune they were about to make.

~ * ~

Richards came down the vehicle bay, squinting a bit. He'd been woken up by the report Dizrell was standing outside the doors.

"What can I do for you?" The Captain asked.

"You have taken another valley. You need to leave."

Richards vaguely wondered how these creatures, who had showed no signs of technology or vehicles, knew what was happening on the other side of their world. "We found something of value. We need to bring it with us."

"You have taken the place where the stars fall. You may not stay there."

Richards was tired, and possibly a bit hungover. "You're not going to tell us what to do. Be glad we don't just blast you to gravel and take whatever we want. You have no weapons. What are you going to do?"

Dizrell regarded him for a long, silent moment. "You have been warned. The spirits will right the wrong."

Richards managed not to laugh. Barely. He'd heard a lot of

threats, and assorted kinds of divine wrath promised. He'd never seen anything happen and wasn't worried. "Well, they know where to find us," Richards said.

Dizzell remained motionless for another long few moments and turned and left. Richards keyed his com unit on. "Yellow Alert," he said. "Full guard shifts at all times. Security takes priority over all other duties." He had no idea what Dizzrell had planned, and he didn't want his crew getting caught unawares. Things were going really well, the loss of the one scoutbike to one side. This would probably be their most profitable trip ever, and might come close to putting them in that golden upper ten percent on the earnings report. That led to a lot of highly enjoyable daydreams. Really, what could a few savages with no technology do to an armed ship with a well-trained crew?

~ * ~

"There isn't another way?" Shaorrell watched sorrowfully as Habicon prepared the ritual.

"They will not listen. They can kill from a distance. They will keep taking if we allow it. They are sick with greed, but that will save us."

"How?" There was a lot she didn't understand. But she knew she had to learn whatever she could in the very short time left. This cavern was used very rarely, and the rite-worker didn't come back from it.

"I do not fully understand them. They have a way to speak across distances. They have not done this, out of fear and greed. So when these takers are gone, none will come to look for them."

"You said the needs of the people come before what we want to do. I'm not ready to guide them without you." It was the best argument she could think of to get him to change his mind. It was the only one.

He turned to look at her, and she thought, for a moment, she might have prevented this awful thing from happening. Then she saw his eyes shift color just the slightest bit. "That is the wisest thing you've ever said, and the best hope I have that you might follow me." The elder finished tracing the circle on the floor of the cavern. "I believe you will do your best, and that no one can do more than that." Habicon reached up with a hand that was still powerful despite his age and pulled the deep purple crystal from his shoulder. He threw it to her. "Take our knowledge. Use it well. Do what you must to make things better for them."

~ * ~

Habicon stood in the center of the circle and let his power reach down. "You must go," he told her, the rumbling, grating voice softer.

Shaorrell fled as the dim cave took on a reddish hue. The circle filled with heat and power, the smallest sample of what it could become. Habicon called to the fire that consumed all. He offered himself, his power, all that he was or had ever been. All it needed to do was what it did best: burn.

Hal sat at the sensor station, bored out of his mind. He was a pilot, dammit. He should be flying overwatch or keeping an eye on the foolish creatures that had actually threatened them. Threatened *them*! VulcanCorp had nothing to fear from some group of primitives who didn't even have engines or weapons. He was jolted out of his daydream of flying an attack mission to teach the natives a lesson by almost his entire console lighting up in alarm.

"Report," First Officer Grayson said, walking over to his station.

"Thermal blooms everywhere. Atmospheric disturbances." He frowned. "I can't see where any of this is coming from."

"Power up the shields," she ordered, then activated her com to ship-wide page. "Captain to the bridge."

Hal moved his fingers in a desperate dance across the board. "Shield up. Some of our crew are caught outside the area."

The ground began cracking, and the *Shrike* tilted to one side. "Launch!" Grayson ordered. Too many things happened at once, and Captain Richards never made it to the bridge, called away from enjoying the company of Scout Mona Chen as they prematurely celebrated their bonuses in his office.

The shields were designed to protect the *Shrike* from particles in space, or energy weapons from a rival vessel. The lava erupting suddenly under it exceeded the energy ratings, and the generators struggled to keep up. Tectonic plates shifted, a horrible groaning, grinding sound filled everyone's ears, and then brilliant purple lighting burst up from the ground, striking the ship in multiple places at once. The generators whined, shook, and then exploded as Hugo tried desperately to bring them back in balance. The shields failed in the moments after the generators blew, and lava burrowed into the hull of the starship. The heat of atmospheric entry was nothing compared to being engulfed in lava, and no hull was built to withstand that. More lightning flared, and what hadn't melted scorched or exploded as the ship both sank into and was consumed by the lava. The new magma vent seethed and began the long process of cooling, flames spurting here and there in a rough circle, similar to the one Habicon had used to summon this destruction.

The remote crew at the second mining point had no shield, fewer weapons, and a limited store of supplies. When Dizrell led some of his people to them, they fell quickly.

Captain Richards' reports about Asatri B643 were never sent. VulcanCorp searched, but was never able to determine what became of the *Shrike*. Space was a dangerous place. Things happened. The accountants made sure the budget allowed for a few such losses every fiscal year. It was just the cost of doing business.

~ * ~ * ~

Wayland Smith is the pen name for a native Texan who has lived in Massachusetts, New York, Washington DC, and presently makes his home in Virginia. His rather unlikely list of jobs includes private investigator, comic book shop owner, ring crew for a circus (then he ran away from the circus and joined home), deputy sheriff, writer, and freelance stagehand. Wayland's novels so far include Tools of the Trade, Blood Of A Nation, In My Brother's Name, and Cadre Clash, the first book in the Wildside series. He has short stories in the anthologies "Cat Ladies of the Apocolypse", "HeroNet Files, Vol 1", "SNAFU: An Anthology of Military Horror," and "Misfits of Magic," among many others. He has spoken on panels at DragonCon, DC AwesomeCon, MystiCon, and RavenCon.

A black belt in shao lin kung fu, he is also a fan of comic books, reading, writing, and various computer games (I'll shut 7 Days to Die down in one more hour. Really). He lives with a beautiful woman who was crazy enough to marry him, and the spirits of a few wonderful dogs that have passed on.

Scorched Earth

DJ Tyrer

"You won't believe it," exclaimed Ron as he burst in through the kitchen door as Martha was busy sweeping up the broken crockery from the night before.

She sighed. "What?"

"Those burnt patches are back. Not just one or two…" He made an excited little noise that caused her to cringe. "I think…" He took a deep breath. "I think it's aliens!"

"Aliens? What on earth are you talking about?"

"Not on Earth, baby—space! I think our farm's being visited by beings from space. We're, like, at a cosmic crossroads or something."

"Really? Aliens? You do know how stupid you sound, right?"

"Stupid? Stupid? You come with me and see for yourself."

He grabbed her arm and dragged her out the door into their yard, then up the lane to the paddock furthest from the house.

"Hey!" she cried, but he ignored her.

She shook his hand off her arm and glared at him.

"Well, look," he said, gesturing across the grass. "Perfectly round, each of them." There were numerous rings of scorched earth where the grass was burnt away.

Martha took a moment to calm her breathing. "So? I've told you before, it's probably kids burning tyres or something." She looked away as she spoke.

"Really? You think so? Because, I don't see any bits of rubber. In fact, I don't see anything, the ground's completely burnt clean. I'm telling you, it's aliens. They're landing their spacecraft here, probably plotting to mutilate our cows."

"We don't have any cows," she retorted. "You sold the last ones because you said milk doesn't pay anymore, remember?"

"Well, that's why they haven't mutilated them, isn't it? They'll probably be after us with their probes when they realise there aren't any cows here, now…" He winced. "I don't fancy that."

She shook her head. "I'm going back. I've got stuff to do."

"So have I—I'm going to call the press and the air-force and the CIA. They all need to know."

"That we've got circles in our grass?"

"Exactly, Honey, exactly."

"Don't…you're going to look like an idiot."

He snorted. "We'll see who looks stupid when I'm on national TV…

~ * ~

As she watched Ron's grinning face leer out at her from the TV screen, Martha was certain the answer was definitely him.

Her husband was out in the paddock, filming live, pointing to fresh rings of scorched earth and making wilder and wilder claims about the aliens he believed had made them and the reasons they had chosen to visit his farm. It was embarrassing to think their neighbours would be watching, the whole country was seeing him make a fool of himself. She wished he'd taken the hint when the authorities had blown him off, but their lack of interest had only convinced him that he was at the heart of some conspiracy.

She'd tried talking to him, of course, but that had only ended with another blazing row, worse than the usual ones about the farm and bills and her need for a life. Out of old cups and plates, she'd resorted to hurling her best tea service at the wall in frustration.

And, no matter how he begged or cajoled, she absolutely refused to be interviewed about the circles. She'd only have said something rude, anyway.

The interview was over and the image on the TV screen cut back to the studio, where the anchor and a couple of guests bantered about little green men. They seemed to have their doubts.

Ron stomped in with a satisfied grin on his face.

"They believe me," he told her.

"Sure," she said. Was it his smugness or the fact he was so, so wrong that irritated her most? Or, fear someone might believe him, investigate?

He said something else, but Martha wasn't listening.

Instead, she paused to pick up a fragment of her favourite teapot, the one decorated with roses, having spotted it in the space next to the fridge. She studied it for a moment, then tossed it into the bin.

"I've got to go feed the chickens," she told him and walked out, leaving him in mid-sentence. He glared after her.

~ * ~

Of course, there was another argument that night. How could there not be? Ron was all over the local news and he was lapping it up, even when it should have been obvious they thought he was a joke. Embarrassed, irritated, guilty at the way she felt, she couldn't help but start to lose her temper.

There was no more crockery left, so she headed straight for the kitchen door.

"Oh, that's right," he snapped after her, "run off to Lillian, as you always do, and tell her what a terrible husband you have." He gave a sarcastic laugh. "You know, if you'd only walk the other way up the lane, you might see the aliens and then, you'd believe."

He said a bit more, none of it complimentary, and, not for the first time, she wondered why she was still with him if she was always needing to get away.

Martha strode through the darkness of the lane, her anger burning inside her, almost oblivious to her surroundings, jaw clenched tightly shut. Every time they had an argument, which meant almost every night, she made the same pilgrimage, desperate to be away from him before she lost control.

Finding herself in the paddock, well away from the house, it was safe for her to let loose her rage. She gave a roar of frustration and a wave of flames surrounded her.

She heard Ron curse.

Surprised, she turned, the flames dying away to nothing.

He was standing a short distance away from her, mouth open, eyes wide in shock.

He'd followed her. He never followed her!

They stared at one another in silence, then he said, "*You're* the alien?"

That made her blood boil. She felt the familiar tickle in the back of her throat.

"I'm not an alien, you idiot. Aliens don't exist."

"But…the fire…"

Smoke was escaping from her nostrils, a flame licking at her lips like a swollen tongue.

"I'm a dragon," she said through clenched teeth, barely containing the fire as she spoke.

"You're a freak! I never should've married you—mama was right!"

That. Was. It. She gave in to the primal flame, let the glamour that surrounded her drop.

Ron screamed as she inflated in size and a wave of fire engulfed her and the entire paddock, rolled down the lane to engulf their home. A moment later, he was silenced, reduced to nothing but ash.

"I never should've married you," she murmured, a little sadly, as she shrank back down into human form. "Mama was right, dragons and humans shouldn't mix, it always ends badly.

The ash that had been her husband drifted slowly away on a soft night breeze as she stepped back out into the lane and into an uncertain future. She wished she'd never accepted Ron's proposal, it had been a mistake for both of them, but most of all him.

Nothing was left of their life together, now, but scorched earth.

~ * ~ * ~

DJ Tyrer is the person behind *Atlantean Publishing*, and has been widely published in anthologies and magazines around the world, such as *Strangely Funny II, III, IV, V, VI, VIII & IX* (all Mystery & Horror LLC), *Destroy All Robots* (Dynatox Ministries), *Mrs Claus* (Worldweaver Press), *More Bizarro Than Bizarro* (Bizarro Pulp Press), and *Irrational Fears* (FTB Press), as well as on *Cease Cows, The Flash Fiction Press* and *The WiFiles*, and in issues of *Belmont Story Review* and *Tigershark* ezine, and also has a novella available in paperback and on the Kindle, *The Yellow House* (Dunhams Manor).

Visit DJ online at:

Author's Webpage: djtyrer.blogspot.co.uk/

Author's Facebook page: facebook.com/DJTyrerwriter/

Atlantean Publishing: atlanteanpublishing.wordpress.com/

LIGHT OF THE KILNS

Danielle Airola

Zolphara's hands trembled as she wiped wet clay onto her apron and stepped away from the table. She glanced at the pot seated on her wheel before lowering her gaze to the floor as the door opened.

Master Haviss cleared his throat. "Here are the apprentices, my lady."

A woman with streaks of iron gray in her dark hair followed Master Haviss into the studio, her gaze sweeping across its occupants. No one spoke as she inspected the apprentices' work. She walked around all the tables and potter's wheels and inspected all of the shelves before she spoke. "Most of these are adequate. Once again, you have reason to be proud of your students."

Master Haviss bowed his head. "Thank you, Guildmistress. We eagerly await your choice. Would you like more time to decide?"

"No." The Guildmistress came to a stop in front of Zolphara. "She is ready."

Zolphara clenched her fingers together so hard they hurt. "Thank you, Guildmistress."

The Guildmistress gave a warm smile as Zolphara looked up at her. "Relax. What I've seen of your work shows me you know what you're doing." She turned to Master Haviss. "Let me know when she returns. I'll come back to inspect the results of her expedition and perhaps choose another candidate."

Master Haviss thanked her several times as he ushered her out of the room. Muttering broke out in the studio when the door closed.

"Out of all of us," someone seethed, "the Guildmistress chose *her*?"

Zolphara squeezed her eyes shut for a long moment before she opened them again and removed her newly thrown pot from her wheel. *I can't expect them to be happy for me.* She kept her head down, avoiding glares and glances as she tidied her workspace.

Master Haviss entered the studio and approached her, clearing his throat with a smile. "We have quite a bit to discuss. Please follow me."

Zolphara wrung her hands in her apron as she followed him into his office. She sat down across from him, but did not meet his eyes.

"Would you like a cup of tea? You look like you need one."

"Yes, please. Thank you."

Haviss continued chatting as he made tea. "I'm not surprised she chose you this time. I couldn't agree more with her decision." He poured two cups of tea and passed one to her. "You've certainly earned it."

"The others don't think so."

"They're speaking out of jealousy. I hate to admit it, but some of them haven't made as much progress by now as I had hoped. Many of their pots and vessels are lacking something."

"They look down upon me because my family is foreign."

"I know," Haviss spoke gently, "but that has never made any difference to me. Their anger and jealousy won't help them improve their craft. You produce quality work and you're ready for the task ahead of you."

"Thank you, Master." She sipped at her tea.

"Now, most apprentices want to leave as soon as they can, but of course you'll have time to pack and prepare. If you'd like to visit your family before you leave, you can do that, or we can send them a note."

She took a long sip of her tea. "I don't want to trouble them. What am I allowed to take with me?"

He shrugged. "That's your decision. You'll find tools along the way."

Zolphara frowned. "I don't really understand what you mean."

Haviss chuckled. "That's part of the challenge. It'll make sense later, I assure you, and I can only give you so much help before you leave."

Right—I'm supposed to figure this out on my own. Zolphara fell silent as she finished her tea. "If I pack tonight, I should be ready to leave tomorrow morning. Is there anything else I need to do?"

"Clean up your workspace and you're free for the rest of the day." Haviss removed the empty teacups from the table. "I have no doubt you can do this. Ignore the others. I can provide you with before information tomorrow."

"Thank you."

He wished her a good evening as she left his office, and Zolphara entered an empty studio. With her apron, she rubbed at the dry clay caked on her hands. Flakes of it drifted to the floor as she shuffled her way to her wheel. She put her pots and her tools away with slow movements. With her workplace tidy, she went to her room to wash up before heading to the kitchen.

The chatter in the dining room stopped as she entered the room carrying her food. Avoiding the gazes of her peers, Zolphara sat down away from them to eat alone. The silence remained until the others finished their meals and left the room. *It's nice in here without all the noise.*

Zolphara ate and cleaned up her dishes as slowly as she could manage, stretching out every moment of the evening. When she returned to her room, she placed clean clothes in a satchel. *I can deal with everything else tomorrow.*

~ * ~

Zolphara avoided the studio the next morning, and it appeared as if her peers refused to glance at her throughout breakfast. *They won't have to see me again after today.* She ate slowly,

trying to put her thoughts in order. When she returned to her room, she slipped a worn, old book into her satchel and slung it over her shoulder. Without looking back, she made her way to Haviss' office.

He greeted her with his usual kind, tired smile. "You look like you're ready to go."

"I don't want to waste your time, and yes, I think I'm ready."

"I'm glad to hear that." He handed her a map. "This will show you most of the way you need to go. The entrance to the tomb isn't marked, you'll have to find that on your own." He pointed to a series of markings between the location of his workshop and the cliffs at the edge of the map. "Each of these towns and cities has an inn where you can stay."

He handed her a disc of baked clay displaying the seal of the Pottery Guild. "Don't lose this, you'll have to bring it back to me. Show this to the innkeepers and any shops you visit. They'll know to send your bill to the guild. Do you have any more questions?"

She slipped the guild token into a pocket of her breeches and shook her head. "I don't think so."

He smiled. "All right, then. Come, I'll take you to the stables. Show the token to stable masters, too, unless you'd rather walk all the way to the tomb."

They left the pottery workshop in silence, avoiding the other apprentices. Zolphara cleared her throat in so rough a manner it caused pain. "They can't try to sabotage my journey, can they?"

He shook his head. "Only if they wanted to risk their own positions within the guild."

I'm not sure that makes me feel any better. They made their way through the city streets until they reached the stables at the city's edge. There, Haviss arranged for her to join a wagon full of passengers headed to the first destination marked on her map.

Haviss cleared his throat as Zolphara turned away to board the wagon. "You don't have to worry about the others anymore. I'm sure you'll return without any problems."

She swallowed hard. "Thank you, Master." With a forced smile, she climbed into the wagon and took a seat amongst the other passengers.

~ * ~

After a week of nothing but wagons and inns, the last wagon Zolphara had hired with the help of her guild token took her closer to the cliffs marked on her map. With the cliffs in sight, Zolphara thanked the wagon driver as she disembarked. She took slow steps toward the cliffs, looming over her more and more ominously as the wagon rolled away and she clutched her map with both hands.

Biting her lip, Zolphara folded the map and stored it in her pack. "This won't help me anymore."

The sun sank lower in the sky as she approached the base of the cliffs, her gaze wandering back and forth along the mass of rocks and stone. "There could be so much hidden in there. How does one hide a tomb?" She came to a stop when she reached the cliff face, extending an arm to run a hand along its surface. "It's certainly not the most glamorous place to be buried. Maybe that's the point."

Twilight streaked the sky with pink and orange as she searched the cliffs. "I'll lose my light if I don't hurry, but there's something there."

She spotted an opening in the cliff face a few meters above her. An exploration of the stone revealed worn handholds once hacked into its surface beneath the opening. "Nothing else looks particularly promising, so I can take this chance." With several deep breaths, Zolphara grabbed the handholds and began to climb.

Her arms ached by the time she hauled herself onto the ledge nearest to the opening in the cliff. Sweat made her clothes stick to her and she wiped her hands on her breeches. "Making pottery certainly didn't prepare me for this. I don't think this is the test I'm supposed to expect."

Taking a long drink of water from her canteen, Zolphara inspected the opening in the cliff face. The stone bore the marks of chisels or pickaxes. "Looks like someone carved this. It's not natural, and it's certainly large enough to accommodate a person."

She glanced over her shoulder as the sun sank in the sky above her. She blew out a deep breath. "This might not be the tomb's entrance." She peered into the opening, finding a hallway cut into the rock. "At least it's something, and it means I won't have to stay out in the open."

With a few steps forward, she plunged into the hallway's darkness. Running a hand along the wall kept her steady as her eyes adjusted to the lack of light. "There's light up ahead coming from… somewhere," she mumbled. "Someone must've made this tunnel for a reason, but how far does it extend?"

Zolphara recoiled as she neared another hallway, this one brightly lit by a series of torches. "Who keeps these torches lit? But someone does keep them lit, so this place must be important." She traced a few fingers over a carving in one wall. It matched the guild token she carried, making her smile. "This has to be the first guild-master's tomb. I've found it."

A blur slammed into her, sending her tumbling to the floor. She scrambled to her feet and found a young woman glaring at her.

Zolphara's mouth fell open for a moment. "Petrella? What are you doing here? I thought they didn't send multiple apprentices to the tomb at the same time."

"They don't." Petrella's fist slammed into Zolphara's cheek. "I'm here to make sure you don't return. Where's the guild token?"

"I don't have to give that to you. It's not mine to give, and I need it to finish my test."

"I'm ready for the test, too! The guildmistress should've picked me, you don't deserve this. What makes your pottery so special? You think you're unique because you're a foreigner?"

Zolphara clenched her fists. "You're trying to make me doubt myself, but you can't do that. Ask yourself if I really stand in your way."

Petrella lunged at her and they collided. Zolphara's head hit the wall, and she slumped against the stone as the world went dark.

~ * ~

Zolphara's head ached as she opened her eyes. Her satchel sat open next to her; its contents strewn across the floor. She slowly re-packed her belongings, accounting for each item. Her hand lingered on her book. "Of course she took the guild token. At least she didn't take this."

She rose to her feet and slung her satchel over her shoulders. "I don't know if I can return to Haviss without the guild token and still pass this test. I'll deal with that when the time comes. It's best if I keep exploring."

A series of hallways led her to what appeared to be a closed stone door. Pushing against it with all her strength made no difference, but her fingers brushed against a carving. She squinted in the light of the nearest torches.

"It's the same image as the guild token, but this carving is deeper than the others I've seen. Could the token be a key of some sort?" Sighing, she shook her head. "I suppose that doesn't matter if I don't have the token. At least there are other passages to explore." Petrella's words echoed in her memory, and she took a deep breath to compose herself. "No. It's not for her or the others to decide what I deserve. I've come this far already. I have no reason to give up."

She wandered until a gap in the floor made her stop. The stone floor ended, and a shaft extended a few meters from where Zolphara stood. Petrella's broken body lay at the bottom of the shaft.

Zolphara squeezed her eyes shut and whispered, "She died because she came after me." She opened her eyes. "I'm sorry, Petrella. Things didn't have to be like this."

She turned away from the shaft. "There's no way to climb out of that, so I won't be getting the guild token back." A sick feeling settled in her gut. "If I return, everyone might blame me for her death. I have to tell them. They need to know what happened."

Slowly, her footsteps took her away from the shaft. *As awful as I feel, I have to keep going.* Her exploration brought her to a room dominated by a kiln. "This seems appropriate for the tomb of the Pottery Guild's first master. Is this my test? Am I supposed to make something?"

She inspected baskets full of clay and shelves of various crafting tools. She stopped when she found a particular item. "A mold for the guild token? That means…" She glanced at the other supplies in the room. "Yes, I can make a replacement token."

Zolphara set to work, lighting a fire in the kiln. The room supplied everything she needed and she plunged her hands into the clay. *This almost takes my mind off what happened to Petrella.* She pressed clay into the mold, smoothing it out with her fingers. When her work satisfied her, she removed the token from the mold and baked it in the kiln. She stared at the token after she removed it from the kiln and waited for it to cool.

"This was a simple enough task, but there must be something behind that door." She let enough time pass for the token to cool before she scooped it up and left the room.

Her wanderings brought her back to the sealed door, and she regarded her new token for a moment before pressing it into the carving. Something made a loud clicking noise, and the sound of stone grinding against stone filled the hallways. The token fell from its place, and Zolphara caught it as the door opened.

Slipping the token into a pocket, Zolphara entered a dark chamber. A sarcophagus stood in the middle of the chamber, surrounded by a dozen kilns and fire pits arranged in a ring. "That other room wasn't the test, *this* is the test." She took a few more steps into the room and fires ignited in the kilns and pits, filling the burial chamber with light and heat. She recoiled, shielding her eyes with one arm.

When she could lower her arm, Zolphara inspected each blazing kiln and pit. A pottery wheel sat at one end of the sarcophagus, and baskets full of clay and miscellaneous items had been stacked against the walls. A shaft cut into the ceiling allowed smoke to escape from the room.

She dug through a basket and pulled out a spoon. "These aren't exactly sculpting tools. Did someone leave them here for a reason?" Shaking her head, she picked up a mound of clay. "Maybe those items will be useful. Making something in each of these fires sounds like a way in which I could try to prove myself. I don't think I'm going to get any instructions from the guild."

Zolphara dug her hands into the clay, but hesitated. *Whatever I create, it needs to be better than anything I've made before.* Withdrawing her hands from the clay, she reached for her satchel instead. She removed her book from her satchel and thumbed through its pages.

In the light of the kilns, Zolphara looked through illustrations and read descriptions of pottery and ceramics from the kingdom from which her family had originated. "The other apprentices mocked me when I made some of these items, and then I didn't make more. It was easiest to avoid the others." She straightened her shoulders." Their opinions don't matter to me anymore."

With the book to guide her, Zolphara let her hands shape the clay. The heat from the fires left her fingers slick with sweat. Working at the pottery wheel soon left her hands and clothing caked with clay. She used the miscellaneous items in the baskets to carve decorations into her creations, blending designs from her book with those Haviss had taught her. One by one, she fired her creations in each of the kilns and over each fire pit. *There's nothing I enjoy more than making these.*

Zolphara placed each finished item on the lid of the sarcophagus. "I don't know what else to do with these, but this feels appropriate." She yawned, exhaustion biting deeply into her bones. She sat down against the wall and closed her eyes.

When Zolphara woke up, all the pottery she had made had been removed from the sarcophagus. Her breath caught in her throat. *Guild members must be here—Haviss did say they'd be watching.* The sound of grinding stones boomed through the tomb as she pushed herself to her feet. The wall opposite the burial chamber's door opened, revealing another hallway lit by torches.

She returned her book to her satchel and ran a hand over a face still filthy with dried sweat and clay. "I suppose that's the way out." She felt the weight of her replacement token in her pocket. "This isn't truly over until I return to Haviss." With a sliver of a smile, Zolphara followed the passage out of the tomb and towards the road that would take her back to the workshop.

~ * ~

A week after leaving the tomb, Zolphara arrived at the workshop. Ignoring the other apprentices, she went immediately to Haviss' office. He greeted her with a smile, and she found her pottery from the tomb sitting on his desk.

He ushered her into the office and made tea. "Welcome back and well done. This pottery is excellent." They sat down across from each other and he passed her a cup of tea. "You're approved for graduation to becoming a fully-fledged member of the Pottery Guild. Congratulations!"

Zolphara swallowed hard. "A-are you sure? There was…there was an incident."

He nodded, his smile fading. "Yes, I'm aware of what happened. The others told me Petrella wished she had been chosen. The tomb's guardians informed me that she followed you."

She wrapped her hands around her cup of tea to keep them from shaking. "Petrella attacked me and stole your guild token. I found her at the bottom of a shaft."

"There are various shafts in tombs of that age. They were added to trap tomb robbers." He paused. "Petrella's death isn't your fault. The tomb's guardians saw everything. I believe you made a new guild token?"

She retrieved the token from her pocket and handed it to him. "You're sure I passed the test? I'm no longer an apprentice?"

"Yes, that's correct. I know it may take you some time to put Petrella's death behind you, but you're free to start your own career now. The Guildmistress is very pleased with your work. I'll send her word that you've returned, and we'll plan your graduation ceremony. You've earned this."

She bowed her head. "Thank you, sir." Zolphara's gaze settled on her pottery. *As soon as I can, I'm going to make more of these.*

~ * ~ * ~

Danielle Airola writes fantasy and steampunk. She lives in Montana.

THE TECHNIQUE

John A. McColley

"Yes! Yes! NO! No fancy turns. This isn't a stage play where you leap over barrels and swing on ropes in the middle of a sword fight, Amblin! This is real. You have seconds to square off, block a flurry of attacks, and find your opening. Just one, deep, strike to a vital, the heart, a lung, the jugular if you must show off, then move to the next opponent. That's war, that's Life!" Greygar was especially vexed this morning. Spittle flew as he attacked Amblin's technique, sent them back to their mark over and over. "Again!"

Amblin slashed and zizzed and magnified the sparks from sliding blades into distracting flashes, sent tiny lightning bolts chasing down their opponent's weapon, summoned the power of the blade to reach out beyond itself, stabbing for one of the circles on Greygar's heavily magicked tabard.

"Better, but I can still see unnecessary flourishes in your blade work. Time spent moving to the side is wasted unless it's a feint. In. In! Stab! You are a ray of holy sunshine, the finger of May piercing her foes!"

"If not May, from whence come the instincts to waver? To spin?" Amblin had asked once, before they had learned not to ask questions during field training.

"Truth does not spin; justice does not waver! We must be direct, fast, and deadly. Strike, move, strike, move, leaving the bodies of our enemies, May's enemies, to feed the land," Greygar had said, punctuating many of the words with prods from a wooden training sword, before the subject of blade magic had even been broached.

Now, the magic was everything, or should have been. While Amblin had a few small tricks up their sleeve, they had been allowed only the rudimentaries of the power sleeping within their blade. The true power of the Rays lay beyond the barrier of the promotion test.

"Now!" Greygar snapped. Amblin realized they had been drawn back to an earlier moment. Something there pulled at their mind. The path to becoming a worthy Ray of May's light lay ahead.

Rumors of invasion always whispered around the eaves. They had grown louder recently on the verge of bursting from the shadows into polite conversation. The nation would need their blade honed, ready.

"Run! Three laps of the grounds, then bathe, eat, bed. Tomorrow is your last chance to show you are ready before the test. If you fail, we will have another year together. I don't think either of us wants that."

The trail wove a mile around the compound. It was grueling, with many hills, including the path to the lookout at the highest part of the compound, beside the waterfall. At least Greygar hadn't ordered them to take a pack.

As Amblin approached the gate from the training field, Greygar cleared his throat. Amblin wheeled around and the man threw a stone the size of their head. The stone, smoothed by the river over endless years, struck them in the chest, nearly bowling them over. Training kicked in and they brought up their hands just in time to hug the small boulder to their belly. They could only imagine the penalty if it had fallen. After the last such infraction, their body was so worn out after the punishment they couldn't rise from bed for two days.

Amblin jogged, trying to set a pace acceptable to Greygar, while still allowing them to complete the course. They soon missed the pack. The stone weighed nearly as heavy, and there were no convenient straps. To pass the time, as running was extremely boring, especially in a place one has run hundreds of times before, Amblin pretended the rock was a parcel they were meant to deliver to the next place they passed. They told themselves they would leave the parcel with the woodworkers, the potters, the smiths, the animal handlers, the bottom of the hill guards, the top of the hill guards.

The mist swirling around the top of the falls cooled them, but made the rock slippery. Colorful rainbows arced before them. *May does work in curves!*

As they turned to descend, they almost let the stone go, to bounce and roll to the bottom under the power of gravity. Almost, but again, they had made that mistake before as well, when they were younger and the weight had been a melon. They completed the circuit, and then another pretending the rock was a head trying to give them advice about sword fighting and running despite all attempts at interesting conversation, then a third as the sun brushed the treetops across the gorge protecting the compound's west side.

By now, all pretense and delusion had drained away. Any distraction from the now massive weight they carried had burned off with the fire flaring up in their forearms, upper arms, shoulders, and back. Their legs had endured this training, with the pack, far more often. Doing this two days before the big test signified Greygar didn't think Amblin worthy to even have the chance to prove themselves. The stone fell at their feet as they crossed back into the training area. It rolled in an arc to the left. Something stirred deep beneath the woolen blankets of fatigue which enrapt their brain as they tracked its movement.

"Don't leave that there," is all Greygar said as he passed by in the other direction.

Bathing was a chore, as their arms would barely respond. Eating was worse. They were late to dinner and only ate because the cooks had mercy on them and poured them some soup and noodles rather than feeding it to the animals.

They slurped up as much cold, saltier than usual, soup as they could, foregoing utensils as their arms hung useless by their sides. Eventually, the sky dark, save for the emerging stars and a thumbnail crescent of moon, they collapsed on their bunk fully dressed.

~ * ~

Amblin found themselves on a great stone plateau etched with rings inside of rings. Smaller circles were pierced by larger ones, except the circle at the center, which sported a crown. Not a crown as one might see it looking at the king or emperor as they spoke, but from above, the points ranging out in every direction.

A grinding arose from the pale brown stone. The space between the large circles crumbled and fell away. Amblin barely leapt to one of the smaller circles. Utter blackness dotted with points of light filled the spaces between the narrow edges of the circles.

The smaller circles began to spin, including the one they stood upon. They spread their feet for balance, lowering their body for more. As they watched, they saw the smaller circles also traveled along the larger circles, all at different rates. At the center, the jagged outline of the circle began to glow brightly. It came into view and vanished again as Amblin spun. A small circle sped by with another even smaller circle on its own path around it.

Again, something wiggled at the back of Amblin's mind. While the worm was not ready to become a butterfly just yet, it dreamed of wings.

~ * ~

Amblin awoke in the thin light of morning, stiff, aching, wondering if this future awaited them every morning if they lived to one hundred years old. Bodies moved all around them, dressing, stretching, bouncing up and down as they waved their arms to get their hearts pumping. The bunkhouse disgorged dozens of acolytes into the cool of early morning only for yawns to turn to cries of alarm.

"To arms! Get your weapons!" someone called.

"The gate won't last much longer!" another yelled.

Battling their own body to even move forward, Amblin recited the techniques they had learned, lunging, parrying, feinting, always stabbing for one target or another with speed and accuracy. They envisioned themselves looking into the eyes of their single opponent, the other falling, then another, and another, as they strode across the battlefield.

Outside, someone screamed. Alarm bells rang, their heavy, slow notes rolling right through Amblin's body. They pulled their shoulders forward, then back as they struggled to walk faster, then begin to jog again. It seemed as though every joined from their feet to their hands ached and complained like old leather needing oil. Finally, they stood at the doorway of the bunkhouse. The left outer compound gate hung by the merest timbers, and men and women in the enemy's traditional battle dress ran and rode through, spears, swords, and nasty spiked flails mowing down Amblin's peers.

"No!" Amblin cried out, trying to run and stumbling down the stairs to the path.

"You go hide. You weren't ready before, and now you're in no fit shape to stand lookout, let alone fight," Greygar growled as he ran by from somewhere deeper in the compound. The potters and woodworkers followed behind him.

Amblin couldn't let this pass. They couldn't run away and hide when even the unskilled fighters were joining the fray. "No!"

Amblin yelled again, urging their body to a shambling jog, then a run as their muscles loosened. Their first enemy fell in three strikes, their second, five. Amblin felt the adrenaline burn through their body, a high, jittery fire searing away pain as they fought off stiffness. One enemy became four, then six. There were simply too many foes to take on one at a time. As if of its own accord, their sword point described a swooping circle, knocking aside the blades of those closest.

Circles. Rainbow arcs. Worlds spinning around May. The images from their dream clicked, aligning themselves with scientific manuscripts they had helped transcribe. Taking a half step back to one side, Amblin dragged the point of their sword along the dry ground, sending up a stream of sparks which quickly bloomed into a ring of fire encompassing them. Completing the technique which had been scratching at the back of their mind, locked behind discouraging words of straight stabs and single opponents, Amblin released a wave of power from the blade. Flame roared outward, forcing a chorus of screams from nearly a dozen throats which all peaked, then suddenly ceased as lungs and armor seared, their owners' spirits returning to May.

The explosion drew attention from all around, and as the circle of flame crested, crumbling like an ocean wave, every eye within fifty yards focused on them. The respite didn't last. Amblin charged forward to stand beside Greygar, who had himself been facing off half a dozen foes and showed wear for it.

The attacking forces faltered. Amblin's Ring of Fire slew seven more, then twenty, before the route came to full bloom, enemies falling over themselves to escape the way they'd entered, or take their chances riding the river over the lower falls.

"Looks like you passed the test, after all," Greygar growled. "And a day early. Let's get that gate back up and then we'll take a day to recover. When the dead are buried, we can begin formalizing your new technique and seeing if any other acolytes can manage it."

"Always straight to the point, eh Greygar?"

"That's the way I learned, the only way I thought served May… I think now perhaps there are other ways, Ray Amblin." Greygar offered his hand. Amblin took it and they limped toward the fallen gate.

~ * ~ * ~

John A. McColley writes from his cave in the woods of New England.

He's a member of the SFWA and has a Patreon where he serializes Scifi and Fantasy novels: patreon.com/JohnAMcColley and spends too much time on Tik Tok @JohnMcColley631.

SMOKE EATERS

Kevin Hopson

"Oh, man," Grayson muttered. "Here he comes."

I stood with my back to the van and crossed my arms as Marcel approached. He was a lanky fellow with thinning gray hair, and he managed the apartment complex where I happened to be parked.

"Rocco," Marcel said, coming to a stop. He looked up at me, which was common for people to do given my height. "What did I tell you about parking here?"

I shrugged.

Marcel glared at me. "Well, let me remind you. This parking lot is for tenants and guests only."

"Come on, Marcel." I grinned. "You know Grayson is a friend of mine. There's no law against chatting with him in the parking lot."

Marcel huffed, resting his hands on his waist. "You're parked here day and night, but you're not a tenant. And I know you're not rooming with Grayson." He glanced at Grayson. "That would violate his lease agreement since he claimed to be living alone."

I watched as Grayson's eyes widened. I definitely didn't want to cause any trouble for him.

"It's true," I pointed out. "I'm not living with Grayson, and I obviously don't rent here. However, I'm assuming guests do visit on occasion, sometimes even for extended periods of time."

"Of course," Marcel replied, "but that isn't the case here." He eyed my van. "If I had to wager a guess, I'd say you're living in your van, and you're doing it on private property."

Marcel spoke the truth, but I wasn't about to admit it. My job provided a decent source of income, so I could afford an apartment. I just didn't need one. I was content living the way I was.

"Have you seen me sleeping in the van?" I asked.

Marcel opened his mouth to speak, then pursed his lips.

A buzzing of my phone interrupted, and I pulled it from the front pocket of my jeans.

"Looks like I'll be out of your hair soon enough," I said. "I have to go. Talk to you later, Grayson."

He nodded.

I met Marcel's gaze one last time. "Enjoy the rest of your day."

Marcel gave me the stink eye as I cracked the door and got behind the wheel. I had a delivery to make. A potentially dangerous one.

~ * ~

Food delivery wasn't typically a hazardous job. Despite automobile accidents being one of the leading causes of deaths and the fact that I sometimes found myself driving through shady neighborhoods, the job proved to be uneventful more times than not.

The thing that made this particular delivery a little daring was the wildfire raging only a mile from my destination. Clearpass lay in the valley with several suburban neighborhoods encompassing it, and the latest wildfire was slowly encroaching the foothills just beyond the city.

Wildfires were an unfortunate norm for this part of the country. And they were becoming more common across the globe, even in places that rarely experienced them.

Some days the sky appeared as if it were on fire. Other times the smoke and ash drowned out the sun, covering the city in darkness. And today was definitely a case of the latter. Though it seemed closer to dusk, it was only half past noon, and many of the streetlamps glowed as I rolled down the road in my van.

I spotted my destination up ahead, gently applying the brakes until I came to a stop in front of the house. I put on my face mask to help combat the smoke, got out of the van, and circled around to the passenger-side door. Two plastic bags rested on the front passenger seat, and I took a moment to scan the horizon before grabbing the food.

I could barely make out flames in the distance given the heavy cover, but I knew the fire wasn't far off. In fact, I wouldn't be surprised if the neighborhood was ordered to evacuate in the coming days. Once the fire hit those foothills, it was only a matter of time.

"Beautiful," a voice said, startling me.

I spun around, and an athletic brunette stared back at me. She stood in her lawn wearing jeans and a t-shirt, a ponytail draped over the front of her shoulder.

The woman took a step toward me. "Sorry if I scared you."

My pulse accelerated, and I let out a breath. "No problem."

She smiled. "It's amazing how nature reclaims its territories."

I deliberated. "Yeah. Sometimes there's a fine line between beauty and destruction." When she didn't reply, I swallowed, a feeling of embarrassment washing over me. I opened the passenger-side door and glanced at the order receipt. "I'm assuming you're Maria Foster?"

"That's me. I appreciate you coming out here. Not many drivers like to make the trip. That's why I offered a fifty-dollar tip to anyone willing to do it."

"I figured it would be worthwhile for that kind of money."

"Do you mind helping me carry the bags inside? I have a bad wrist."

I eyed the wrist brace on one of her hands. It wasn't normal for delivery drivers to go inside a customer's house, but the request didn't seem out of the ordinary given her situation.

"If you're uncomfortable doing it, I'll understand," Maria said. "I can probably carry both with one hand."

I shook my head. "I don't mind."

She pulled a phone from the back pocket of her jeans and tapped away at the screen.

"There." Maria's lips stretched into a grin. "I just sent your tip, plus a little extra for the service."

I slid my phone out and, sure enough, a payment of sixty dollars had just come through.

"You didn't have to do that." I deposited the phone in my pocket. "Thank you, though."

"You're welcome."

I grabbed the bags and closed the van door, following Maria to the house. She opened the front door and stepped aside, allowing me to enter.

Maria raised her index finger and pointed. "The kitchen is right through there."

When I entered the kitchen, my mouth hung agape. Two people were seated at a round table. One was a male with cropped dark hair and pale skin. The other was a woman. However, she was gagged and appeared to have her hands tied behind the chair.

"What the hell is this?" I asked.

Maria pulled a gun from the waist of her jeans. "You can put the bags on the table and have a seat."

I gently lowered the bags, resting them on the table. Then I plopped my butt down in a hard, wooden chair.

"Keep your hands on the table where I can see them," Maria ordered.

I obliged.

"This will go smoothly as long as you don't fight me on it. Do you understand?"

I nodded.

"First things first," Maria said. "Piper needs to eat. And so do you, Blake." She looked at the woman. "I'm going to have Blake remove your restraints so you can eat, but I'll be holding this gun the entire time, so don't get any ideas."

Piper bobbed her head, and Blake got to his feet. He untied the cloth around Piper's mouth, then removed the thin rope that bound her wrists. Piper panted, keeping her head down. She didn't dare lock eyes with Blake or Maria.

Maria glanced at Blake. "Piper has the turkey sandwich."

Blake walked back to his chair and hunched over the table, perusing the bags. He handed Piper a sandwich and took another for himself.

Maria eyed me. "You're welcome to eat. I bought enough food for all of us."

"I can't say that I'm hungry," I replied.

"And I can't say that I blame you."

Maria held the gun in her right hand. Her left hand had the wrist brace.

"Is the brace just for show?" I asked.

Maria shook her head. "No. I have carpal tunnel in my left hand." Then she grinned. "But it gave me an excuse. It got you to help me, didn't it?"

Unfortunately, she was right about that.

"Look," I said. "It's obviously none of my business, but what exactly is going on here?"

"You're right," Maria responded. "It is none of your business, but I'm going to be straight with you anyway."

"I appreciate that."

"Blake is my brother, and I just met Piper yesterday. She's homeless. Well, she was until we pulled her off the street."

She could have fooled me. Blake looked the more homeless of the two. His face was sunken in, and he was rail thin. Piper was slim, too, but at least she had a glow about her. It complimented her brown eyes and curly black hair.

"But how do I play into this?" I inquired.

"We're going to need your van," Maria replied. "My car won't run. Not since we got back with Piper last night."

I glimpsed Piper. She slowly chewed her sandwich, still staring at the table.

My brow furrowed. "I don't understand. You could just steal my van. You don't need me."

"I like to be in control of the situation, and I feel better if you're with us." Maria paused. "We're smoke eaters. Me and Blake."

I'd heard that term before but couldn't recall where.

"It sounds familiar," I admitted.

"We're a group of believers."

"Believers of what?"

"That fire will consume the Earth, and our only path to salvation is by appeasing the gods."

Great. A cult.

"What about Piper?" I asked.

"What about her?"

"Is she a smoke eater?"

"No."

"Then what's her deal?"

"She's going to appease the gods."

I had to mull that over for a moment. "You're going to sacrifice her?"

"Yes."

How original. What is it with cults and sacrifices?

I looked to Piper. If Maria's admittance shocked Piper, the woman certainly didn't show it. She knew what awaited her and had no intentions of fighting it, if the defeated look on her face was any indication.

"So," I said. "You figure no one will care about a missing homeless person. No one would even notice it, right?"

Maria nodded. "The less attention she draws, the better." She took a step forward. "But we can arrange for you to take her place. Or maybe we can throw both of you to the fire."

That didn't sound very appealing to me.

"We cleaned her up," Maria continued. "We got her some fresh clothes and some food in her belly."

"Well, that makes all of this acceptable. It's very humane of you."

Maria put the barrel of the gun to my head. I probably should have kept my mouth closed.

"Sarcasm isn't going to win you any points," she commented.

"Noted," I said. "Would you mind if I removed my mask? It's getting a little warm in here, and I'm prone to hyperventilating."

Maria extended a hand and pulled the string loops from my ears, removing the mask. "Better?"

"Much better, thanks. You can keep it if you'd like."

Maria tossed the mask at a nearby trash bin. It missed the mark, landing on the kitchen floor instead.

"Your keys," Maria demanded. "Nice and easy."

I slid the keys from my pocket and dropped them in the palm of her hand.

"Blake," Maria said.

He looked up from his sandwich, still munching on a mouthful of roast beef.

"Keep an eye on them," she instructed, handing the gun to Blake. "I'm going to back the van into the garage so we're ready to go." Maria eyed me. "Behave yourself."

"Of course," I replied.

Maria turned and soon disappeared from view. Blake pointed the gun at me. I was obviously more of a threat than Piper.

I couldn't help but think. Was there a scenario where I could come out of this alive? Maria had revealed everything to me. And they certainly weren't going to drop me off at Grayson's place when they were finished with all of this. I figured some meaningless banter could help lighten the mood, at least.

"How's the sandwich?" I asked Blake.

He titled his head and shrugged. "Not bad. The beef is a little tough at times. Maybe you could do something about that."

"How so?"

"You know. Talk to the manager or something."

"I don't work there. I pick up orders from different restaurants and deliver them." I pondered. "But tell you what. I'll mention it to the manager if it makes you feel any better."

"That would be cool."

As if I would be able to follow through on that. I'd probably be dead within the hour. Then I noticed something scurrying across the kitchen floor.

"I don't want to alarm you," I said, "but there's a cockroach near the table."

"Where?" Blake shouted. He pushed his chair against the wall and stood on top of it.

"Near the edge of the table."

Piper finally looked up. She scooted her chair away from the table but remained seated.

Blake aimed his gun at the floor. "If I see it, I'm going to shoot it."

"Relax," I said. "They're fast, so shooting it won't work. But I can kill it if you want."

"Okay. Just keep your hands in the air."

I raised both hands. "I'll smash it with my shoe."

I approached Piper, coming to a stop near her end of the table. Then I stomped my shoe against the floor.

"Did you get?" Blake asked.

"I can't tell. I think so, but they have a pretty hard exterior, so it might still be alive."

"Stomp it again!"

I obliged. I wasn't really stomping the cockroach, but Blake couldn't tell from his angle.

"What about now?" Blake said.

"I still can't tell. I'll have to bend down if you want me to make sure. I'll keep my other hand in the air, though."

"Okay. Just be quick."

I dropped to one knee, keeping my left hand in the air while I shooed the cockroach away with my right hand. As it scurried toward the sink area, I gripped the edge of the table with my right hand, forcing it on its side and putting a shoulder to it. I used both of my hands to push the table toward Blake.

The table collided with Blake's chair, and I heard him stumble, the chair sliding out from under him. Something else hit the floor, too. Perhaps the gun, but the table was dividing us, and Blake was likely pinned against the wall. It was now or never, so I clutched Piper's hand and led her out of the kitchen.

A blast came only seconds later. Debris grazed the back of my neck as the bullet went through the foyer wall, thankfully missing me. We'd made it to the garage. When I opened the door, Maria had just finished backing the van in. I tugged Piper's hand, guiding her down the steps.

Maria spotted us, her eyes bulging at the sight. I let go of Piper's hand and circled around to the driver's door. Maria went to lock it, but I managed to open the door before the clicking noise ensued. Maria wasn't wearing a seat belt, so I grabbed her arm and yanked her from the seat. She hit the car next to us and slumped against the door.

"Get in," I shouted to Piper.

She went to open the door. It wouldn't budge. Crap. I forgot that Maria locked the doors. I slid into the driver's seat, the keys still in the ignition, and closed the door. I unlocked Piper's door, and she immediately got in. Maria was starting to get to her feet. I locked the doors and put the van into drive, not even bothering with the seat belt.

There was a banging on the window. It was Maria. I put my foot to the gas, and the van jerked before barreling out of the garage. I caught a glimpse of Blake in the rearview mirror.

"Down," I shouted.

Piper listened, and I ducked as much as I could while still driving. A shattering of glass followed. First the back window, then the windshield. The bullet missed both of us. I turned the steering wheel hard and sped down the street. When I looked back, I didn't see Maria or Blake. We were finally safe.

~ * ~

Two days later...

I sat behind the steering wheel, parked in a grocery store lot, when my cell phone buzzed. I accepted the call and put the phone to my ear.

"Hello," I said.

"Mr. Hobbs?" It was a woman's voice. "This is Detective Burton."

"Good morning, detective. How are you?"

"Not bad. I just wanted to give you an update on the case."

"Okay." I was curious about something, so I had to ask. "How is Piper?"

"About as good as she can be given the situation."

"Is she out on the street again?"

Burton hesitated. "Unfortunately. But I've connected her with some emergency housing services and places where she can receive free medical care. It's the best I can do at this point."

"I understand. Thanks for doing that."

"It's no problem."

"And what about Maria and Blake?" I asked.

"That's what I wanted to talk to you about. We haven't been able to locate them."

"So, they're on the run?"

"Most likely. But we found some documents in their house, including a members list for the group they belong to. It's possible one of the members has taken them in, so we'll be running down all of those leads."

"Anything else?"

"Yeah. How are you holding up?"

I took a breath. "Okay. My van needs some repairs but, other than that, I'm fine."

"I can send you contact information for someone I know. They do good work at a reasonable price."

"I appreciate that."

"I have to follow up on another case of mine, but I'll be in touch."

"Thank you, detective."

"You're welcome, Mr. Hobbs. Take care of yourself."

"Will do."

I disconnected the call and contemplated. I'd probably have to stay in the area just in case I needed to testify or further assist with the investigation. However, once that was behind me, I planned to move on. Maybe visit another state or even the East Coast. I'd had enough of wildfires and, though few places were immune to them, a change of scenery would certainly do me good.

~ * ~ * ~

Kevin Hopson has dabbled in many genres over the years. A few of his stories have been contest/award winners, and Kevin's work has appeared in more than twenty anthologies. You can learn more about Kevin by visiting his website at kmhopson.com.

THE HAZAMESAM SÉANCE

Robert Bagnall

When I was sixteen years old, Father O'Shea said, "Brian, there's been a death at the Kavanagh place. Go and sit. Make some tea. Listen. At a time like this, it all helps."

The Kavanagh place was a laborer's cottage on the edge of farmland, shadowed by a curtain of trees, far removed from the village. I set off at dusk. In the dark, I knocked tentatively. The door opened, and a figure filled the doorway, silhouetted by a dull fireplace glow. Then the figure stepped back, and the additional illumination of an oil lamp revealed Mrs. Kavanagh, hunched over.

"Father O'Shea sent me. He thought you'd like me to sit with you."

Mrs. Kavanagh held the door for me. "He's a good man, Father O'Shea."

She made tea. I wanted to ask what had happened, how it happened, but death felt too enormous and Mrs. Kavanagh too placid. I didn't want to remind her of what must be overwhelming her every thought. I feared the wrong word or a glance at the bedroom door would bring it all home to her.

"He's a good man, Father O'Shea," Mrs. Kavanagh repeated as though she was the one struggling for conversation.

"He's a man of God."

"Is that what you want to be? A man of God?"

"Yes."

I don't think anybody had ever asked me so directly. I was taken aback by the firmness of my answer.

"Is Father O'Shea a good man *because* he is a man of God, or a good man who *happens* to be a man of God," she mused.

"I think he became a man of God because he's a good man. That's his way of doing good."

She nodded thoughtfully. "Can you be a good man without being a man of God?"

"Of course, otherwise Father O'Shea would be the only good man amongst us and there are many good men in the village. Father

O'Shea says in Dante all those people who died before Christ was ever born are in Hell because they were heathens. But if they came before Christ then they never even had the chance to be Christian. That doesn't seem fair."

After we'd both taken a bit more tea, she calmly told me she used to believe in God. The Father, the Son, and the Holy Spirit. "Which makes me a fool."

"You can't say that," I said, in genuine shock.

"When I was young, eighteen, don't laugh, I was eighteen once, I knew some people, certainly not men of God. They asked me to look after things for them, a bag of things. I looked in the bag. Jewelry, rings, gold, diamonds. A nice haul. I knew they were stolen. A jeweler's shop in Waterford. A brick through its window in broad daylight. Scarves around their faces. A King's ransom, apparently. Knowing the jewelry did not yet belong to anybody made me feel better. They hadn't stolen anybody's memories."

I goggled. Seeing my comical expression, she added, "I should have gone to the police. But I didn't. They were my friends. But my friends never returned. I never saw them again from that day to this."

Was I receiving confession? Father O'Shea had never warned me to expect this.

"I know what you're thinking, what did I do with it? That was sixty years ago, my dear." She laughed softly. "Sixty winters, sixty autumns, summers, springs. Sixty years of scraps and scraping by. The answer is nothing. Absolutely nothing. But I'll tell you what should have happened to that jewelry. I should have worn those rings and trinkets. Or sold them and spent it on good living. That's what I should have done. Do you know why I didn't?"

I shook my head.

"Hell. I feared going to Hell. But I know now there is no Hell. Except the Hell we make for ourselves on Earth."

My jaw sagged in amazement.

"Don't gawp, boy. Go to Tramore. Look for a grave named Maguire. He died on my birthday, April the fifth. That's why I picked it. A foot from the gravestone over the body. Six inches down. That's where you'll find the bag. I buried it. But be careful, it'll be rotten by now."

She looked outside. "The rain has eased. You should be on

your way."

Suddenly I was no longer so convinced of my future as a man of God.

~ * ~

Tramore is a seaside town, steep-sided, looking down onto a sweep of low dune and, beyond, a crescent of white sand holding back the sea. From my vantage point I watched a courting couple walking on the otherwise desolate beach. They strolled, unhurried, the woman hanging on the man's shoulder. At an arbitrary point they would turn and walk back. There was no purpose to their promenade, other than promenading itself.

I trudged on. There was drizzle in the air. It was late, I was hungry and had no idea where I would sleep. I trusted church doors were kept unlocked in town as in the country. More than once I had found somebody asleep, the collar of a threadbare coat pulled up to their chin, hat down over their eyes. Father O'Shea encouraged me to give them comfort, but at the same time to encourage them gone. I struggled to square the circle of such contradictory instructions.

I trailed around the graveyard of Holy Cross Church looking for the resting place of a Maguire who had died on the fifth day of April, frustration growing, before remembering it was a name both Catholic and Protestant could lay claim to. I had disregarded Tramore's Protestant church, not even thinking it an option to the pious Mrs. Kavanagh-to-be. But sure enough, there I found, staring back at me from a granite slab, the name 'Maguire'.

"What are you up, boy?"

He wore a light grey raincoat, belt hanging loose, white dog collar visible underneath. Younger than Father O'Shea, his hair was slicked back, with Brylcreem more than rain.

"I'm tending the grave of my uncle," I said. I'd yet to remove sufficient earth for this response to be ridiculous, my gardening merely looking incompetent.

"You'll have more than just weeds out at that rate. Leave the dead to rest." His terseness did not come across as convincing. I recognized a voice deployed at Sunday school, a tone he had learnt by imitation. "Are you hungry?"

"No," I lied.

Frowning, he considered me, the pile of earth, my muddied

hands. My answer had freed him of the obligation of Christian charity. He nodded and turned away.

I watched him go, counted to ten, and resumed scraping at the soil, kept loose by the Irish rain. But just inches below the surface it became compacted, and I needed a flat stone to work it.

My task absorbed me. I was dimly aware of rain dripping from my hair, of damp patches on my knees. But not of the two people standing above me. I twisted around to find silhouetted against the glowering sky the young reverend and Father O'Shea.

"Tending the grave of your uncle," the reverend spat sarcastically.

Father O'Shea said nothing.

As I struggled up, my legs having gone to sleep, I saw it. The corner of a cloth bag poking through the soil, brown with age, the weave camouflaged by earth. It was at the very edge of where I had been digging. In the gloom, I had missed it.

Then everything happened at once.

I reached for the bag as the reverend and Father O'Shea reached for me.

My fingertips expected rough hessian but, instead they felt velvet. The mouth of the bag had become the hem of a sleeve, earth giving way to clean blue fabric, a wrist and hand twisting from the soil, sprouting, coiled, like the beans we had grown in school.

I screamed, but the hand, emerging from the ground, whipped and gripped tight hold of my wrist. I could feel the two men wrapped around my legs and waist, holding me firm.

All at once, where the protruding limb had loosened the soil, the very earth began to glow, furiously backlit, as if the clods of turned earth had been scattered loose over an inferno, roaring white and yellow, only now revealed. A ring of fire. I was being pulled into a ring of fire.

I could hear the two men shouting, but their words were deadened to me, muffled beyond my hearing. I glanced behind and those two men of God, one from each church, had become hideous insect forms, with yellow-green scales and obsidian eyes wrapped around their skulls with as many facets as the chandeliers that hung in Lord Loughran's ballroom.

My forearm was pulled into the furnace, pushing the soil with it as it went, the packed ground like an eggshell crust with nothing below it.

Nothing but fire and brimstone.

Hell.

HELL.

I was screaming, but couldn't hear myself. I was entering the very gates of Hades.

But this furnace was neither hot nor cold. It didn't roar, except with all-pervading silence. And the Devils were behind me, trying to keep me on God's Earth, so this could not be Hell,

But if it wasn't Hell, what was it?

My elbow, then my upper arm, and next my shoulder, were hauled into the brilliance. The bone-like arms around my knees could not hold fast, the grip of the claws of the things once disguised as preachers slipped. I entered the light with the ease of a river baptism, a light so bright it pained me, even with my eyes screwed tight. Was this heaven? Was this death?

White gave way to black.

I found myself slumped in a full-length reclining seat, soft leather enfolding me, as if I had been plucked from drowning and deposited. My body tingled, twitched. I smelt the caustic sweetness of charged air, as though sparks were about to arc and crackle. My vision swam, a flickering dance of yellow amid shadows.

I blinked and blinked again. My head felt like it had just been released from a vice.

Slowly the scene resolved.

I was sitting in the gloom of some enclosed industrial space. All was grey metal, exposed reinforcements, bulwarks, struts, supports. I decided I must be far underground, that this engineering was to keep the graveyard above from crushing us like bugs.

A face loomed in from out of nowhere, pulled at an eyelid and dazzled me with a torch. I tried to screw my eyes shut, turn away, but I was admonished in a language I didn't recognize.

Words were exchanged in meaningless guttural sounds.

I struggled up in my seat, bringing wide-eyed incredulous faces into view. They all wore military uniforms of a kind I had never seen. More figures, all with weapons drawn, not quite pointing at me, but readied, stood in the shadows. And, in the center of the space, within a transparent glass cube ten feet in each direction, stood a woman massaging and manipulating a licking, dancing flame with no obvious source, half her height. I had been staring at the ceiling, the yellow glow in a sea of shadow the reflection of the flame in the dull metal.

The woman turned to reveal her face.

"Mrs. Kavanagh," I reeled back into my seat, a sand-dry throat making words difficult.

A woman in a military uniform stepped forward and in the incomprehensible hubbub I was suddenly aware of addressed me with a single word I couldn't understand.

She read confusion in my face and repeated what she said. "Commander?"

I looked down at myself. I was wearing a similar uniform. I took in my hands, my arms. These were not those of a callow youth, used to lighting candles and reciting prayers. These were sinewy, strong, experienced. And I could understand everything being said around me.

Like every single person in the room except Mrs. Kavanagh, the woman brandished a weapon of a kind I had never seen, long like a shotgun, but thick, black and bulbous, meshed with tubes and wires. Her finger wavered near the trigger. Something told me she would not hesitate to use it. But not on me. I was the subject of her protection.

She smiled with relief at my understanding. "Welcome back, Commander."

I looked again at the woman I knew as Mrs. Kavanagh, fighting to control the floating flame in the glass cube. She looked younger, regal, chin jutted, a power in her eyes. She wore a suit of the same blue material as the hand...her hand, I realized. She had pulled me through... Through what? To where?

The pseudo-Mrs. Kavanagh leant forward and placed her hands together around and within the flame. When she drew them apart the flame grew to fill the void, becoming a distended eye of swirling white, red and yellow. I recognized it as the blaze I had mistaken for the entrance to Hell.

And then she reached into the slit of light that hung above the table, her arms up to her elbows vanishing into the violence. Screwing her eyes against the glare, unseen by us all she began to do battle.

As I watched through near-closed eyes, head turned aside, I

tried to make sense of the last few minutes. Like a dream, but vivid and fully formed, I had been a child, a youth, in rural Ireland of the 1950s. That had been my life, and I could remember and recite my entire life. Whereas this…

I knew I stood in the antechamber to a space vessel's air lock. We were in deep space, not underground. Here I had suited and booted a hundred times, gone through pre-mission checks, locked and loaded my weapons. I knew the truth, yet how had this come to be?

None of this made sense. Who was I? Which was I?

The woman, the younger so-called Mrs. Kavanagh, dragged her arms back through the scar of light. And in her hands were the two things.

The color of pus and bile, I had only glimpsed them before, behind me, snagging me. Now I saw them in their full horror, their dozen legs clawing at the air, their distended skulls, the bulging eyes, the pulsing gills. The size of dogs, they writhed and thrashed as they emerged. They were two of the most hideous things I had ever seen.

I rose in my seat, instinctively wishing to intervene.

Lieutenant Tiersen—how was it I now knew her name?—bade me stop. "There is nothing we can do to help her, until…"

The Mrs. Kavanagh-that-was-not was fighting them. A hand locked around the throat of each, she was choking them. Lips pulled back, the sinews in her neck standing, veins blue, she slowly robbed them of life. The two creatures kicked and swung their twelve limbs, but gradually the fight went from them. Spasming, they wilted.

Mrs. Kavanagh dropped to her knees.

Doors to the glazed cube opened, armed guards fell upon the creatures, seized them with pincers around their throats, around their legs, carried them warily, as if they were toxic.

Mrs. Kavanagh levered herself up, brushed herself down, and stepped out of the cube. "Their means are limited in this dimension." There was a great weariness in her voice.

"To the airlock," somebody ordered.

Tiersen turned to me and grinned. "We've prepared a surprise for them. Acid and fire."

"I don't understand."

"You did it, Commander," she reassured. "You lured the Hazamesam. We have them now. They cannot harm us any longer."

"The Haza…"

A device I did not recognize was pressed against my arm. I felt a sharp stab.

"My name is Brian Mulcahey," I said, as much to myself to fight this insanity as to any of those around me. My breathing labored. "My name is Brian Mulcahey. I am sixteen. I live in the parochial house at Ballyantrim, County Waterford." I felt myself lifted onto a gurney. "The year is nineteen fifty-five. Costello is Taoiseach…"

Somehow my name, the names of people, of places, had become nothing but nonsense, baby-babble, in the language I now spoke. The reality that all those memories, fading as I spoke, were illusory, there was no Father O'Shea, neither the parochial house nor the Kavanaghs' cottage ever existed, there was no Ireland, crystalised.

As darkness closed in on me, I heard voices.

"An entirely constructed world, consistent in every detail. Fabricated by the Hazamesam to harvest minds. He's going to be disorientated for some time. The level of illusion these creatures can achieve on dimensions we cannot easily access is incredible. To anybody trapped within their web everything is real. Totally real."

"But he's going to be okay?"

"It's too early to tell. He took a great deal of calling back. Nobody has ever gone as deep as he did…and lived."

~ * ~ * ~

Robert Bagnall lives in Devon, England. He is the author of the sci-fi thriller '2084 - The Meschera Bandwidth', and the anthology '24 0s & a 2', which collects 24 of his 60 or so published stories. He can be contacted via his blog at meschera.blogspot.com.

A Peach for a King

Cheryl Toner

1

Peaches swung from the beam, the rope creaking woke her. In a haze, she surveyed the decrepit room. She smelled hay. Dust tickled her nose and a dog barked in the distance. Farm smells wormed into her sinuses as memories of her abduction surfaced. She glanced above her head to her strung-up wrists, rubbed raw and bruising already. Peaches' shoulders ached and her head throbbed with every heartbeat. Itchy hay clung to the heel of her sock. Her toes swept the floor. Where were her shoes? She sucked in breaths deeply, a feat in the hot air. Humidity sat on her like a mattress.

What had she gotten herself into? Her vision slowly darkened before she passed out.

2

Two days ago

Peaches always knew she was different.

First came her name. She looked nothing like a peach, all round and bright and oozing with goodness. Actually, she looked like the opposite of one, with her dark hair and eyes, olive skin and angular body. "All knees and elbows," she heard more than once. Not graceful at all.

Second, and even more indelible on her soul, was where she came from. Peaches had no idea. A dark hole sat in the middle of her chest, where kisses goodnight, family vacations, piano lessons and birthday parties with loving parents should have been. Instead, an aching void set up camp there.

She grew up in the foster system, bounced around homes, to families and back. Nothing stuck. From institutional dorms and prison-like routines to grubby trailers and shabby houses on crumbling cement blocks. Peaches lived at the mercy of ratty, rotten people who gamed the system for a few extra dollars every month. Funny, she thought. How horrible must she be to not fit into one of the dysfunctional or downright dreadful foster homes she cycled through?

But today would be different. Her palms were slick with sweat as she gripped her black garbage bag in one hand, her bus ticket in the other, waiting for her ride to freedom. She was heading south to bigger and better things.

Peaches spent her entire eighteen years just north of New Orleans. A mere sixty miles away in Sunbush, Louisiana, and it may well have been a thousand miles away. She never went to New Orleans for a day trip, sports game, concert or festival. Oh, to be that lucky. Some of the other kids sometimes told stories of Mardi Gras and crawfish festivals. Those stories were as real to her as the Voodoo, Hoodoo, and any other late-night conjuring of monsters to scare children into staying in their beds. It all sounded like a fantasy to her.

But today, Peaches was on the precipice of her new life. Peaches Thibodeaux turned eighteen years old today. She bit her lip, watching the bus pull into the bus station. Butterflies swarmed in her stomach. One little ride over Lake Pontchartrain and she'd peel off the bayou like a soiled band-aid. No more state or government rules. No tossing and turning on a musty mattress, trying to fall asleep as her stomach growled because her foster "parents" only kept her around for the money. She finally felt free of her miserable, suffocating childhood and she did not plan on spending one more day in the Louisiana backwoods.

Air brakes hissed and the bus doors swung open. Weary travelers slowly disembarked, rocking the bus as they stepped off. The humid air seemed to wrinkle, droop and moisten everything and everyone around her. Peaches bottled up the urge to yell at everyone to get off the bus. She bounced from foot to foot from her street-view vantage point, scanning the interior of the bus for the last of those disembarking. Time's a-wasting!

3

"What do you think of her?" Jean Paul nodded at a young lady in a dowdy brown dress.

Alphonse shook his head no, his broad shoulders and thick neck showed the hours he spent in the gym. The two watched buses coming and going in the New Orleans terminal, the windows reflected in cheap sunglasses. The men waited, but not for anything so pedestrian as a bus.

Jean Paul and Alphonse perked up when they saw a lanky teenager with dark hair step off a bus. Her ill-fitting pink and white tie-dye t-shirt and blue jean shorts screamed of rifling through thrift store racks. She looked around, surveying the tall buildings, highway overpasses and church steeple a few blocks away. She smiled, paused, and stepped with confidence toward the terminal.

They glanced around. Amazing how quickly the area cleared out once the bus doors opened. An unattended bags announcement echoed through the halls, fluorescent lights flickering. It was near dusk and, with the exception of a homeless man with an overflowing shopping cart nearby, nobody lingered. Jean Paul and Alphonse looked at each other, nodding.

They were fishing, and this young lady had no idea they planned on reeling her in.

4

"Oh!" Peaches stopped short. Two fit young men stepped in her path, smiles plastered on their faces. Sunglasses kept her from seeing their eyes. They were well-muscled white men with gelled hair, dressed in cargo shorts and polo shirts.

"Hey there little lady. You just arrive in town?" Jean Paul pointed to her garbage bag.

Peaches faltered, glancing back to the empty bus and then over their shoulders to the terminal. Somehow, the bus driver and the couple dozen or so bus riders seemed to have vanished. "Uh, yeah." She stepped back a step, her pink flip-flop askew. "Can I help you?"

"Oh no darlin, we're here to help you." Alphonse's smile matched his partner's. "You see, we're the unofficial welcome ambassadors to the Big Easy." He spread his arms wide, muscles flexing.

Peaches glanced back and forth between the two men. She burst out laughing. "Oh, that's funny! You know, I read online about this sort of thing. Looking for some simpleton, a babe in the woods, gettin' off the bus and just scoopin' her up for some type of sick, sexual stuff." She wagged a finger back and forth. "Not today, gentlemen."

"Okay, you're right," said Jean Paul. "We're not really ambassadors. You got us! But we are definitely here to help. Why would you think we'd have an ulterior motive?"

"Pluuuuease," Peaches dragged the word out, hip cocked. "I know I'm from the sticks, but we got street smarts where I come from. Now get out of my way."

"Please, let us help you. What's your name?" Jean Paul asked.

"Peaches," she replied defiantly, chin jutted out.

"Where are you going Peaches?" Alphonse asked. "I mean, what's your plan? That trash bag says you ain't rollin' in the dough, so maybe we can help you out." He smiled at his partner. "Maybe you need a ride?"

Peaches shook her head. "Sorry gentlemen, I'm on my own path." She turned to walk around them.

Jean Paul reached out, roughly grabbed her arm and pulled her toward the parking lot. "No, sorry goes to the lady," Jean Paul growled. "We have plans and you're exactly what we need."

Peaches yelped and struggled, grabbing Jean Paul by the hair. Before she could scream or cause a bigger scene, Alphonse took a 9mm from the back of his waistband and hit the back of her head. As she started to fall, she sensed Jean Paul toss her over his shoulder.

5

What the hell is this? Peaches' blurry vision could only make out cobwebbed and dusty rafters above. Her head throbbed and her arms and shoulders ached. She twisted her neck, her body following. As she blinked and twisted a bit more, she realized she was strung up from the rafters.

Sunlight streamed in through poorly boarded up windows. Dust motes floated lazily through shafts of light. Peaches gazed around. She dangled in some sort of large workshop or barn. Her toes grazed the rough cement floor. She dangled above the center of a red painted circle, about six feet across. Directly below her the cement was a mess, all charred and ashy.

Her eyes darted to the circle, the charred cement, the rafters, her chafed wrists and throbbing hands above her head. The gravity of her situation cleared the fog from her mind and spread like the cresting sun. Peaches began to feel suffocated, struggling to breathe. "Helllp…she whimpered, too weak for a proper shout.

Her lungs cried for air. She struggled, yanking her arms and kicking feet, but the effort and magnitude of the situation overwhelmed her. She sucked in one more breath and fainted.

6

"Look at her." Jean Paul chuckled, tapping the monitor and swiveling back to Alphonse. "Same as the last one."

The men relaxed in the dining room of Jean Paul's aunt's house as they watched their victim struggle in the barn out back. The house, nearly as old as New Orleans, had been built west of the city along a bayou.

His Aunt Delphine, well, she embraced being a crazy old bird, and her house reflected that. People driving by would see all the tools of her trade, from a plethora of yard statues mixed with junk, to a "Psychic" neon light in a window and hundreds of wind chimes hanging with the Spanish moss in the nearby trees. Customers had to weave their way through the broken furniture in the yard to make it to the front porch. Astonishingly, to Jean Paul and Alphonse anyway, Aunt Delphine made enough to get by with her psychic readings and occasional rituals.

And that's why Peaches hung in the barn. The waxing moon would crest in two days and Aunt Delphine needed a young innocent for her Ring of Fire ritual.

Jean Paul turned the monitor off. "No one's going to come looking for this piece of trash."

Alphonse looked up from his phone. "Think we can go back into town? This old house always gives me the creeps. I want to hit up Frenchman Street. You know, that jazz bar. Check out the ladies. We can get some good grub there too."

"Sounds like a plan. Let's go."

7

Upstairs, Delphine scraped her yellow teeth with the end of a small stick as she watched her nephew Jean Paul and his friend back the dark sedan with tinted windows out of her driveway. She wrapped herself in a colorful flowered robe over her nightgown, her fine, white hair a victim of a restless nights' sleep. She sat in front of a dresser covered with candles and tchotchke, perfumes, lotions and potions. Musky incense thickened the air.

She didn't like the friend. Never did since Babette birthed him. His beady eyes and pointy nose made him look like a rat. But, since his mother was one of Delphine's oldest friends, and his mother needed help, well, she knew she'd have to put up with the young man.

Babette and Delphine couldn't have been more opposite. How they became fast friends began as a fluke. Delphine hung out in her mother's spiritual store and Babette came in with her mother. While the adults talked, Babette discovered a basket of commercialized voodoo dolls. The doll's fat little purple bodies with copious white stitching made Babette laugh and she searched for her mother to show her what she found.

Instead, she found Delphine.

Babette's stature screamed "city," with her smoothed back golden hair, pigtails, button-up white shirt, plaid skirt, and properly buckled Mary Janes. Delphine, not so much. She was a mirror image of her mother in a flowery, summer dress, her wild dark hair held down by a bedazzled headband. Her feet were bare, the bottoms black with dirt. Both were miniature versions of their older selves with Babette's freckly arms and nearly translucent skin, a contrast to Delphine's golden brown.

The ten-year-olds ran, stopped and rifled through bins around the store, Delphine pointing out what she liked, all the new trinkets, and the use for various objects. Through their laughter and talking, the two girls realized they went to the same middle school. From that day, they were inseparable.

Fast forward ten years. Babette married an uptight gentleman from the Garden District. Kingston was a man with soft hands who wore tailored velvet suit vests and bowler hats. He inherited his posh lifestyle from his ancestor's plantations, never having worked a day in his life. Being just twenty years old, Babette became smitten with his manners and generous gifts, but didn't realize until after the nuptials it was all window dressing. Her husband was a dictator, a drunk, and a philanderer, all disguised as a southern gentleman.

Babette's husband didn't fancy Delphine at all. The feeling was mutual. Delphine's flowy, mystical style was in complete contrast to the man's entitled behavior. And, as it happened, Babette's joy at being married dwindled over the years. Just the sound of his voice churned acid in her stomach. Turns out, she wanted a partner, not someone lording over her, passing out on the floor, or coming home smelling of another woman's perfume.

So now, after being married for two decades, Babette asked Delphine for help. And Babette wasn't asking for something little. She requested a permanent solution to her marital woes.

Delphine glanced to her backyard, worry wrinkling her brow. She hated doing the ring of fire ritual. Not that she cared much about the young lady hanging in her barn. The girl made no difference to Delphine.

Delphine worried about her nephew. Family was the closest bond. Blood over anything else. She had to bail him out of jail a couple of times in the last ten years. Just minor stuff, but Jean Paul knew the inside of a jail cell before he could drink. Alphonse? He was Babette's son and Jean Paul's closest friend. Frogs on a log and all that. Delphine needed at least one of them to help. The ritual took a lot out of Delphine. The last time she did it, she literally aged a decade. But, if her best friend needed her help, Delphine would do just about anything. That's what best friends do.

8

Jean Paul and Alphonse parked on a side street, a short walk from Frenchman Street. As they sauntered to the jazz club, they encountered a couple of barely twenty-one young ladies.

"Hey there guyssssss," slurred the blond one, a two-foot-tall pink drink clutched in one hand. "We found the drinks! Now where's the party?"

Jean Paul held out a hand to stop Alphonse, while holding the other hand to his chest. "Us?"

"Of course, you." The other young lady giggled, her dark hair cut in a bob, much of it covering her sweaty face. She shook it out of her eyes. "We want to dance!" She then whirled around, her own tall, pink drink sloshing over the rim. "Where's the party?"

The men glanced at each other. They already had a girl for the ritual, so meeting up with these ladies, well, who wasn't up for just plain fun? They both grinned, a nearly ear-to-ear smile on everyone's faces.

Alphonse bent at the waist and extended his arm. "Come this way ladies. We know the perfect place."

9

Babette lounged in silk pajamas on silk sheets, a nail file aimlessly running over the tips of her nails. From her second-floor bedroom she could hear traffic and pedestrians out front. All the houses on her street were McMansions with a respectable distance between each structure. With enormous, multi-floor balconies and floor to ceiling windows, they were a sight to behold from the tree-lined street.

Inside, they were just as grand. The sweeping staircase, soaring ceilings and high-end touches throughout were breathtaking, even to Babette. She came from an upper middle-class home, yet this updated piece of architectural history made jaws drop. That's why she stuck it out as long as she did. She certainly didn't do it for love.

Her husband, Kingston Eli LaBlanc, inherited the material things, but not the gentleman part. Sure, he put on a show socially and obviously for her. It was the biggest bait-and-switch Babette ever fell for. Their wedding night proved that. A dominating narcissist, Kingston drank so much the ugly came out, then treated her like a prostitute. It's been like that ever since.

She thought things would change. She did her best to placate Kingston when he came home liquored up, and sometimes it worked, but usually it didn't. And that frame of mind came about daily. Why wouldn't it? Kingston didn't have to work, so he focused on what he called his social game, which included drinking to excess and inappropriately groping and talking to any lady nearby. The women often fell for it, hammering another nail in the coffin of her crumbling marriage.

The men in their social circle looked the other way but talked about him behind his back, plastering fake smiles and uttering, "How are you doing?" to keep in his good graces. After all, Kingston was New Orleans royalty.

But Babette had two decades of his crap. She finally reached her tipping point of being treated like an object, "shushed," cheated on, and just generally a feeling of sadness. Catching her husband in bed with a coed became the final straw. She screamed at them and threw the lotions and whatnot from her nightstand at them. The coed ran half naked downstairs, through the house and past the cook. Totally mortifying for Babette. Kingston later passed out on the bathroom floor. Rather than help him to a bed, not hers, of course, she kicked his bloated stomach and stepped over him. Babette wouldn't bend forward two degrees and extend one hand to help out that drunken lothario.

After the most recent "incident," Kingston forced her to see someone, weaving a story of how his "fragile" wife couldn't function because of depression. After all, it wasn't like he acted any differently. He thought a good bourbon could fix nearly any problem, but Babette's doctor only prescribed sleeping pills. She was prescribed nothing for depression. Realistically, to fix depression, she'd have to get rid of the problem. That, she knew.

"Chere!" Kingston yelled from the bottom of the stairs.

Babette sighed, pausing her nail filing. *Speak of the devil.* Just two more days, Delphine had promised her, and then her problem would be gone.

10

The next morning Delphine pulled one of her books from the shelf by her vanity. The edges were brown and brittle, the pages yellowed with time. She opened the book and it filled her lap, the page size large enough to stay open on its own. She gently flipped through the words and diagrams, searching for The Ring of Fire spell. She did this spell before. Her mother had taught her.

She smiled nostalgically, finding the spell. Two facing pages were filled with a circular design for the floor and just a few phrases to recite. That's it. Delphine absentmindedly ran her fingers around the circle, scanning the words. *This is a good one* she told herself.

She looked up and breathed deeply. Gratitude filled her, knowing she could help out her friend. After the ceremony tomorrow night, Babette would be a happy, rich woman. Not that Babette's husband would die. This spell had something even better coming his way. Delphine smiled and nodded. He surely deserved it.

11

The sound of car tires crunching on gravel jerked Peaches awake. She moved, trying to stretch in her awkward, hanging position. Car doors slammed and voices headed her way. Her reptile brain sounded all alarms, causing Peaches to twist even more, despite her knowing her actions were fruitless.

A side door opened, the setting sun spilling into the nearly empty space. Bales of old hay were stacked waist high on the opposite end of the small barn. A well-muscled young man held the door open as two stooped old women shuffled in. She remembered him from the bus station.

Peaches rolled her head to the side. She wanted to demand an explanation, but could only utter, "Water."

"Oh Alphonse, you didn't feed or water this young lady?" The old lady with the "palms read here" look about her asked the man after he closed the door. "We can't have that." She walked forward, extending a water bottle to Peaches' lips. "Here chere, drink."

"What you care about her for?" asked the man. "Your nephew's in jail. That's who you should be worried about."

Delphine looked back to him. "Mind your place now." She looked to the other lady. "Babette, is that how you taught your son to treat women?"

Babette shook her head. "You know me. This issue right here," she waved her hands in circles towards her son, "is alllll Kingston. Why do you think we're here?"

Alphonse shook his head and tsked. "Ain't nothing wrong with me. After all, Miss Delphine, I ain't the one in jail right now."

Delphine looked back to Peaches. "That may be, but the both of you should've been here, not fightin' in a bar. You should'a made sure this little lady was ready for the ritual. I can't have her on death's door."

"Whatever." Alphonse shrugged. "She's still twisting the ropes. There's plenty of fight left in her."

"Anyway." Delphine motioned away with her hands, leaving Peaches hanging. "We got to get this ready. Alphonse, can you go in the house and get the rest of the stuff I laid on the counter? I have most of it here." She pointed to a box on one of the hay bales. "Mind you, be careful with that book."

Alphonse nodded and left.

"So, you're sure this will work?" Babette looked from Delphine to Peaches. "I mean, you don't know what I had to do to get Kingston out here tonight."

Delphine nodded. "Of course, chere. When have I not worked my magic on something?" She cackled, her voice rough with age.

"Okay, well you know I've been waiting for this forever."

"I know dear." Delphine walked closer to Peaches, studying her unlined face. "I'm certain your husband will be brought to his knees after tonight."

Peaches eyes grew bigger and her heart raced. She twisted again, fearful of whatever was coming tonight.

"Don't worry dear." Delphine patted Peaches cheek. "It'll be over before you know it."

12

Jean Paul picked the crusted blood at the corners of his mouth. He sniffed and held back tears. He couldn't believe he got thrown in here last night for fighting. He didn't even start it.

The smell of piss and body odor permeated the space. His two cellmates were from the streets, finding their bunks in the cell comfier than a greasy, airless alley. Jean Paul nicknamed them in his mind, The Big One and The Little One.

The strangers also discovered that Jean Paul acted quite the fancy pants and not so tough on his own. The Big One shoved Jean Paul off one of the cots last night and, when Jean Paul dared to stand his ground, The Big One beat the consciousness out of him.

Jean Paul woke on the floor, aching all over. He scooted to the wall opposite the toilet, knees to his chest, nursing his wounds. On the inside, his blood roiled with rage. He vowed he would get even, if it came in his last dying breath. And it wouldn't wait. He'd do it here, in this very cell. After all, living with his auntie taught him well.

13

"Why in tarnation did I have to come out here?" Kingston bellowed his displeasure as he crunched along the pebbled drive. "Not even paved," he muttered, dismayed at the slipperiness of his soles and the dust settling on his shined oxfords. Kingston's driver nodded as the rotund man passed him, bourbon glass in hand. "Don't go too far. I can't for the life of me understand why the wife wanted to meet for dinner out here…" He continued picking his way to the front stoop, finding fault in every inch of Delphine's yard, pathway, creaky steps and porch. "Does this woman live in a junkyard?"

Delphine waited for him after hearing his car ease into her driveway. She swept open the front door and moved to the side to let Kingston in. "I see you remember where I live."

Kingston sipped his drink as he stepped over the threshold, judgment coloring his face as he scanned the woman's living room. "Not really," he chuckled. "My driver did though."

"Well, good enough." Delphine plastered a smile on her face. "I see you've already started with an aperitif." She nodded to his drink.

Kingston took it as a challenge, upending his Old-Fashioned glass, smacking his voluminous lips. He patted his heavy stomach. "I have. I don't suppose you could refill this for a gentleman."

Delphine huffed, turned and walked to the kitchen. "Close the door behind you. We're in here."

Kingston followed, disgust turning his lips down. Incense filled the air and cobwebs clung to corners. He smacked the back of the flowered sofa on the way through the room and a plume of dust caused him to cough. *How could anyone live in this hovel?* He never understood the relationship his wife had with Delphine. He needed to find Babette and get the hell out of here and back to civilization.

14

Peaches moaned. She remained awake, wondering why the trio left her hanging without any answers. She only knew something was happening tonight. Peaches rubbed her wrists together while trying to gain purchase on her toes. There had to be a way to get out of these ropes, she thought.

15

"Your drink, sir," Delphine handed Kingston's filled glass back to him and she retreated back to the kitchen. He pulled a chair out in the adjacent dining room and sat at the set table. The top half of the walls were papered with faded, flowery wallpaper while chipped, creamy white wainscotting ran around lower half of the perimeter of the room. He dismissively brushed the plate, silverware and napkins to one side, but then spied freshly baked rolls in the center of the table.

He grabbed the drink with one hand and used his sausage-like fingers to scoop up a roll, alternating between eating and sipping. Smacking, he nodded in approval. "Looks like you've been baking, but I don't see my wife around here. Not that she'd help much in the kitchen. As a matter of fact, I don't even know if she can bake. Or cook."

"Married twenty years and you don't know if Babette can cook?" Delphine sucked in a deep breath. She muttered under her breath.

"What did you say?" He looked at her expectantly, an eyebrow cocked, as if an insolent child had dared to get smart with him. He popped the remainder of the roll in his mouth.

Delphine looked at Kingston. "Really?"

"'Really?', what? You ever seen her cook?" He thunked his drink on the wood table. "I'm not feeling this whole situation. I don't even know why I'm here. Where's my wife?"

A host of retorts ran through her mind, but Delphine thought how easy he made it for her. Such a jerk. "She's out back. If you want, we can call for her."

Kingston threw back the rest of his drink, washing down the roll. He paused, looked at Delphine and then glanced back to his empty glass. "Somein's funny with dis." He shook his head, trying to clear his mind. He clumsily set the glass on the table.

Delphine crossed her arms and leaned against the laminate kitchen counter, watching the sleeping pills take effect. He was too busy judging her home to notice she slipped a truckload of Babette's sleeping pills into his drink. She smiled. "Sure is."

"Wha's dat mean?" Kingston shook his head again, fighting the weight of his head as it bobbed forward.

Delphine surmised he'd be out in less than thirty seconds. "Babette! Chere! You can come in now."

Babette came around the corner from the other side of the kitchen. She watched Kingston as he melted off the chair, slowly sliding to the floor. He put up a good fight, his head being the last thing to hit the floor. "Whaaaa…"

"I don't know how you listened to that gasbag all these years." Delphine walked to the chair, pushed it aside, and tipped Kingston to face up. "Alphonse! Come on! We need to move him."

Alphonse came into the dining room and the three of them worked around Kingston's body. Alphonse's gym time paid off as he took the head and shoulders and the ladies took one leg each. They carried the unconscious windbag over the tile, maneuvering him through the back door and into the barn. They dumped him unceremoniously at the sacrifice's feet. Alphonse kicked an errant arm inside the red circle.

"W-who is that? W-what are you doing?" Peaches tried to curl up, sliding her feet away from Kingston.

"Just wait and see," said Alphonse. "You're in for a real treat."

16

Jean Paul continued to work himself up. Dinner sucked, if you wanted to call it that. An anorexic soggy sandwich and coleslaw just minutes from turning sour, ordered from a mom-and-pop place around the corner. His cellmates still hogged the bunks, so he sat with his legs crossed on the cold floor.

His festering hatred of the two men churned his lunch into acid in his stomach. The saving grace from the crappy lunch was it came with about twenty packets of salt. An idea formed as he dumped the packets next to him, slowly pushing them around on the dirty floor.

17

Their live sacrifice whimpered and her eyes skittered around the barn as they filled the room. Kingston remained unconscious at her feet.

"Relax child." Delphine shushed her. "Alphonse. Get a couple of bales of hay over here so's I can sit down."

Alphonse dragged two bales a few feet from the circle on the floor. Both Delphine and Babette sat on one bale while Delphine brought out her book of spells and placed it on the other bale. Opening the book, she ran her gnarled fingers down the words. "Alphonse, be a dear and run back inside. I forgot the salt."

"Salt?" Babette looked over her shoulder. "You didn't use it last time. Plus, it won't burn."

"The last time we didn't have all this hay out here. Don't want to burn the place down. It's all the same anyway. Fire is dramatic, but I just need the circle, salt, and words."

Babette pursed her lips. "Okay. But you know how much I need this. If Kingston wakes up like this," she waved to him on the floor, "he'll kill me, and you too!"

Delphine shushed her. "I got this."

Peaches continued to whimper.

"You shush too." Delphine looked at Peaches, studying her closely for the first time. She stood, slowly walking toward the dangling girl. Picking her way around Kingston, Delphine leaned forward and stuck two bony fingers in Peaches' mouth, forcing her lips open. "By the looks of this dear, you ain't never seen a dentist and," stepping back, Delphine looked her up and down, "your clothes tell me you like a deal at Goodwill."

Peaches mumbled, "What do you care?"

Babette laughed from the bale of hay. "We don't care about you. We just want Kingston to get what's coming."

Delphine chuckled as Alphonse came back.

"What'd I miss?"

Delphine waved her hand at him. "Nothing. Now give me that salt so we can start."

18

Jean Paul's cellmates looked warily at Jean Paul. He started babbling to himself earlier and now Jean Paul spoke even louder. He opened the salt packets one by one and poured them on the concrete floor.

"...in all that I know, I command you to leave...leave this ring of fire ..." He rocked, eyes closed, face to the ceiling.

Jean Paul barely heard The Big One say, "We musta knocked the crazy into him," as both his cellmates watched from their beds.

Jean Paul continued rocking and chanting, pouring more salt on the floor.

19

"…in all that I know, I command you to leave…leave this ring of fire…" Delphine chanted, walking the perimeter of the red paint and salt circle around Peaches and Kingston. She raised her arms to the ceiling.

Delphine made eye contact with their sacrifice while their offering screamed. Kingston drooled on the barn floor, straw clinging to his bottom lip.

Delphine chanted louder. "…in all that I know, I command you to leave…leave this ring of fire…"

20

Both the Big One and The Small One pulled their feet up, trying to get away from Jean Paul. As Jean Paul chanted, storm clouds formed outside their diminutive cell window. They glanced to it, then back to Jean Paul as he continued to rock and chant, his eyes rolled back.

21

Peaches closed her eyes, willing herself to be somewhere else. *Anywhere, anywhere but hanging from the rafters.*

She saw one of the old ladies watching, smiling, leaning forward in what seemed anticipation. The wind whipped up outside, gusts shaking the barn. It howled through the cracks in the walls as lightening flashed and thunder split the air.

Peaches watched the other lady as she continued to walk around the circle, chanting and raising her wiry arms. She yelled and yelled some more. Finally, Peaches heard, "I command you to LEAVE!" On the last word, the lady cast salt on her and the old man at her feet. "LEAVE!"

22

Jean Paul stood in his little salt circle, arms cast to the ceiling and shouted, "LEAVE!"

A final round of thunder shook the jail and the lights went out. Jean Paul fell to the floor.

23

In the deathly quiet, Jean Paul heard a dog bark in the distance. Waking, he opened his eyes. It took him a moment to realize he lay under someone hanging from the ceiling. His eyes darted in confusion, not comprehending what he saw. It was the girl they had kidnapped. Hanging there. But how could he be laying on the barn floor? He smelled the hay, but he was in the jail cell, right? It was all wrong.

Babette walked close and kicked Kingston's butt. "Did it work?"

Jean Paul craned his neck to the old lady. "What? Why are you kicking me?"

24

Babette and Delphine looked to the body on the floor and then back to the one hanging. Delphine poked the girl. "Wake up, you old coot."

Coughing erupted from the body hanging. "What in tarnation are you two old bats doing to me?"

A smile spread across Babette's face. "It worked! Woo hoo!" She jumped up and started dancing around the two in the circle, her hips swinging from side to side. "Delphine, you did it! My miserable husband is going to know what it's like to be a piece of worthless property."

The young lady's body struggled, but the words that came out of "her" mouth were that of Babette's husband. "Get me down. I'll kill both of you old bags with my bare hands!"

Babette stood next to Kingston's body, joy radiating from her being. She bent over and grasped his hand. She knew her life would be much better with a grateful, malleable young lady inside her husband's fat body.

25

"Thank you, Babette. And Auntie, I channeled you from my jail cell," said Jean Paul, taking Babette's hand, looking for help to get off the concrete floor. "I wanted to get even with a couple of lowlifes I got stuck in a cell with and, and, I made a circle with salt and I thought of you and chanted and now I'm here!"

Delphine's mouth fell open and Babette froze, both looking at Kingston's as he smoothed his hair back.

"Jean Paul?" Delphine covered her mouth, her eyes connecting with his rheumy eyes.

"Yeah, I'm Jean Paul. Who else would I be?"

26

Peaches woke, the cold floor feeling soothing, but the smell offended. Sweaty men and sewage, that's what filled her senses. While she wasn't hanging anymore, her shoulders still ached from the memory and her entire body felt hot.

Through a haze, she looked around. Flashes of memories swirled in her mind. She recalled falling through a ring of fire. Now she lay on the floor in a cell. Two men stared at her.

The Big One looked at her and shook his head. "I don't know what kind of hoodoo voodoo crap you did, but try that crap again and we're gonna make you wish you'd never been born."

"I'm in jail?" Peaches slowly scooted up, looking at the bars and the metal toilet with no privacy. She rubbed her face, the rough five o'clock shadow alarming her. Something was definitely wrong. "How did I get in jail? I didn't do anything wrong."

The Little One laughed. "Yeah. We're all innocent in here."

The Big One chortled from his top bunk, leaning down to high five The Little One. "This one, he catches on quick, don't he?"

27

"If you're Jean Paul, then where is the girl?" Babette looked to the three expectantly.

Jean Paul dusted off his pants. "I always knew your drinking made you fat, but geez old man, I can't even breathe easy. Your gluttony is gonna put me in an early grave."

"Oh no!" Babette looked at Delphine. "Jean Paul is in Kingston's body now? And Jean Paul was in jail, so I guess the girl is now in jail?"

Delphine nodded.

Babette mulled the situation over, looking at the girl and her husband, who were now Kingston and her nephew, respectively. Kingston was a young girl with no money and bad teeth. Jean Paul was now Delphine's age, technically a rich fat man with cirrhosis of the liver.

Babette shrugged. "This isn't what I asked you to do, but do you see a problem here?" She looked at Delphine. "My 'husband' is now a teenaged runaway. He can go back to the bus station. No one is looking for that girl anyway.

"Also, Jean Paul's body is in jail, but does the sacrifice even know Jean Paul's name? She woke up in a body that's not hers, and she has no idea why she's in jail. We could leave her there. It's not like you won't have your nephew around, albeit in an older body. I always enjoy Jean Paul's company. Now you, me and Jean Paul can visit without worrying about my domineering husband."

Babette twisted her wedding ring around her finger. Her husband is now a young man on the inside. Babette smiled at Delphine. "I see absolutely no problem here."

Delphine nodded. "Alphonse, cut this 'young lady' down and take her back to the bus station. She'll have a wild story to tell and nobody will believe she's from one of the richest families in the city. I mean, look at those teeth."

Kingston's eyes watered, he sucked in a deep breath and expelled a howl. "You can't do this to me!" He twisted on the ropes. "People will know! They'll believe me. You can't do this! They won't believe you two old biddies!"

"Oh, they'll believe us. "After all, I am your wife," Babette said. She pulled her new and improved husband near her. "And yes, my dear, we can do this. We just did."

28

Delphine liked visiting Babette in the city these days. They usually took tea on the veranda at the back of the house. Babette's cook brought out a silver tray laden sweet tea and peach cobbler today.

Delphine, Babette and Kinston, who they called JP these days, rocked back in their cushioned, wrought iron chairs. Their glasses ran with sweat, the heat nearly too much for the trio.

"Mmmmmm, this is such a treat," said JP. He took a bite of the cobbler and put his fork down. "Not too much, you know. I'm trying to lose weight."

Babette smiled. "You look slimmer already, dear. So much better than before."

Delphine shook her head. "I don't know if I should be happy for you both or disgusted, but it looks like your marriage has been revived." She nodded to their entwined fingers, where JP pulled Babette's hand to his lips and kissed her red nail polish.

Babette giggled. "You should definitely be happy for us. All of us, as a matter of fact. Kingston, that 'run away' in her Daisy Dukes, has never made the news and," she pointed with her other hand to the side of the house, "we have a mighty fine gardener these days since your nephew was young and fit. And he does a great job with my roses."

They heard the clip of pruning shears. JP laughed. "I still can't believe you got me, er, well, you know, her, out of jail. They would've let 'em out soon enough."

"Well, my dear nephew, now that wouldn't be very southern of me to leave 'family' in jail now, would it?"

All three laughed and sipped their tea.

~ * ~ * ~

Cheryl Toner is a world traveler, having spent nearly three decades in the United States Air Force. Living outside of the United States for about half of that time, she drew from the local cultures. From living in Europe and Korea, to being deployed to the Middle East and Africa, among other places, and working in the pentagon, she weaves her experience and knowledge into her stories. She generally writes in the murder mystery/police procedural genre but has occasionally veered off into other types of tales.

Cheryl has one grown son and lives in northwest Louisiana with her husband Frank, her dog Chanel and cat Cammie.

KATE

R. Joseph Maas

When I was a senior in high school, I fell in love with a woman. It seems odd saying that because we were both just kids at the time, but there was an important distinction between a girl and a woman I had not yet made at the time. In fact, it would take some twenty years more along with a failed engagement to one woman, and a failed marriage to another, before that simple bit was sorted for me since I hadn't managed it on my own.

Yesterday was my twentieth high school reunion. I had made a mental list of things I wanted. Some were comfortable: seeing old friends, having a good meal at the dinner gathering, spending the day with my closest friend with whom I had graduated alongside and who had somewhat reluctantly come along as moral support, and the opportunity to revisit my old school; to soak in its familiarity and revel in the changes it had seen through the years. The drastic nature of the last one came as a surprise because what had once been a dark and lonely place had become much more inviting; windows had once been rare, but now filled entire walls, cramped hallways had been widened, and while some things were familiar, there was so much new in the place I could get lost when relying on memory to take me where I wanted to go. The school had become a metaphor for my own growth in the intervening decades. It too had become brighter, more open, more welcoming, and was different enough, it was hard to recognize without careful scrutiny.

There were harder things I wanted too. They were things like validation, a sense of belonging, and a reference point for where I sat in the world now against where I had been. I found some of these easily enough. I heard no unkind words directed at me from the people who had once treated me so poorly. I ran into a few old friends whom I had kept track of on social media, but for whatever reason had failed to interact with. One of which I made plans to join for dinner in the coming weeks.

As for the latter, I found myself akin to a photo where the subject is well in focus, but the surrounding landscape is irreparably hazy. I could see me clearly; the changes to me having happened so slowly they might not have happened at all without proof of what I once was, a yearbook photo in this case, against the reflection of who I am now in the mirror. Looking at the younger version of myself, I can still see me hiding in the image; there was a face that had to shave much less frequently and body with far less of a gut, but my eyes have not changed.

Most of the others were so different I could not find the ghosts of who they had once been. An errant tooth in one man's mouth matched with this one I used to know. This woman's cheekbones are so strong now, I don't recognize her at all, but her children could so easily have been someone I once knew. Or that guy, sitting away from the rest of us wearing a tag with the name of one who once upended me in a toilet. While I know his face from nightmares I still have today, he bears no resemblance to the monster in my memories. There were little details strewn about the group reminding me of acquaintances and tormentors alike, but it was like they were in costumes. Camouflaged children pretending to be adults.

There were new faces too, of course. The wife of one of these shadows, a man I once knew who has since become covered in thick, dark hair whose only recognizable feature were his brown eyes shining beneath bushy brows, managed to give me one of the greatest compliments I have had in years. After she finished eating, and as her husband and her were departing the table to mingle, she told me, "Of all the people I have spoken with tonight, you are by far the most kind, entertaining, and conversational one." I couldn't help but smile and reply, "That, I assure you, will go straight to my head." We both laughed. Before I left for the night, she gave me a warm hug when saying farewell. It was an interaction I will cherish even though I have already forgotten her name.

Alcohol was prevalent and over the course of the evening, I had imbibed a glass of red wine followed by a glass of white. Fortunately, it had helped keep my occasionally strong social anxiety (a trait I had picked up during the aforementioned failed engagement) under control. As its effects wavered over time, it helped less and less. While I had burned up my two prepaid drink coupons, the option to get further intoxicated remained open for cash, but I was saving for a trip to Mexico and an excessive bar tab was a complication I didn't want. There were cheaper ways to make a fool of myself without alcohol's aid.

As the event sped past 9:30, most folks were deep in conversation with old friends. Even the one who came with me had managed to reconcile with a man he'd had a falling out with back in middle school. Quite the opposite, I was growing a nervous need to again leave this part of my life relegated to the safety of my memory. Earlier, I had been complimented by one old friend for having gotten into the food first since he was hungry and no one else cared to break the taboo of transitioning cocktails and conversation into dinner time. Emboldened by his comment, I was growing excited to be the first to leave as well.

My friend agreed to go knowing well my issues with crowds. I reminded my friend polite behavior dictated we give thanks and bid adieu to our host before disappearing. She was a girl I once had a crush on and had in my bolder days even asked to the homecoming dance. She married a boy who often bullied me in middle school. Somehow, it was nice seeing both of them. She gave us both a hug and thanked us for coming. She also made sure to invite us to the next reunion in ten years.

I turned to leave and there was Kate.

In the list of things I wanted for the day, there too had been a list of people I wanted to see. I knew Karlee was not coming. I asked her months ago while playing against her in an online game. There were a few sophomores I knew while I was a senior who I would have loved to seen who would never have been invited our class reunion. There was also a group of friends who had joined the military after we graduated and were still serving far from home. In fact, almost none of the people I actually wanted to see were coming and the whole event was me testing if I could even survive such a gathering. At the top of the list, well above anyone else on the list, and in her own special category, was Kate. I had completely lost track of her since graduation. I wanted so badly to see her once more, to know she was well, and to say something I had kept in my head and heart.

And there she was.

An hour spent touring the school. No Kate.

Over an hour in a park with more and other old classmates waiting for a fancy pizza truck that never came. No pizza. No Kate.

Two and a half hours at a dinner, mingling on a concrete patio at a bar in downtown Denver. No Kate.

Suddenly, there she was. Not an arms length away. She had managed to sneak up on me.

"Hey, Robert! I'll bet you don't remember me," she said.

Not true.

~ * ~

Senior year of high school was difficult. And I did everything in my power to make it more so. Every kid has their goofy phase. I had leaned into mine with a sort of frenetic abandon that may remain unmatched until the end of days. Glasses, not too thick, but bad enough. Braces until after graduation. T-shirts adorned in characters from science fiction and cartoons both domestic and foreign. Shorts with crew socks pulled all the way up and never rolled or folded down. I was the spitting image of perpetual virginity. When you add on a know-it-all personality and all the social skills of the worst nerd/geek/dork hybrid, it was impressive I had any friends.

I made excuses for my lack of popularity. By parental decree, I was not allowed to work and had no allowance. No money was a pretense for not dating. Denialism at its finest. The truth was much simpler; I was a gangly, awkward oddball who looked goofy on my best days.

So when it came time for Valentine's Day, my perpetually romantic mind was desperate for love and my hands were left empty. One of the extracurricular business programs at the school had decided the normal humiliation wasn't enough and had set about fundraising by selling gourmet lollipops to be delivered in the middle of various classes throughout the day. It was a very public gift giving event.

Time has taken many things from my memory. I don't remember what class we shared nor when Kate and I decided to get each other one of those candies. I don't remember why she thought she wasn't worthy of one but she somehow knew she wouldn't get one days ahead of time. I do remember skipping lunch to have the funds to buy her one of the treats never doubting her sincerity or dedication to the plan.

I also remember when the group came to deliver them in fifth period. I remember them handing me the one she had bought for me. I also remember the tears of joy I cried when I was alone that night.

Most of all…

~ * ~

…I remembered Kate.

Two decades had passed between us. A few new laugh lines had appeared on her face and she had only grown more beautiful with them.

My brain sputtered and my heart jumped. Years of either retail employment, self-doubt, or a blend of the two still sent my eyes darting about to find her name tag. I had to be sure, I suppose. If I swooned at the wrong woman, my heart would never recover. My embarrassment remains as I write it. I found her name tag on the left side of her chest.

Confidence restored, I found my tongue, "You're Kate. And I have been looking for you." It should have been something less insane. Something like, "I was hoping to run into you," would have sounded less like I had been showing up in random bushes around town outside of people's homes, but I was happy I hadn't just gone straight to "I love you."

I continued, ignoring my own stupidity. "You look beautiful! I actually had a list of people I had hoped to see today and you were at the top." Those three words pushing harder at the back of my throat.

"That's so kind," she returned.

Putting all of my weight into the fact she had come up to me, her last name was the same as it was in high school, and those words were continuing to gnaw at me, "I'm sure you came tonight just to see me, right?" I grinned widely. Clenching my teeth helped keep my heart below my tongue instead of on top of it.

One of my classmates laughed and answered for her, "Actually she got real excited when she thought she saw you, and asked me if that was you."

My cheeks were hot, my hands were shaking, and the "I love you" strained to break free from behind my front teeth. It very nearly escaped when a man started squeezing his way towards her out of the corner of my eye.

I swallowed hard, and while my heart stayed in my throat, the important part was it stayed. His name tag clearly read his name and below it, parenthetically, "Kate's Husband".

The next breath I drew was as sharp and as painful as none ever had been before. But I managed.

I spoke with them both at length. How they met. Their two kids. Their home in California. His job as a nurse. He struck me as a genuinely good guy. I am glad she has him. At some point I recounted to them a truncated version of the lollipop tale, he laughed and asked, "How close of friends were you?" There was no jealousy, just amusement.

One of my most distinguishing characteristics is a circle of gold that unevenly flares out from my pupils into my otherwise blue irises. I joke about it being a ring of fire burning from my soul. For a moment, I saw that fire of mine reflected in her eyes as they looked back at me. A gift from the universe. An opportunity to see myself once again with someone I have loved for so many years; to imagine what could have been if things had gone different.

The whole interaction delayed me from leaving the party by only eight or nine minutes. I held her twice and met the man she loves.

Our host took a picture of us and posted it to a website. While her husband isn't in it, we are still separated by two other people. Poetically, the photo has her just out of reach. Regardless, for that captured moment, we are together. I am still wearing glasses, a t-shirt with a cartoon logo, shorts, and crew socks (thankfully folded down). It is as close as I have been for years and may ever be again to Kate. I have it saved to my phone.

So, what is it that makes her a woman and not just some girl I once knew in high school? After all these years, her kindness has remained. The girls I knew back then have grown to be better people and to treat others better. It wasn't a lesson she needed to learn.

I wonder how different things would have been had I called out to her instead, had I seen her first, had my heart escaped my throat. How badly I could have ruined what became such a beautiful moment. I imagine she too came with a list of people she wanted to see. And somewhere on it, was my name.

Since I could not say it last night, let me write it once more now and never again. I love you Kate. Thank you for everything. You have been a light in my life since I met you.

And while my love will remain forever unrequited, it will also remain unforgotten.

~ * ~ * ~

R. Joseph Maas has been writing since he was 7 years old. After decades of practice, his first published work was released in March 2014. As a single father, whenever he is not playing with his daughter, he is inevitably indulging in the worlds he imagines. He even occasionally writes some of what happens in those places for others to read. He continues to work on the "Tales of the God-Hand" and has been lucky enough to see many of his short stories in print.

Follow him if you like at facebook.com/talesofthegodhand.

THE YEAR OF THE DYING FISH

J.B. Polk

The lake slashed the canvas of the forest like a silver knife. A mass of slivers, resembling shattered glass, glimmered on the surface, but every now and then the water shuddered, the ripples advanced farther inland to lick the hills. With each quiver, the shards rocked and submerged only to appear again an instant later.

Above the lake, the conical funnel of a volcano belched out a woolpack of smoke, vomited tongues of orange fire, making a curtain of smut rain on the foliage already coated by a layer of powder.

"Another one," Vega said.

"The third one in an hour. More than a hundred in the last week or so. You think it'll blow up?" He looked askance at the other man hoping that he would say no.

"It will. And it's going to be a great one. The whole summit will disappear, and all that earth will slide down to the lake. I'd better send a telegram to San Marcos," Gallego, the geologist said.

He was a small nondescript man with the kind of face that filled up crowds in busy cities, the kind one tended to forget.

"The Indians must be evacuated." He dug his heels into the mud bubbling around his riding boots.

Vega laughed without mirth.

"Evacuated? You must be kidding."

"They'll have to go." Gallego glanced at the shimmering mass bobbing up and down then shook his head.

"Look at the fish. They are dying by the thousand. There must be an underwater connection. I saw it with the Hudson a few years back. Sulphur leaked into the lake and poisoned the water. But the flooding was worse when the whole top just toppled into the lake. The blast was as powerful as the Hiroshima bomb. And it wiped out all the hamlets within ten miles around. Nothing was left, not a single hut. Not one man or woman or child alive. Could have been avoided if someone had paid attention."

Vega snapped off a tree branch and cleaned the leaves one by one with a finger.

"They'll not move. It's their home. And they have nowhere else to go."

"You're not listening, Vega! If Tacana blows off its top, it'll be the end of this place. And of the people. So don't give me this carp that they will not move. They simply have to go."

"It's you who's not listening!" It was the tone rather than the words that conveyed Vega's exasperation.

"I've lived here long enough to know they'll not budge as much as an inch. For them, Tacana is not a volcano, but a God. A hungry God who's got bored with the monotonous diet of lake eel. A man drowned there last month and his body's not been recovered. They believe Tacana's got him, and it has whetted his appetite for human flesh. Do you think it is the first time? I'm telling you it's not. Every time someone drowns in the lake and is not found they are certain Tacana got to him. It's been like this for hundreds of years. So you can drop your modern talk and instead listen to me!"

Gallego cleared his throat and spat into the water.

"You're talking about another century. They can't be that backward…"

"Another century? Not here. Time has stopped here or at least the clocks that measure it must have jammed. For you Tacana is a geological formation with an opening to the Earth's crust. For them it's a hungry monster that has to be appeased. And there is only one way that he will be appeased."

"That's for others to decide. I can't let these people die. We don't need another El Chichon. Nine villages were completely destroyed. Two thousand dead. We don't need this. Not now. Especially with the elections coming up. The president has taken a personal interest in the whole thing. He'd have my head if I didn't do anything."

The geologist walked towards a circular clearing in the forest where two dapple grey horses nibbled on clusters of white-coated grass. He patted one on the rump and freed the animal from a tree it was tied to.

"I'll take care of the brass. You go and tell the Indians. And do it now. Before it's too late."

He pushed himself up onto the saddle.

"And remember, Vega. Your loyalty is where your cheques come from."

Gallego spurred the animal and trotted off with a muted clop of hooves.

Around the lake all was silent. Even sparrows, normally chirpy and flustered at this hour, seemed to have vacated their nests.

Vega strode towards the remaining horse and patted its neck. The gesture had a practical value—to reassure it and let it know he was about to mount. But it also fulfilled a need. The need for a physical closeness even if the recipient was a beast of burden used to harsh treatment and steep mountain paths.

It was not the first time Vega felt rootless—a mestizo not of blood, but of culture." Scratch the townie enamel and you'll find a country lout," he laughed to himself.

I'm an Indian with a smattering of education, kept at a distance by both my own and by those whose lifestyle I crave, he thought with a taste of bitterness.

He jumped onto the horse and rode through the hushed forest towards Chaual, a haphazard swarm of shacks leaning against each other in an order less row.

Two skinny mongrels barked at the horse without much conviction or interest then lay in a puddle of shade, salivating muzzles resting on bony paws.

From the end of the row, the slurred lyrics of a reggaeton song leaked out mingling with the desolate mooing of a cow.

Vega approached the third hut and parted a threadbare, stiff with dust curtain protecting the interior from the glare of the sun.

The shack was just one room. Rolled-up bedding was stored against one wall, the other part was cluttered by a wooden table on spindly legs and assorted junks whose purpose or utility he failed to establish. On the far, windowless wall hung a picture of the Virgin side by side with a 2014 Coca-Cola calendar—an amalgam of the old and new, the pious and the irreverent.

Just like this village, Vega thought. *A radio transistor spewing out reggaeton side by side with their belief in hungry lake Gods.*

As always when entering one of these dwellings, apart from a nostalgic stab to the heart, he became aware that in the silent decrepitude human figures were no more than part of the room's artifacts.

A woman kneading a ball of dough stood by the table. She sprinkled the table-top with a blizzard of flour, her gestures resembling those of a peasant sowing seeds.

"*Buenas,*" he greeted her. "Your husband?"

She pointed her chin in the direction of a dim corner without releasing her grip on the dough.

In the penumbra Vega could see the form of a man slouched in a chair, elbows resting on his knees, the head bent. He seemed to be in a kind of a trance, his thoughts taking him away from this squalid room and this sad village.

Vega grunted to signal his presence.

The man gazed up, his eyes dark pools embedded on a chess piece face.

"You seen them, Vega…" his voice barely rose above a whisper. "Dying."

"I've come to help." Vega said.

Something like a spark of interest ignited in the dark pools, but quickly burnt out.

"You need not worry. It'll be taken care of…"

The smothering heat of the fire or maybe it was the first flush of fear slapped crimson patches onto Vega's cheeks.

"Taken care of? You can't do it! You have no right! It's barbaric!" he shouted.

The man exposed pink toothless gums in a grin.

"How much did they offer you, Vega?"

"You should know better than that. All I care about is your safety." Vega tried to control his annoyance.

"I told you; it'll be taken care of."

Vega turned to the woman.

"And you, Maria? You are a mother yourself. What if it was your child, your daughter? What would you do, then?"

The woman slapped the dough on the table where it rested bulging and grey like a bloated carp about to spill its guts.

"You want to know? You *really* want to know?" She mouthed the words distinctly, each accentuated by a hiss.

"If it was my daughter, I'd not hesitate for a moment because it is for us! For the community! We've done everything. Old Villas even offered his goat. But Tacana's not a fool. He didn't fall for it. No. No-one can cheat him. He knows what he wants, and he'll not rest until he gets it. And we must give it to him, or we will all die."

As if to prove her right, another tremor fluttered the curtain and the full-breasted girl on the Coca-Cola calendar appeared to come to life.

"I spoke to Gallego. He thinks you people must leave. He's waiting for the go-ahead from the president himself," Vega said.

The man got up abruptly from the chair, straightened his shoulders and confronted Vega.

"Gallego! Another pompous ass from the capital! He thinks what he's told to think. He's not a K'iche like me."

He added after a hesitant pause," Or you."

He strode towards Vega and grabbed him by the shoulders, their faces nearly touching.

"What matters is the fish. We're dead without it."

His fingers tightened their grip.

"Have you forgotten who you are? Your roots, traditions? Has the little education they hammered into you wiped out everything? We are fishermen—without the fish we are nothing. You used to think like us, but now…" His voice trailed off and he waved his hand with exasperation.

Maria looked at her husband with calm eyes then returned to the dough separating small pieces then using an empty wine bottle rolled them into thin cakes.

Vega disengaged the restraining hands.

"You can't really believe it's going to help. You are too smart for that. You know how to read and write. You know the old legends are just a lot of baloney."

"It doesn't matter what I believe. *They* expect me to do it. They trust me. Because I'm the village elder."

"And your conscience? It's human life…Life you are trying to protect…You can't…" Vega spat out a deluge of broken sentences.

The man kept his unblinking stare fixed on the floor as if a sudden rush of sadness had come upon him.

"I must," he said, then covered his face with his hands.

Vega turned on his heel and left the hut.

The sun glistened in the sky like the fly on a fisherman's line and the village, seen through a film of dust, had an odd nakedness associated with abandonment. The shacks resembled ancient burial mounds and, if what Gallego had predicted was to happen, that's what they were going to be.

Behind the village, on a knoll covered by grass and green bushes, he spotted a group of children, noisy, puppy-like, flailing their arms and legs in a make-believe game of cops and robbers, or whatever it was Indian children in Chaual played.

"Bet you can't catch me!" One of the boys shouted as he tugged on the pigtails of a small girl.

"Bet I can!" She shouted back and chased after him with as much effort as her short legs would let her.

Vega didn't wait any longer. He turned his back to the bucolic scene and started walking towards the clearing where he'd left the horse. He knew he could do nothing else—nothing for Chaual, nothing for the children. As he mounted, he wondered if the child chosen to feed the hungry god was among those he saw playing on the hill.

~ * ~ * ~

Polish by birth, **J.B. Polk** is a citizen of the world by choice. Her first story short-listed for the Hennessy Awards, Ireland in 1996. She became a regular contributor to Women's Quality Fiction, Books Ireland and IncoGnito. She is also the co-founder of Virginia House Writers, Dublin, and helped establish the OKI Literary Awards. Her creative writing was interrupted as she moved to Latin America and started contributing to magazines and newspapers and then writing textbooks for Latin American Ministries of Education. Since she went back to writing fiction in 2020, 49 of her stories, pieces of flash fiction, and non-fiction have been accepted for publication in anthologies and magazines in Australia, UK, Germany, the USA, and Canada.

BUBBLE GUM

Moira Richardson

Timmy Anderson loved bubble gum. He loved his Mom, sure, and his Dad was alright. His baby brother was kind of a terror, but he was okay enough, despite all the crying. So Timmy liked life well enough, but what gave him a reason to get out of bed in the morning was bubble gum.

He preferred the name brand, Bubble Yum®, the big rectangle squares that burst with flavor when he bit into them. On a really bad day, like today, he'd chew two. Two was too many, really, making his jaw ache from the effort of chewing, and after a few minutes, he'd end up spitting out half of it once the best of the flavor had faded.

He'd forgotten to do his homework last night. It was stupid, and he knew it, but he wasn't the smartest kid in the room most of the time, and he knew that, too. It used to bother him more, but then he'd turned to bubble gum and stopped caring as much. Luckily, he rarely ran out.

He rationed his supply carefully by skipping lunch twice a week so he could use the lunch money his mother gave him to feed his habit. He stopped at the small corner store after school twice a week to refill his supply, and most of the time, they had the exact kind he wanted and if they didn't, well, he wasn't all that picky. Even the individually wrapped, rock-hard kind that cost ten cents a piece would do the trick.

Mrs. Peters didn't know he'd forgotten to do his homework yet, but she'd figure it out soon enough. Timmy opened his desk, while she was writing on the white board, to sneak a new piece into his mouth while he had a chance. Chewing gum during the school day had been banned ever since an older kid had stuck a large gob underneath a teacher's gradebook. Timmy wasn't a rule- breaker, most of the time, but he didn't see the point of him not being allowed to chew bubble gum during class. It wasn't like he was going to stick it underneath his desk when he was done, like Johnny always did, and he certainly wouldn't dream of throwing it across the room like a spitball because he wasn't a monster. Timmy was a responsible bubble gum chewer.

When he looked into his desk, there was something there that wasn't supposed to be. A glowing ring of fire sat right in the center, flames spitting up in a circle around his unopened pack of gum and as he watched, the flames grew larger. He slammed the desk shut, without even meaning to do it, and when Mrs. Peters turned around from the whiteboard, he did his best to look innocent, which wasn't that difficult since he really was clueless most of the time. Only it didn't work this time because his desk was starting to smoke now, thin tendrils of wispy grey trekking up out of the edges of the desktop. Please stop, he silently begged the desk, because he didn't want to get in trouble again, but he saw Mrs. Peters' eyes narrow as she looked out across the room.

"Is there a problem, Timmy?" she asked, staring directly at him now. He looked down at the notebook on his desk and held his jaw frozen so she wouldn't know about the bubble gum. He didn't say a word, but it didn't matter, because the smoke grew thicker and thicker and soon she was striding towards him. "Timmy Anderson! What in the world?"

He finally looked up. Mrs. Peters was right in front of him, but the smoke was so heavy now she was partially obscured. He could smell the wood on the desk beginning to char, knew the pack of bubble gum was definitely a goner, and before she'd even started yelling at him, he stood up without a word, because he knew the drill. "Principal's office. Now!" She snapped, her voice, angry and sharp. "Anton, get the janitor! Tell him to bring a fire extinguisher."

Timmy didn't stay to hear more. He grabbed his bag and headed out of the room, lamenting the loss of seventy-nine cents, and worse, a fresh pack of Bubble Yum®. He walked to the principal's office, slowly, dragging his feet and barely noticed the scuffle behind him as the rest of the students exited the room. Mrs. Peter's yelling faded as he turned the corner. He continued walking, slower and slower but still moving, and by the time he reached the principal's office, he was a nervous wreck. The last time he'd been here had been for chewing gum, which was harmless enough, but this time he'd left the classroom in flames.

He pushed open the door and stared at his feet when he reached the secretary's desk. "You're here again?" The secretary's voice sounded nice enough, but Timmy wasn't fooled by her tone. "I'll let him know." He didn't bother taking a seat and just stood there until the principal's door opened and he heard his name called. He shuffled his feet and took a familiar seat in the black seat in front of the large wooden desk where the principal sat.

"What happened this time?"

Timmy just sighed. He didn't look up and just stared down at his knees. He watched as one foot, and then the other, bounced slightly up and down, shoelaces swaying with the movement. "You know the rules, Timmy."

Timmy didn't say anything at all. What was the point? "No bubble gum during the school day."

"I know," he said, finally. "But this wasn't that."

Timmy could feel the principal's eyes on him, but he didn't look up, not until the phone on the desk rang. He snuck a peek as the principal was talking, taking in the man's large body that always seemed to be trying to escape from his bulging dress shirt and the mostly bald head that was always shiny no matter the temperature. Mr. Gonzalez looked nice enough, but he didn't like bubble gum so he couldn't be trusted, even with his jokes about being your pal. Timmy knew better.

He watched as the man hung up the phone and looked over the desk at him. "The Reckoning snuck on me this year," he said, as a weird expression Timmy couldn't read passed over his face. "I would never have expected you…but it's always a surprise."

Timmy didn't know what the man was talking about, but he didn't understand grownups half the time. He understood the words, most of them, but it was the combination of them that left him confused. Plus, he didn't know what reckoning meant, that was a word he hadn't heard before, but it didn't sound good. His Dad was always shouting about Timmy wrecking the place when he got home from work.

"Well, I suppose we better get on with it then."

"Sir?" Was he finally being kicked out of the school? He'd heard that happened sometimes, with the really bad kids. He didn't think chewing bubblegum was on the same level as punching somebody in the bathroom and making their nose bleed, but grownups had funny ideas sometimes. He didn't really like school, but he didn't think his mom and dad would be very happy if he were kicked out.

"You have been chosen, Timmy."

Timmy looked up to find the principal staring directly at him. Timmy matched his gaze for a beat, then looked back down at his bouncing sneakers "Chosen?"

The principal sighed and looked off to the side, out the window that looked out over the parking lot. Timmy didn't see anything but cars out there, but maybe the principal could see something he couldn't. "Why did it have to be you?"

"I didn't do anything," Timmy said, feeling indignant. Chewing bubblegum was one thing, and he knew he wasn't supposed to do it and he kept on doing it anyway, but he didn't know the first thing about starting a fire, and even if he did, he wouldn't have done it at school. He was dumb, but he wasn't that dumb.

"Let me tell you a little something about this school, Timmy." The principal stood up from his desk, groaning a little under the effort of it, and came around to sit on the other chair next to Timmy.

This was a strange development. Despite all his pal talk, the principal had never done this before. He was so close that any one of the straining buttons on his dress shirt could pop off and shoot right at Timmy, and Timmy could even smell the man's cologne mixed with the tiniest bit of sweat. Timmy wasn't sure what to think.

"When this school was founded," Mr. Gonzalez said. "The founders made an agreement with a dragon who ruled over the land at that time."

"A dragon?" Timmy had seen pictures of dragons in his story books. They were fearsome creatures with beady red eyes and green skin and massive wings that let them fly over castles where they kidnapped princesses and other such things. "But dragons aren't real?"

"Dragons are indeed real," the principal said, his voice growing deep and serious with intent. "And they are terribly smart, Timmy. Terribly, terribly smart. And this dragon, well, he had certain tastes that are frowned on in all forms of polite society."

Timmy could understand that, at least he thought he did. Bubble gum was considered rude at the dinner table at home and banned during the school day, but it was still Timmy's favorite taste.

"Each year one student is chosen to go on a great adventure... This year, it seems, that student is you." Timmy felt the principal's eyes on him again and looked up then down quickly. "It could be very dangerous, Timmy. The last...tribute didn't return. But if you succeed, you will receive all the riches you desire."

Timmy liked the idea of this. "Like bubble gum?" He imagined a drawer full only of bubble gum. A room stacked to the brim with boxes and boxes of bubble gum. A whole house full of the stuff. This sounded pretty good to him.

"Sure, kid, all the bubble gum you want." The principal sighed and rubbed the top of his shiny head. "Listen, you do have a choice here. That's the agreement. You can choose to go, or you can choose to stay. If you choose to stay, someone else will be chosen, and honestly, Timmy, maybe that would be for the best. Because the dragon…"

"Dragons aren't real," Timmy said again. The man was trying to trick him, somehow, he could sense that, even though grown-ups were supposed to be trust-worthy, except for the ones who were strangers; that's what his mom always said anyway. If you get into trouble, you find an adult to help. But this grown-up kept talking about dragons so Timmy was confused.

"Look, here's the deal. If you choose to accept the quest, you'll face a great challenge. If you succeed, you'll get all the bubble gum your little heart could ever desire, but if you fail…well, listen, Timmy, I think you should just go back to class, okay?"

"But…" Timmy couldn't stop thinking about a whole house full of bubble gum. He looked up, meeting the principal's gaze directly and holding it this time. "I want to go."

"Are you sure, Timmy?" There was that look on the man's face again. Timmy couldn't help but feel the principal was a little bit glad he'd said he would go even as he was trying to talk him out of it. The truth was Timmy wasn't sure, he was hardly ever sure about anything except for wanting bubble gum all the time, but if this man didn't want him to go, then maybe he should go. Plus, all that bubble gum…it was impossible to resist.

"Yes, sir," said Timmy. "I'll go. Does this mean I won't get a detention?" This last statement was about as mischievous as Timmy had gotten in his entire life, but he sensed, somehow, that he had a tiny bit of power in this situation, as small as it was, and if he could avoid another hour after school with the bad kids, he'd be happy about that. He watched as the principal hid a small smile behind his hand.

"Sure, kid. Tell you what…you make it back and I'll see to it you never get another detention in your life and you can chew bubble gum all day every day in school."

"Okay!" Timmy stood up, before the man could even think to change his mind. "Where do I go?"

Mr. Gonzalez stood up again and gestured for Timmy to follow him toward a doorway at the back of the office. Timmy had always figured was there for storing supplies, but when the principal unlocked it with a large rusty old key, it opened to a dark stone hallway lit with burning flames along the sides. A smell, soft and pleasant, drifted into the room from the open doorway. Timmy recognized the scent from one of the incense sticks sold at the corner store, but he didn't know the name.

Timmy looked from the hallway up to the man, whose face glowed terrible in the new light. "You confirm that you are accepting this quest of your own free will?" The principal's voice sounded dark and heavy, somehow, and seemed to boom through the large space.

"Yes, sir," Timmy said, cringing a bit as he heard his words echo back to him through the cavern. He felt a slight push on his back as the principal stepped back and a rush of air as the door slammed behind him.

"Nice knowing ya, kid," he heard through the doorway.

Timmy paused for a second then began to walk along the glowing rock walls. As he walked, the floor sloped downwards and the room opened up, larger and larger with each step, until he was standing in a large cave glowing with flames all around the edges. The smell was stronger now, but it wasn't unpleasant. Two large wooden doors stood at the very back of the space and in the center of the cavern was a large black lump that turned as he walked close to him. Timmy froze in place because looking at him now was a dragon come to life, twice as tall as a school bus as it stretched up into a sitting position, with glowing red eyes and a body full of scales that sparkled and shined in the firelight.

As Timmy watched, it flicked out a long tongue the exact same color as bubblegum. "Ahh," the creature said in a voice that seemed to boom inside of Timmy's head rather than coming from outside of it. "A new tribute." A hand surprisingly human-like, but black with long silver claws that looked impossibly sharp appeared on the creature's stomach. "I am quite hungry."

Timmy considered offering the creature a piece of his bubble gum, but judging by the size of it, even a whole pack wouldn't be enough, and Timmy wasn't willing to share that much. The creature's mouth opened and Timmy saw its teeth were just the same as its claws, only larger. The pink tongue flicked out again along with a little puff of smoke this time. Timmy watched as the smoke flowed up to the ceiling dotted with hundreds of crystals that flickered and glowed from the firelight. His mother always said when he met someone new, he should say something polite, such as asking after their health or if they've been enjoying the weather lately, but he wasn't sure what was polite to a dragon so he decided to say nothing at all.

"Has the situation been explained to you, child?"

"Not really." Timmy decided to be honest. "My desk caught on fire, and I ended up here."

The dragon's laughter echoed inside his head and throughout the cavernous space. "As is often the case." The dragon's head seemed to wave through the air and ended up very close to him, pink tongue nearly touching his skin and one large eye right u next to his face. "You must choose a door, whichever one you'd like. One door leads to all the riches you desire and a life well-lived. The other…well, if you choose that door, I win."

Timmy didn't like the idea of the dragon getting all of the bubble gum. He could practically taste it already. He'd start with three pieces, mostly because he never chewed that many at once and his mouth watered already at the idea of it, even if he knew it would be nearly impossible to chew. The decadence of it appealed to him since he could never afford to chew that much regularly, unless he skipped lunch an extra day and his mom had already said he was getting too skinny.

"Each door is guarded by one of my minions," the dragon said, and as he spoke, he snapped his clawed fingers and two armed guards appeared in front of each of the doors. They were very tall, taller than any man Timmy had ever seen, and they wore black armored chest plates. Each also held a long double-bladed staff. He couldn't see their faces behind the metal helmets, and they looked kind of scary, but his mom always told him not to judge a book by its cover so he tried to be brave. "One guard always lies. The other always tells the truth. You may ask one guard one question and then you will choose which door you will enter."

Timmy knew the dragon was trying to trick him. It probably wanted to keep all of the bubble gum to itself, so he had to be careful now. He wasn't sure what kind of question the dragon meant for him to ask—the whole thing was confusing, —but he knew the decision was an important one, if he wanted the bubble gum, which he did, more than anything.

He thought for a long time. He wondered if the dragon had any rules about chewing bubble gum, but if it did, it didn't say so.

Timmy really wanted a new piece, but he was worried he'd have to share if he asked, so he kept gnawing on the old gum in his mouth, flavorless and grown tough, but it seemed to help him think. Finally, he made his decision. He pointed at the guard on the left. "Do you like bubble gum?"

There was silence for a moment, just the sounds of the firelight crackling throughout the large cavern, and Timmy was almost afraid to breathe. The guard tipped his head to the side, just the slightest bit, but he didn't say anything for the longest time. Finally, he answered. "No."

Timmy didn't hesitate. He pointed at the door behind the other guard. "I'll take that one," he said.

"Are you certain?" the dragon's voice said in his head. There was something about the tone of it that seemed unhappy and Timmy knew he'd made the right choice. He wouldn't waver now. "Yes," he said, and before the dragon could say anything else, he went to the door as the guard stepped aside and he pulled it open, stepping through.

He was surprised to find himself back in the principal's office. The principal looked up from his desk and the look on his face told Timmy he was surprised to see him, too. The man began to stand, but before he could, the room began to fill up with packs of Bubble Yum®, hundreds of them, thousands even, and the principal sat back down without saying a word. Timmy knew, without anyone telling him, they all belonged to him, and there'd be more, infinite packs, whenever he wanted them. He grabbed a fresh pack and tore into it, spitting out the old gum towards the surprised principal, who'd already promised him no more detentions so what did it matter now? Timmy shoved three unwrapped pieces into his mouth and grinned as the delicious flavor hit him. Boy, did he love bubble gum.

~ * ~ * ~

Moira Richardson is writer and artist living in Southwestern Pennsylvania with her husband and three grumpy cats. This is her first fiction publication.

MY BIRTH GOD IS ANUBIS

Zary Fekete

When my family still lived in Egypt I attended the El Dahar primary school. One of the things the teachers taught us was which constellations matched with which Egyptian mythological gods. They also talked to us about which constellations marked our day of birth. My birth god is Anubis, God of the dead. That's a nifty thing to say to a six-year-old girl.

We moved to this stupid American suburb just after I turned twelve. Dad got a job at an American university because they were intent on hiring foreign professors. So, I had to leave the El Dahar schooling system behind (no big loss) and start re-learning everything in American English. We don't learn about Egyptian gods anymore, but nothing here prevents me from feeling like my life is still overshadowed by some kind of stupid astrological curse. I'm seventeen now, and I could actually use some help from a divine being.

I would start by asking for some mythological help with my body. My face is so round. I hate it. No matter how I turn in the mirror I can't see any sculpted lines. There is no definition to my chin. I have no cheekbones.

Mom always tells me, "Ramla, all the women in our family have bodies like you. It's part of your heritage." I know she's talking about my extended family in Egypt. But the only girls I see around me are these cookie-cutter, blond, texting, fake air-kissing Barbies. They tease me about my body and my name. Ramla means "one who predicts, future". I can tell you one thing…I don't see anything good on my horizon.

Ugh, Sandra doesn't have this problem. When she came into English class today David noticed her right away. The afternoon sunlight lit up her cheekbones perfectly and suddenly she was a radiant goddess dazzling us in front of the blackboard. How was David NOT to notice her? The other thing about Sandra is she doesn't wear a bra. Once Mr. Peterson asked the class for a declarative statement for the English lesson. Sandra said, "Bras are a tight strap of patriarchy which depress women's sexuality and lower their place in society." She earned some points with the boys. One day I was bored so I looked up what the name Sandra means. Turns out it stands for "defender of men". Irony?

Last year when Sandra found out I liked David she sent him some of her "top-shelf" selfies just because she could. That certainly got his attention. If I tried to take a selfie of my upper body my arm wouldn't be long enough to contain all of me in the frame.

When English class was finished, I followed Sandra up the hallway and watched her ponytail slide back and forth across her back like a metronome. I was kind of hypnotized. It seemed like David was hypnotized, too. He walked up next to her and they started talking. I couldn't really hear what they said. I think he asked her to the Freshman Formal. He also stared at her chest a lot.

When I got home I decided to start work on my history homework. We are supposed to write a paper describing our personal family history. I started to google some information about El Dahar, and that's when I saw the web advertisement. Google must have figured out I could speak Arabic because one of the first search results was for an Egyptian weight loss pill. It was called Tawahal, which means "transform". The slangy Arabic in the ad made the pill sound like it was different from other weight loss products. *"Magical measures, bury your old self, resurrect into the new."* Something about removing water from the body, transforming the mind, and ancient Egyptian healing. I was curious so I clicked on it. They deliver to the United States, but shipping was over one hundred dollars! Forget that!!

It didn't take me long to get bored with my history homework. I looked out the window. It was getting dark. I felt like I needed something to take my mind off the day. I went into the backyard and lay down on the grass so I could see the night sky. That's one thing I like about living here. I can see the stars. Back in El Dahar there was too much light pollution. Here I feel like I can sort of lose myself in the darkness above. It reminds me of something else the weight-loss ad said, *"Embalm yourself in beauty."* And there was something else my primary school teacher taught me about Anubis, my constellation god. His name has more than one meaning. Some people know him as the god of the dead, yet he is also sometimes called *"he who is in the place of embalming."* It seems like more than a

coincidence. If only my name meant more than just "one who predicts the future". Why not "one who realizes the future"!? Then
maybe I would order that Tawahal pill and finally be on my way real
transformation...

I finished looking at the stars and went in to bed.

~ * ~

I did it! I woke up this morning, and I ordered some Tawahal.
I used Mom's card. She won't check it before the order goes through
and then I'll have to make something up. Oh, well, I'll have it by
then. I guess the one-hundred-dollar shipping really works. It's
coming from Egypt, but it says it will arrive tomorrow. Fast!

As far as I'm concerned it can't get here fast enough. In gym
class today Sandra purposefully asked Mrs. Hutchins, our gym
teacher, for shorts two sizes too small. In the locker room I snuck
a peak of her squeezing into them. What can I say? They work. It
was like she was wearing body paint. She strutted around David for
a couple of minutes and then I heard her ask him if he would help
her with her English homework. He said yes. She batted her eye-
lashes at him. But his eyes weren't on her lashes, they were on her
hips.

~ * ~

The Tawahal pills arrived! They came in a kind of elegant,
expensive velvet box. The outside of the box was dark red with
pictures of stars and moons and the inside was bright yellow with
lots of images of the sun. Clever, a transformation from night to
day. The inside of the box smelled like it was flavored with some
kind of perfume. It also smelled dry. Kind of like scented sand.

Inside the box was a bottle made out of deep purple glass. The
only other thing in the package was a list of ingredients and a small
set of instructions. I didn't recognize any of the ingredients...
intybus, angustifolia, apricot kernel, zeolite.

The instructions said to only take one pill per day. They also
said, "Hark, manifest through thought the things desired. Cleanse yourself
before your own eyes lest another cleanse you." I was not entirely sure what
the words meant. Was I supposed to meditate or something? I got
a glass of water and took out a small, white pill. I placed it on my
tongue and swallowed it.

Then I went out into the backyard and tried to lose myself in the night sky. I could see the Anubis constellation. It might have been my imagination, but it seemed brighter than usual. I spent some time thinking about myself, my body. I also had some more thoughts about Sandra; I couldn't help it. I thought about her in those ridiculous, tiny shorts. How would she feel if those shorts shrunk and crushed her?

Eventually I got sleepy. I took a shower and then went to bed.

~ * ~

Wow! That was fast. When I woke up in the morning I lay there for a couple of seconds wondering what was wrong. I usually avoid touching my tummy because I hate that jiggling sensation that follows my every movement. I moved my hands down there, and I think it felt firmer. I thought I must have been imagining it. I went to the bathroom and looked at myself in the mirror. No, not my imagination. I could tell immediately. My face looked different. Usually it's round and plump with the occasional zit. Today it was bright and smooth and, something else. It almost seemed like it was someone else in the mirror looking at me.

Then something rather strange happened. As I stared at my face I felt like the rest of the bathroom sort of faded into the background…almost as though the lights were turned down on everything except me. My skin shown with a fierce brilliance and my eyes dazzled in a way that surprised me. Also delighted me. It was as though I was on display, and, for the first time in my life, I wasn't ashamed. I actually wanted people to see me. I really wanted David to see me. I felt courageous. I decided to wear a dress today instead of jeans. I only have two. I picked the yellow one, yellow like the sun. To match my transformation? Oh, I hope so!

In English class I sat in the front row, next to where Sandra usually sits. I got there early. Mr. Peterson came in with his arms filled with English books. When he saw me he smiled and said, "Very bright today, Ramla. New hair cut?"

The rest of the class began to arrive and, even though I kept my eyes forward, I could sense everyone noticing me. I could hear whispers and feel glances. Finally, Sandra and David came in. The moment David looked at me he stopped talking and just stared. Sandra stared too. She didn't say anything. When she sat down next to me I could feel her staring at me sideways. David sat behind us and halfway through class I felt something brush the back of my arm. I looked down. David was handing me a note!

I opened it and it said, "Gee, girly! Nice dress!!"

I looked back at him. It was very weird. I kind of felt like I had a little bit of power coursing through me. I lowered my head when I looked at him and stared into his eyes. His mouth dropped open.

~ * ~

After school, I went out to the backyard again. I tried to think all the same thoughts I had last night. I stared up at the stars. There was no doubt about it. The Anubis constellation was intensely bright, far brighter than usual. I looked around me at the trees and the starlight was actually casting shadows. As I looked back up at the sky I felt as though the world around me began to ripple gently. I lay on the grass and felt the sensation of the earth revolving below me through the dark expanse of space above. It was absolutely delicious. I don't know how long I lay there. Finally, I got up, took a Tawahal pill, and went to bed.

I had a strange dream. Sandra was in the dream. She was small, almost like she was a little doll. The doll was dressed in a tiny version of her gym outfit. I reached down in my dream and picked her up. Her body was twisting and writhing. She wanted to get away. I held her intently and looked into her little eyes. Slowly, I began to squeeze her. I could feel the tiny movements of her elbows and knees as she tried to fight against my enclosed fingers. I didn't let go. Gradually the movements slowed until she lay limp against my palm. I felt a faint stirring of a breeze around my body, and then a wind came out of the darkness and began to blow. There were strands of sand and a kind of incense smell that seemed to be coming from everywhere. A moment later the Sandra-doll started to come apart in my hands, like dust. The dust floated up into the dark sky. There was a deep moaning sound as the Sandra-dust drifted up into the sky toward the Anubis star cluster. Her essence was dried and pinned against the heavens.

~ * ~

In the morning when I looked at myself in the mirror I couldn't believe it. My face was entirely mine but richly different. I was seeing another woman. Even my eyes looked deeper. They were swirling with different colors. They contained a kind of ancient depth which went far beyond years or age. I was looking at the eyes of mythological female creation rather than a girl.

I delighted in my new appearance. I kept turning and examining my hourglass figure with flawless olive skin. I skipped school and spent the day on my computer, saturating Google with search words: Anubis, Tawahal, Ramla, Egyptian mythology, magic ingredients, anything I could think of. I learned quite a lot. About the ingredients for Tawahal, for example. Most of them are natural herbs. But apricot kernel is sometimes used to make cyanide. And zeolite is used in desiccant packets to keep clothes from getting musty. Its main purpose is to dry and preserve something to its intended state.

I also googled the instructions that came with the pills. They were taken from an ancient Egyptian text called *The Wisdom of Anubis*. The text is supposed to provide fortune for those who quote from it and spite for one's enemy. It touched on the Osiris myth, one of the key founding stories for Egyptian mythology, the myth in which Anubis allows the wife of Osiris to restore her husband's body through mummification. The myth revolves around the concepts of order and disorder, sexuality and rebirth, death and afterlife. Quoting from it is supposed to grant the speaker their deepest desires. I wrote some of the lines in my notebook.

That evening I went out under the stars again. I didn't need to look up to know the Anubis cluster was blazing. Maybe I was imagining it, but the backyard seemed like it was lit with an otherworldly luminance.

I took out my notebook and by the light of the stars I began to chant softly,

I shall see light-land, I shall dwell in it…

Make way for me, that I may see Nun and Amun! For I am that Akh which passes by the guards…

Whoever knows this spell…she will be like Osiris in the netherworld.

She will go down to the circle of fire. She will open the portal! She will touch the flame…

I took a Tawahal pill and lay down in my bed. My body was vibrating as I fell asleep.

~ * ~

I woke up earlier than usual and went directly to the mirror. I took off all my clothes and just stood there. I looked like a statue carved from ancient marble, yet alive, lithe and virile. My skin seemed to flicker and pulse similar to dappled sunlight, sand imperceptibly moving beneath. And something was moving almost imperceptibly beneath the surface of my skin…shifting lightly like blown sand.

My face glowed, my eyes shining with amber fire. My full lips, which I hated before, now full and ruby. My hair rippled, never ceasing to move as if the wind shifted it.

I wore my other dress. The red one.

I didn't go into English class today. Instead, when the buzzer rang for class to let out, I stood in the center of the hallway. When the students came out of their classes they turned to look at me as they passed…my body was parting a sea of onlooking and rapt gazes. David came up the hall toward me. When he saw me, he dropped his books. I walked toward him. He started to say something, but I held up my finger. He stood there, wide-eyed. I twisted my lips into a little smile and touched my finger against his lips. The saliva on his lips was wet beneath my finger…and then it dried under my touch.

I felt power come of my body.

~ * ~

I took two Tawahal pills that night. After I swallowed the pills it felt like my body started to shimmer. The floor beneath my feet was shifting sand on a beach. I walked to the mirror. The girl looking back at me was me. She was also a dark princess with wind swirling around her like a mirage. I felt like I could hear deep voices chanting and churning. I went to my bed and fell asleep.

I dreamed I floated above a desert floor. The sand below me was covered with thousands of people who had come from distant lands to look up at me. They brought things with them to offer me …baskets of dried flowers and crushed leaves.

I had never seen those things before, but, somehow, I knew the names. Intybus and belladonna and myrrh. Jerusalem leaves and pyrena shells and thorny resin. They laid them at my throne as they bent down to worship me.

On the horizon a storm flashed lightening, creeping closer, thunder rolling across the sand. The constellations moved and grew larger as if Anubis traveled closer.

When I awoke in the morning I didn't look in the mirror. I didn't need to anymore.

The clothes in my closet were all gone. Anubis had replaced them with regal garments and beaded strands of pearls. I chose a transparent purple sari. When I walked out the front door of my house the people in my neighborhood were all lined up on each side of the street, waiting for me. They were all naked. As I walked down the street, the people bent and swayed and moaned softly.

I went to the highest hill in the downtown city park. The rest of the town had already gathered there, their heads tilted back in a rictus of admiration as they stared up at me. As I waited I saw a column of people carrying a funeral pyre. Sandra's desiccated body lay on it, her eyes crusted white. Cyanide had leaked from beneath her lids and dried there like salt. Her embalming was completed.

I looked down on everyone, opened my mouth and a low call came from my throat. Soon the town was writhing and holding their hands up towards me. The torches touched the pyre and Sandra's body was in flames. I saw David in the midst of the crowd. I pointed at him and beckoned. He was drawn forward up the hill. When he reached me, I turned to the attendants on either side of me. Somehow my thoughts spoke to them. They removed David's clothes from his body and wound a linen cloth around his hips. His eyes were on me the entire time. The attendants brought him to me. I took him into my arms and felt a great power surge within me, as though a billion voices were stored within my heart. I looked out at the crowd, and with a cry of great force, I pointed at the sun.

Jagged lightning flashed followed by crackling thunder. The sun's brightness surged in the sky. In a flash the town below me dissolved into sand and there was nothing left except a magnificent desert. The heat was brilliantly intense, and I could feel the sun's rays penetrating my skin. I breathed in deeply and felt solar energy in the air liquify and fill my eyes.

Then the sun tore across the sky in a flash and fled beyond the horizon. In a split-second daytime was replaced with the brilliance of a night sky absolutely inflamed with stars, the brightest of which was the Anubis cluster. I continued to breathe and I felt the light of day and night enter my eyes, my face, my waiting body.

I suddenly knew things, great things, dark things, ancient things. I understood who I was. I stood before the world, a cosmic Queen. I contain within me all love, sapphic, achillean, eros... All people bowed before me. Anubis, God of the Dead, Embalmer, rested his scepter on my brow.

"How did you find me?" I asked.

"I heard your call," he answered.

I am Ramla. I have become my name. I see my future. The world is at my feet.

~ * ~ * ~

Zary Fekete...

...has worked as a teacher in Hungary, Moldova, Romania, China, and Cambodia.

...has been featured in various publications including Zoetic Press, JMWW Journal, and Intrepidus Ink.

...has a debut chapbook of short stories out from Alien Buddha Press and a novelette (*In the Beginning*) coming out in May from ELJ Publications.

...enjoys books, podcasts, and long, slow films.

Twitter: @ZaryFekete

DRAGON BLOODLINES

Bruce H. Markuson

bloodline | ˈbləd͵līn |
noun
an animal's set of ancestors or pedigree, typically considered with
regard to the desirable characteristics bred into it.

"Jamey, read me another story about Dragons." Bai was only a
nine year old girl. The daughter of Dr. Ling. Dr. Ling, had hired me
as an intern for a geneticist's position.

When he hired me, I'd just turned seventeen.

I had worked with my father in his independent genetics
business for years before he passed away. I knew more about
genetics and gene splicing than almost anyone else in the world. I'd
planned on taking over his business. I quickly learned I needed
more real-world experience before people would take me seriously.

A new volcano had formed just outside of Coban Guatemala.
Dr. Ling, from China was studying new life forms living around
volcanoes. He opened his new facilities in Coban. However he had
a hard time finding people who would work in that part of the
world.

So when offered an internship to work with Dr. Ling, I jumped
at the opportunity. There was one caveat. Dr. Ling, also told me I
might have to fill in as a nanny for his daughter Bai until he could
find a full time nanny. As it turned out, this became my full-time
job for the first few weeks of my internship.

Bai is a very nice girl and I loved taking care of her, but this
wasn't what I was hired for. One of the first things I noticed about
Bai is she is obsessed with Dragon stories.

"Jamey, read me another story about Dragons." Bai asked
again.

"Bai did you brush your teeth and take a bath like I asked you?"

"Yes Jamey, I did. Now can you read me the story of the Futs-
Lung Dragon?"

"Ok Bai." I said, as I tucked her into bed. "The Futs-Lung

which means 'hidden treasure Dragon' lives deep within the earth."

"It lived between the lithosphere and the asthenosphere of the Earth's crust. It can live in the lava" Bai interrupted.

I continued. "Where they jealously guard their precious gems. The most valuable of which is a pearl of wisdom hidden beneath their chin."

"It grows there like a pearl in an oyster." Bai interrupted again.

"It takes a thousand years for them to hatch from their egg. After five hundred years they grow a carp like head. Then, after Fifteen hundred years, they grow a tail, legs and claws. After Two thousand years they will grow horns. The Futs-Lung is not considered an adult until after it has reached the age of about three thousand years. They can shrink themselves down to the size of a mouse, or expand until they fill the space between heaven and earth."

Bai interrupted. "It's not true they live in the space between earth and hell."

"Bai, who is telling the story here?"

"I'm sorry, Jamey, please continue."

"The Futs-Lung is a benevolent Dragon unless it is offended. Volcanoes have been formed when the Futs-Lung temper is unleashed."

I added, "Maybe it is a Futs-Lung who caused the volcano here in Coban. Could something live in a volcano."

Bai interrupted again, "No the Futs-Lung died out a thousand years ago when the underworld flooded. There aren't any left."

"Ok, Bai, I think you have had enough for tonight. So where is your father?"

"He's out walking Musket."

"Every Thursday and Friday, like clockwork, he takes his dog for a long walk. The he comes back with just the leash and collar. I always thought it's a strange name for an English sheepdog. How did he get his name?"

Bai told me. "When he was a puppy he used to pick up old cigarette butts, and spit out the sparks. So, Daddy called him Musket."

"I see, a musket. It's cute?"

All of a sudden we heard a police siren go off. Bai screamed. "It's the Camazotz. The demon men with bat-wings."

"Now Bai, let's not jump to conclusions. Maybe I have been reading too many Dragon stories to you."

"No Jamey, it's true! According to Mayan mythology, the Camazotz, which means 'death bat,' lives in the underworld called Xibilba 'the place of fear' ruled by the Mayan death gods."

"Bai, a Camazotz is a small leaf-nosed bat which probably scared someone so much they imagined it as human size."

"Jamey, it's true! It's the same as the Gallu in Babylonian and Assyrian mythology. They are also bat-winged demon men who take people to the underworld."

I tucked her in and turned off the lights. I checked the news and went to get the gun before I slept on the floor next to her.

Later, Dr. Ling, walked into the room holding a dog leash and dog collar. "Jamey, how is Bai doing?"

"Dr. Ling, there was another attack. The evening news reports a person was ripped to shreds. There have been hundreds of cases reported around here."

"Yes, I know Jamey. They say it was a Chupa Cabra attack. Isn't it just awful? Don't worry, there is no such thing as a Chupa Cabra. It is probably some kind of wild animal. I have closed the fence. I also secured the steel doors and window covers around the house."

"Dr. Ling, if you prepare this house for wild animal attacks to such a degree why do you go dog walking in the middle of the night every Thursday and Friday? By the way, where is Musket?"

"Musket is back at the lab."

I asked Dr. Ling, "What is wrong with musket? He walks funny and his fur is all misshapen."

"No, he is not quite right. Musket has been part of my genetic research. Don't worry, I feel safe at night with Musket. Good night."

"Dr. Ling, have you found a full-time nanny for Bai?"

"Not yet Jamey, but please keep reading the Dragon stories to her."

~ * ~

The next day Bai and I talked more about Dragons before bedtime.

Bai pointed out the page in her book about Dragon scales, she told me, "The color of Chinese Dragon scales have special meanings. A black Dragon is in charge of lakes. A red Dragon is in charge of rivers. A blue Dragon is kind and brave. A yellow Dragon can talk to the gods and a white Dragon means a disaster will happen."

"What kind of disaster?" I asked her.

"A white scaled Dragon means there is something not right with the Dragon. Meaning there is something not right with the environment. Often floods, famine or other major catastrophes will happen. Can we read the story of the Shen-Lung now?"

I told Bai the story of the Shen-Lung Dragon, "The Shen-Lung, which means 'god-Dragon,' is a spiritual Dragon who comes from the realm of steam and mist. It controls rain, clouds and wind."

"The realm of steam and mist." I said to myself.

I went on reading, "It is said the offerings to the Shen-Lung Dragon assure a bountiful harvest. If the Shen-Lung Dragon feels neglected, his anger may be aroused causing floods or drought."

Bai interrupted me, "It was the Shen-Lung Dragon who went to war with the Futs-Lung Dragon. In the battles, the Shen-Lung Dragon flooded the underworld rendering them both extinct."

"Bai, the Shen-Lung Dragon is a spiritual idea. When bad weather came people would simply say it was the Shen-Lung Dragon who caused it. There are many Dragons in Chinese mythology."

Bai interrupted, "I know there are other water dwelling Dragons like the fei-lung; "flying Dragon" a winged Dragon which rides on clouds and mist; the ying-lung; "Responding Dragon" a winged Dragon associated with rains and floods, and the ti-lung; "Earth Dragon" the controller of rivers and seas. But there are also the fire dwelling Dragons like the ch'ih-lung; "Demon Dragon" a hornless Dragon or mountain demon. And the chu-lung; "Torch Dragon", also chu-yin; which means "illuminating darkness". It was a giant red draconic solar deity in Chinese mythology. It supposedly had a human's face and snake's body. It created day and night by opening and closing its eyes, and created seasonal winds by breathing."

I continued, "In Christianity, the devil is referred to as a Dragon."

Bai added, "In India, hell is called Patala where souls of wicked humans are sent. They are guarded by Dragons."

I kept reading silently to myself about Dragons. The Chinese, Korean, and Japanese Dragons had some similar origins like the Japanese "Ryujin", the Dragon god of the sea. The flag of Bhutan, Welsh and Moscow has a Dragon on it.

Dragon mythology itself was widely spread all over the world. From Viking "Drakkar," or Dragon ship, to the story of Beowulf and the "Fire Drake". St. George and the "Wyvern". The Greek "Hydra," a multi headed water dwelling Dragon. The Indian "Vritra," a three headed water dwelling Dragon. The "Jawzahr" from Islamic mythology. The "Naga" from Hindu and Buddhist mythology. In Poland the city of Krakow is named from the story of Kraks fire breathing Dragon. The Russian "Gorynych" a three headed fire breathing Dragon. "Humbaba," who turned into a fire breathing Dragon in the epic of Gilgamesh, 2600 BC the most ancient stories in the world. Even the pre-Columbian Mesoamerican deity "Quetzal Coati" a flying serpent god. It could not have any connection to Dragons on the eastern hemisphere.

The examples just went on and on. These weren't just fairy tales. These stories are deeply imbedded into a diverse range of cultures throughout the world.

Bai spoke up, interrupting my silent reading, "The legends say anyone eating Dragon's heart would be able to understand the speech of birds. Eating Dragon's tongue gives one the power to win any argument. Drinking Dragon's blood provides protection against injury from swords. Glass was once thought to be solidified Dragon's breath. Daddy said the Dragons evolved in the areas of the hydrothermal vents under the ocean where the temperature is almost 800 degrees Fahrenheit. He also said there are whole different varieties of life at those temperatures. All the plant life and animals who evolved there are from another life system not living off the sun but living off energy of the earth itself. At some point, the Dragon's bloodline separated. Some of the Dragons moved to the oceans and became water dwelling Dragons, while other Dragons moved into the earth itself and became fire dwelling Dragons."

"Yes Bai, I have also heard about the hydro-thermal vents under the ocean. It is a completely different ecosystem different from anything else on earth."

"It is why the Dragons and the Camazotz are so different. Daddy has most of the Dragon's blood samples."

As I read, I noticed a lot of similarities of Dragons throughout the world. Some fly, some breathe fire, some have multi heads, some are benevolent and some are absolute evil. And yes, I also noticed there are two groups of Dragons which are often depicted as similar. The fire dwellers and the water dwellers.

"Bai now listen closely," I said. "Do I have to keep telling you? Dragons are only mythological creatures. Now Bai, go to bed."

"Daddy said they have no magical powers. There not mammal or reptile. They're a species all their own."

I tucked Bai in a bit early that night. The sun was still up, but she was tired and upset from last night's Camazotz attack or whatever it was. All of the sudden there was a knock on the door. I looked through the window, opened the door, and said. "Mrs. Lopez."

"Jamey." she replied. "I just spoke to Dr. Ling, on the street. He asked me to stop by and give you a break."

"You saw Dr. Ling, on the street?" I asked.

She replied, "Yes he was at the corner walking that bizarre, strange dog of his."

"Thank you, Mrs. Lopez. Bai is in bed I need to go." I ran out of the house.

I saw Dr. Ling, walking Musket. It was Friday night as usual. Mrs. Lopez is right the dog is bizarre and strange. He walks funny and his fur is just not quite proportionate for an English sheep dog. I was wondering where he takes Musket when they go for a walk. I followed him, I kept my distance so he would not see me. Dr. Ling, walked Musket up the hillside which led to the volcano.

"Where could he be going?" I asked myself.

Dr. Ling, ducked under some yellow police "do not cross" tape and headed up the volcano. Still I followed him. He went all the way to the top of the crater. He stopped, picked up the shaggy old English sheepdog and threw him in.

"Dr. Ling, stop!" I yelled, but it was too late. Musket was already gone.

I continued, "How could you? How could you do such a thing? Just because your genetic experiment went bad doesn't mean you can throw him into a volcano."

I surprised him, "Jamey I...I..." he stuttered back at me.

"That's it, Dr. Ling, I will be flying home tomorrow. You can find a new genetic intern and a new nanny for Bai." I started walking down the hill.

"*Crunch*" I stepped on it. A curious little thing. It must have fallen off of Musket. I picked it up. It got me worried. Very worried.

I turned around and spoke to Dr. Ling. "It was a baby Dragon. It is adaptable to the lava. You have been cloning Dragons from the Dragon blood. You disguised it as an old English sheepdog under all the fur."

Dr. Ling, replied. "Musket was old. I put him out of his misery. Where do you hear such things."

I continued, "The Camazotz, the legend came from right here in Guatemala. They live in the hot underworld between the top of the Earth's crust and the mantle. Due to the flooding of the under-world a thousand years ago, they have lost their natural predators. Now the Camazotz are massively overpopulated, leaving this vol-cano to feed in this world. Feeding on livestock and humans. Now you wish to reintroduce their natural predators, mainly Dragons."

"Has Bai been telling you stories?" Dr. Ling, asked.

"Dr. Ling, I think you made a mistake with the Dragon blood-line. The Futs-lung should be red scaled. It takes a thousand years under natural conditions for a Futs-Lung to hatch. I have been timing you. You would take away a sheepdog or two every week. You are accelerating the growth too quickly. Think in terms of months instead of weeks. The Futs-Lung is quite adaptable to the extreme heat. It must have evolved from the hydrothermal vents under the ocean. You need to look at it like dog breeding. Only some traits need to be input into the hybrid Dragon just enough to make it adaptable to the change in environment, mainly the flood-ing. I believe the Futs-lung may have been a water dwelling Dragon at one point in time and has lost those traits when it obtained the ability to adapt to lava. If I could extract just enough of the genetic traits of the Shen-lung and maybe the Ryujin, I may be able to reintroduce the water dwelling trait back into the Futs-Lung DNA. Then it will be a super hybrid. It should be able to withstand the high temperatures and be able to live in the water as well. The world of fire, steam and mist.

"From now on I will be doing the gene splicing. I will need to see a complete record of the Dragon genealogy you have found and have complete access to all your equipment. And I will need to review all of your genetic samples of Dragon's blood."

Dr. Ling, let out a breath of air. "Yes Jamey, you are one of the world's foremost geneticists and you are as skilled at gene splicing as anyone in the world. I desperately needed your opinion. I couldn't tell you outright and let you think I was crazy. I didn't want to scare you off from working with Dragons. So I had Bai tell you all of the stories to see what you thought. Jamey, what was it that convinced you?"

I held up a clump of old English sheep-dog fur glued to a white scale dripping with Dragon's blood.

~ * ~ * ~

Bruce Markuson is married with two children. He lives in Milwaukee WI. And has a number short stories published. Bruce is also working on a number of series.

He enjoys writing and often finds himself with writer's obsession. He says the best way to write is to have an ending then write to that ending.

BRAVE

Todd Woodman

"See? I told you he'd come. My father is brave!"

"Mmm, yes," Cantree said, watching little Ronta hop from foot to foot in front of the wall monitor at the head of the class. In a room built for thirty students, their two voices echoed. In an earlier age, she would never have permitted any of her pupils to ignore their lessons the way she spoiled this lonely boy.

"He's not afraid of the blue demons!"

"The blue demons don't exist, Ronta. Nor do the gods, or the spirits, or any of the other thousand and one silly superstitions you came to me with."

Ronta smirked, a clear sign he'd thought of something clever, by his estimation. "But my father still believes all those silly things, so for him to climb the wall is an act of great courage."

Cantree nodded, then frowned as the boy picked up his tablet. Six weeks in, and the former savage still hadn't mastered the art of summoning. He could simply choose to be in another location within the construct and be there instantly, yet still he thought in terms of going from place to place by foot or vehicle, as if the City were just another locale. If only he could focus on any one lesson. Instead, his active mind leapt about from concept to concept.

"I want to go see him," he announced.

"Of course. When he's ready."

"He's almost over the wall now. How much longer do I have to wait?"

"He'll need time to adjust to the City. As you did. And I believe you're forgetting something?"

Ronta turned away from the screen, his face screwed up in confusion, before he smiled and mockingly slapped his forehead. "Time expansion. I can't seem to keep it straight. How much time passed for my father?"

"A few weeks since I took you from your village. Four days since we reached the City, which for you feels like a month and a half."

Ronta blinked, nodding. "Right. Ten days for one, more or less."

"More, in fact, not less. But close. When your father arrives at the crèche room, I'll have to meet him there."

"He'll kill you."

"He won't. I'll be wearing another body."

"He'll say you're a soul stealer, then, and kill you anyway."

Cantree smiled. Ronta's father had a few decades of experience with hunting, fighting and killing. Cantree would download a complete suite of martial arts into a perfectly honed athlete-body. The boy's father would stand no chance. Ronta had much to learn and unlearn.

~ * ~

Ahnkeh lowered himself to the ground on the inside of the wall. He squinted up at Father Sun one last time, holding up his hand to block the orange disk and its wobbly, red ring. "Give me strength," he prayed, before padding silently through the open door. The building, made of a substance like rock, though smooth sided and slightly warm, hummed like a living thing. No sign of demons, or soul stealers, or his son. It helped his courage, he knew, to enter during the day, when the blue light from the demons within would not reflect off the undersides of the trees above the wall. That he could not see their light, however, did not mean they were not there.

He entered; spear leveled. Within, flashing blue lights lined the walls, like twinkling stars trapped in stone. His gaze went to the center of the circular room. The lair of the blue demons contained six coffins unlike any burial vessels he'd ever seen. With sides made of silver, and a top made of some unknown material—colorless, like air, but solid as stone—three lay empty in the bare-floored lair. One held a warrior, muscled like a god. The second held the witch, wizened and wiry. The last held Ronta.

He dropped his spear and threw himself atop Ronta's coffin, wailing and tearing at his hair. When at last his grief subsided a little, he wiped tears and snot from his face and gazed at his only child's deformed face. Even as an infant, little Ronta had trouble nursing, his mouth twisted around a lump on his jaw which had grown with each passing year. The evil tumor had swollen so much the boy's right eye no longer opened, and his speech slurred. For the last few months before the witch had stolen him away, Ahnkeh had chewed Ronta's food for him, dribbling gruel into the corner of his mouth. He'd lost the ability to walk the day the witch arrived in their village, posing as a traveling healer.

Long, thin, shiny hairs attached themselves to the boy's head and bare chest, leading to the inside walls of the coffin. A thin black snake entered his mouth. His chest rose and fell, but Ahnkeh knew his son was no more. The body lived, just as the stories told, but the hairs and the snake had stolen his soul.

He looked closer. Had the tumor shrunk? It had! His boy's body was getting better, yet the improvement gave him no cheer. Of course the witch would heal him. Soon, she would return to live in his son's body. He stood with purpose, snatched his spear from the floor, and strode to the witch's coffin. He slammed the flint spearhead against the clear part of the coffin with an overhead swing. Again and again he struck the coffin, and after each he strike he checked for damage. A scratch, a chip, anything. After the fifth strike, his spearhead shattered.

"Damn you, soul stealer! Witch! Give me my son!"

Instead, the warrior's coffin opened. The fighter leapt from his silver box, a giant standing fully six feet tall, muscles rippling under his skin as he moved to place himself between the coffins and the exit. Ahnkeh hefted his broken spear, now a staff, twirling it in his hands. The warrior dropped into a fighting crouch; his hands empty of weapons.

"Your son will be returned to you," the warrior said, in the tongue of the People.

"Witch!" Ahnkeh advanced. The warrior slipped sideways at the last moment. He slapped the staff from Ahnkeh's hands. The warrior swept Ahnkeh's feet from under him. Finished by spinning him onto his belly and pinning one arm behind his back.

"I won't allow you to hurt me. Or yourself. I told you your son would be returned. I did not lie."

Ahnkeh struggled, but the warrior-witch's muscles held him firmly. With a warbling cry, he ceased struggling. "You said you would heal my son, soul stealer! Liar. Filth. Witch."

The warrior stood in one fluid motion, moving again to block his retreat. "Ronta is healing. His mind lives, but not in his body. Once his body is whole again, he will be returned. No one will wear his body. You have my word."

Ahnkeh wanted to hurl the witch's lies back into his face. Her face? What did it matter? He was too late. "What will you do to me?"

"I can take you to your son." The warrior moved to stand by one of the coffins. He touched its side, and the top opened with a whoosh. "Ronta tells me you are brave. Are you brave enough to go to him now?"

"Where is he?" Ahnkeh whispered.

"In a world where there is always warmth and shelter and comfort, where food is plentiful, and disease never strikes. Come, join him there. And when he is healthy, you can return here with him."

Lies, all lies. The witch offered death, and heaven. He looked to the ceiling, imagining he could see Father Sun through the building. *Should I go? If I stay, I will never know.*

He strode purposefully to the coffin, saw depressions within it in the shape of a man. He climbed in and closed his eyes. Hairs slithered over his body, piercing his flesh. Blackness.

~ * ~

Cantree watched as Ronta bounded over the neatly trimmed grass to his bewildered father. They embraced, Ahnkeh lifting his son in his arms and twirling as they laughed together. "Is it you, Ronta? Is it really you?"

"It is, Father! It's me! Look at my face! I'm perfect!"

Ahnkeh set the boy down and looked into his eyes, running his hands over the boy's face as tears steamed over his own. "I have never seen your face like this. How can I know you are my son, and not some witch wearing a body that looks like yours?"

"Ask me something," Ronta prompted, "something only I will know."

The father's face set into a stony mask. He opened and closed his mouth several times before speaking. "When your mother died, what did I say to you?"

"You said you would not let me suffer the way she did, if I caught sick. You said you would sooner smother me in my sleep."

Cantree blinked. Ronta smiled as he repeated his father's words, as if their content was not horrible. His father swept him up into another embrace, his entire body wracking with great sobs. When he'd regained his composure, he said, "I thought you were gone. Your soul…I can't believe we are both whole and healthy. Have you seen Father Sun? Have you been given leave to climb to his throne?"

"We're not dead, Father. This isn't heaven. It's just a simulation. You can't tell this place from the real world, but I know it isn't heaven. When my body is whole again, I can go back to it."

"Those are the witch's lies. She's corrupted your mind."

"No, Father. Look at the sun. There is no Ring of Fire. It isn't real, so this can't be heaven."

Now Cantree waved away a temp screen that had been hiding her and cleared her throat. She wore her own body inside the construct, but not the wizened hag she'd been when last outside. She appeared as she saw herself, not young necessarily, but early middle age. Comfortable, lithe, with just a hint of gray at her temples, crow's feet not too deeply carved, not a hint of the arthritis which had once plagued her ancient body. That body lay in its crèche, to be restored to youth for the last time. Even if it weren't for the impending end of everything, she knew her body could not stand many more rejuvenations. Even the most advanced medical technology had its limits.

Ahnkeh saw her and dropped Ronta, who fell surprised onto his butt. The father sprinted toward Cantree, his face twisted with rage, fists clenched tightly. He meant to beat her to death, clearly. She stood calmly, awaiting his onslaught.

He slowed, anticipating some trick. She remained still. He swung to strike her face. His fist passed through her as if she were made of smoke. His momentum threw him off balance, and the witch reached out to give him a slight shove. He landed on his side.

"Ronta would have died," she said. "Here, he can heal."

Ahnkeh ignored her, striking again and again, kicking, trying to tackle her, shouting curses all the while, and each time his assaults had as little effect as his words. Finally, exhausted, he slumped to the ground. Ronta moved to stand near him, hand atop his father's head.

"I told you, Father. This place isn't real. It's just a place where our minds can wander, learn new things, live and grow and play. You can't hurt Cantree. Neither can she hurt you, once you learn to control the construct. We're perfectly safe here."

Ahnkeh would have none of it. He wailed, cried, and began

chanting prayers to Father Sun. It would be eight days before he could speak rationally. Cantree and Ronta waited him out.

~ * ~

Wandering the fields within sight of the city, Ronta showed his father some of the wondrous things he'd discovered in his free time. A waterfall many times higher than a strong man could shoot an arrow. A cave that ran back into the earth for what seemed forever, with luminescent streams, fantastic rock formations, and blind, white fish larger than a man. A field where long extinct animals roamed, including giant sloths, velociraptors, and unicorns. All of it safe, warm, pleasing to the eye. He showed him plants that bore all manner of fruit, including things neither had tasted before coming to the construct, bananas and star fruit and kiwis on the same branch as more familiar apples and strawberries. Other plants grew tubers that, when cooked, were indistinguishable from pork, or beef, or venison.

These things his father could understand, since they were merely versions of the world he already understood. The auto-kitchen, capable of producing any taste or texture a human could possibly experience, remained beyond Ahnkeh's ken for now, and so they avoided the City. To say his father wasn't ready for aircars and fully immersive fantasy realms and AIs was a bit of an under-statement. Even Ronta's young and flexible mind had trouble with some of the concepts, he'd admitted to Cantree. She watched the two primitives from her office, popping in and out of existence near the pair whenever they ran into trouble. Ronta hadn't yet fully grasped that even a charging saber-toothed tiger posed no real threat, and that even the most psychologically troubling situation could be wished away in an instant.

But Ahnkeh knew. It took only a couple of days for him to realize how harmless the apparent dangers really were.

"This place blunts the edge of my blade," he said to Cantree one evening. The three of them sat around a fire, roasting vegeta-bles and a root that tasted like bison. "I want to hunt. I want to teach Ronta to hunt. There are dangers in the real world he will encounter once he is healed, pain and disease and death. This place is all you claimed it would be but living here forever would make me fat and careless. I want better for my child."

"Yes!" Ronta said, leaping into the air. "Can we do it, Cantree? Can we hunt and build shelters and live like real people?"

"Of course," she said with a smile that threatened to expose the grimace underneath. And so she coded an exact replica of the world outside the City, complete with feral dogs, inclement weather, tigers, disease, poisonous plants, and hostile humans. When she announced herself satisfied with the simulation, she released them with a single warning. "You can suffer here, right up to the moment of death, when you will be restored to health in a safe place. That's the most I can do if you really want realism."

Ahnkeh smiled and led his son into the world. Cantree watched them go, hoping there would be time to entice the father to stay in the end. Over the course of the next few months, she hardly saw the pair in their primitive training world. Others watched from the city, and their adventures became one of the most popular programs on the net. People began clamoring to be allowed to join them in this 'dangerous' world, so similar to the real world outside their construct. Cantree wondered if anyone else saw the irony that any one of them could at any time rent a body and experience the real world in the flesh. She refused their requests, leading others to build their own versions of the outside world, which enjoyed a brief burst of popularity. The trend waxed and waned before she spoke to her student again.

Ahnkeh stood over his son's crèche, gazing down at a face now nearly symmetrical. Ronta stood a little behind him, gazing down at his feet, oddly unwilling to look at his body. Cantree gave them their space, but she too watched the boy's healing body within the construct. So close now. Another month, and then decision time. The father then went to stand over his own crèche, frowning at his body, now free of scars and graying hair and wrinkles.

"I will look young again," he said.

"You will be young, not merely look it. Your body will feel as it did when you first became a man, and you will live a full adult life." And not die in a handful of years, when you reach your mid-thirties, Cantree did not say aloud. In the world outside the construct, people routinely died before reaching forty. In all her time as an itinerant healer, she'd met only one person, a woman, who claimed to be fifty, though she suspected the claim to be a lie. Regardless, the woman had died not long after they'd met. Even with all the changes wrought in the crèche, Ahnkeh might still die before forty of some otherwise preventable accident or predator's attack.

Ahnkeh looked at his feet, then placed his arm over his son's shoulders as he spoke to Cantree. "If all of what you say is true, I will owe you a great debt."

"You will owe me nothing. I heal the sick because it pleases me to do so. I bring those I cannot heal here, so they can be restored. It brings me joy."

"But…there is a payment you seek, isn't there?"

Cantree shook her head; the perceptive primitive had surprised her.

"Don't lie to me, witch. Speak your payment. If Ronta will truly be returned in the flesh, healthy as he has never been, I will pay. Or try, at least."

Now was not the best time, she knew, but she had little choice. "Mother Earth is dying, and even Father Sun cannot save her. The earthquakes you've felt over the past few years, the times when your body has felt heavier or lighter than it should: these are all signs of impending doom. The Ring of Fire, as you call the ring around the sun, is just another sign the end is near. All the wonders of our science cannot stave off the death of Earth."

The primitive surprised her again, nodding his acceptance. "Thus it is told. I hadn't thought I would see the end in my lifetime."

"You don't have to see the end. Not in person, that is. Stay here with me, in the simulation. There are others here, more than you can count. They will all stay here, and even when the outside world dies, we will live on."

Ahnkeh frowned at this. "What you speak is…abomination. When Mother Earth dies, we are meant to die with her. To live on in this pretend world…I won't do it."

"Everyone you know will die. All the animals, the plants, everything will be swallowed in a final, mighty quake." Cantree's description wasn't exactly accurate, but how could she explain the black hole set loose in Earth's core when the Future Circular Collider came online in the late twenty-first century? How could she explain the alien ring, the artifact that had kept the black hole in check for centuries? The best scientists in the City could not explain the ring.

"It wouldn't be bad, father," Ronta said. "We could live in this part of the simulation, where there's real danger. It would be just like home."

"Don't you want to see our real home? The people of our village? Your mother's grave?"

Ronta nodded toward his feet, unable to meet his father's eyes. Cantree willed the child to keep arguing in favor of survival. The boy stood silently, resting his head against his father's chest. She still had one card to play.

"Will you let me come with you, then?"

Ahnkeh frowned, opened his mouth to speak, closed it without breaking the awkward silence. After a full two minutes, he found his voice. "Why would you do this? Do you wish to die?"

Careful, Cantree warned herself. "The payment I seek is the survival of your people. Let me come with you, to speak to the others of your tribe. To ask if they would come here, to stay when the Earth swallows itself. I only want to ask them." She carefully did not say Ahnkeh would be her greatest asset. The hunter who braved the blue demons and survived. That he would return with his son, hale and whole, and himself looking younger than ever, might bring her closer to her goal.

Ahnkeh nodded reluctantly.

~ * ~

Ahnkeh frowned. His son, though healthy, still tilted his head to one side, as he had for years. The witch claimed that though his mind knew he was no longer afflicted with the horrible tumor, his body had yet to learn the difference. "Hold your head straight," he snapped.

"Sorry, father," Ronta said. He could hold his head upright if he concentrated.

Cantree glanced at him, held her hands up in a placating gesture. Ahnkeh looked away, ashamed at his anger. What hunter, leg bitten by a wild dog, would not have trouble with the injured leg even after it healed? Ronta's unfamiliarity with his newly healed body was nothing to be ashamed of. Ahnkeh knew, deep down, his own shame had another source, though he shied away from naming it.

His kinsmen were not so shy.

"She lives," Ormann, his dead wife's cousin said. "You said you would return with her scalp."

Ahnkeh pointed out, as patiently as his shame would allow, the witch had not harmed Ronta, indeed had only healed the boy.

Ormann nodded. "Yes, his body is whole. What witch lies within him? What blue demon lives behind his eyes?"

"I am myself, Uncle," Ronta said, speaking out of turn. Ahnkeh should have cuffed him for such insolence. How could he bring himself to strike his son? Another show of weakness, he knew, but what of it? The others would make their own decisions.

Ormann looked at the boy, then cocked his head at Ahnkeh, the unasked question clear to all: *Are you going to tolerate this behavior?*

"Ask me something, Uncle! Please, something only you and I would know, that I may prove I am still me."

Ormann ignored the boy. "It would prove nothing. Should I believe a witch could heal your son so completely, and not know his thoughts and memories? She healed him, yes, for her own evil purposes. She was old when she came, but now she lives in a child's body."

"She has healed herself, and now lives in her own body, young—"

"You are no man, Ahnkeh. You let a witch live, and now you believe her lies. How do we know you yourself are not a witch?"

Ahnkeh could stomach no more. He pulled his flint knife from his belt. "Speak ill of me again, Ormann, and I will cut out your tongue."

Ormann stood with fists on hips. Ahnkeh watched with great sadness as his other cousins stood behind Ormann. Honor would not allow them to fight him all at once. With his newfound youth and strength, he could probably kill a dozen of his kin. But to what end? Should he kill all the men in his tribe, just to…to what? He put the knife back in his belt. "I won't harm my kinsmen."

"You are no kin of mine, witch-man."

"I invite you all to come to the place where Ahnkeh and Ronta were healed," Cantree said, breaking her silence. "All of you may be healed! Blind Zhen! Do you not wish to see again? Old Trovha! Would you like to hunt again, to run with the youngsters with a spear in your hand? Ormann, do—"

Ormann surprised Ahnkeh, spinning and hurling his spear at

the witch with a speed he had not thought his kinsman capable of. The witch was faster. Cantree slipped to her left, slapping the shaft of the spear as it blurred past her face. "Perhaps you do not need my healing," she said. "You are plenty fast enough as you are."

"Speak again, witch, and we will kill you. Perhaps you are faster than I. Are you as fast as all of us? Leave, and take these two with you. They are no kin of mine."

Ahnkeh sighed. "I will do as you wish, Ormann. But the witch's offer is mine as well: come, and be healed. All are welcome, and none will be harmed."

The tribe would not listen. The women left, returning to their crude huts and lean-tos, while their men brandished weapons and made devil horns with their left hands, waggling the signs behind them.

~ * ~

Ahnkeh's gaze shifted from his son to their surroundings, and back again. Ronta wept silently, softly. Ahnkeh trudged along, staring at every moving thing they spied during their walk back to the witch's lair. There a puma, lounging in a tree. There a flock of birds, wheeling in the sky like a single living thing. In the distance, a herd of cattle, ambling along the steep-sided banks of a muddy river. As they entered the forest, he heard a boar snorting. Would he ever see such beauty again, living in the 'simulation'?

Perhaps he should just stay, then. Live the life of an outcast, waiting for the end of the world. What matter that his own tribe had rejected him? They would all be dead soon enough, if the witch spoke truth. If he could not live alongside them, he could still die with them. And what then?

He looked at the witch, who led them back to her lair. She had taken everything from him.

Except Ronta. Ronta lived. He was healthy and could live a full life as a whole man.

Unless the witch told the truth about the death of the world. Who could say?

"Witch," he called. She stopped, turning to look at him. "When will Mother Earth die?"

"It's hard to say exactly. The...demons within the Earth are devouring the planet from the inside. The crust—the part of the

Earth upon which we live—will start collapsing soon. Probably not less than a month, almost certainly not more than six months."

Ahnkeh placed his hand on his son's shoulder. How he wanted his son to live, to experience all that a man should see before climbing the ladder of heaven.

Just then a thought struck him, one he'd never had before.

"Ronta? What do you want?"

His son looked up at him, his perfect face tilted to one side. Ahnkeh opened his mouth to correct him, closed it with a snap. He would learn, in time.

"Father? I...I want to live. Here, in the real world. For as long as we have. I want to prove that I have learned the lessons you taught me in the simulation. I want to hunt, and fish, and build shelters, and tan hides." His son smiled, a perfect, symmetrical smile.

Ahnkeh turned to the witch. The woman stood with her head bowed, shoulders slumped. "As you wish," she whispered.

Finally, Ahnkeh understood. Truly, she was no witch, though the powers at her disposal were mighty and terrifying. She wanted to possess no one, steal no souls. She only wished to save them, that they might live for all eternity with her. He knew, however, that she was wrong.

"Your simulation won't last forever, will it?" he asked. "It will outlive Mother Earth, but one day it, too, will die."

She nodded, then spoke carefully. "The simulation, housed in a satellite, has insufficient power to reach the nearest star. Still, the City and its residents might live for centuries. Forever? No, not forever."

"Ronta?" he said to his son. "I will go with you, no matter your choice. A short life in the real world, or a long one with...with Cantree."

Ronta smiled. He took his father's hand and pulled him to stand closer to the woman. Ronta took Cantree's hand as well. "I want to live in the real world, with both of you. I want to help find other people, people who don't know us, and won't think we're possessed. Maybe we can convince some of them to go to the simulation, to live with Cantree when the world dies?"

Ahnkeh swept his only child into his arms, weeping with relief that his son had chosen the real world. And with grief, for the loss of his kin, and the coming end of everything.

~ * ~

Cantree watched the two primitives embrace, and made her choice as well. Aside from their village, where they would find no welcome, the nearest human settlement was several weeks' march from here. The crust might collapse before then. Or they might find a tribe willing to follow her, only to die with them before reaching safety. Maybe there would be enough time. Not likely.

Ahnkeh set his son on his feet, and the boy smiled at her. "Will you come with us, Cantree? We'll tell any people we meet you're a healer."

"She doesn't have to stay, my son. She isn't of our world. The simulation is her home. Isn't it, Cantree?"

"I've spent more time in the simulation, certainly," she said. Was it her home? She supposed it was. It was not, however, her calling. "I will stay with you, so I might convince others to live. If we're to have time to try, we must begin immediately."

"Lead on," said Ahnkeh. "We will follow."

Ronta's smile grew wider. "You see, Father? She is brave, too. I told you so."

~ * ~ * ~

Todd Woodman has a degree in history which he has never used in any professional sense. Instead, he is a postal worker eagerly awaiting retirement. Todd's only previous publishing credit came in 2021 when his short story Cold Comfort appeared in the anthology New Exterus. He has self-published one fantasy novel, entitled Souls of Steel and Stone, which came out in early 2022.

THE MOON'S TALE

Sean Jones

An olive-drab helicopter flies over low hills to the east and lands on our soil, stippled in reds and browns, our *gobi* that is not desert, but not grassland, not hilly, but not flat. Two men disembark as the chopper stirs ocher dust while its spinning blades glint in a ring like pale fire and wap-wap-wap to stillness. The visitors stride across the sunlit plain, sidestepping my neighbors' furtive children and my teenage daughter, the two men wending toward my *ger* through other circular, white-felt tents festooned with electrical hookups and satellite-dishes.

And, so, another Westerner, traveling with Batu Ganzorig, my country's former president, arrives in my village to take something. Westerners fail to understand Mongolian customs.

In the visitor's homeland, they may have told him this shaman's word is law, though he will not know *Tengri*, the Great Father in the sky, has tasked our nation to protect *Gazar*, the Earth. In my village, we know the treasure buried here encases the soul of the world.

I stand outside my weathered, wooden door and Ganzorig, clothed in khakis and wearing gold-rimmed Ray-Bans, introduces his companion, a Dr. Henry Painted Horse with the Bavarian Paleontological Institute, a man in a coral-red shirt and faded jeans. His shoes are rustic and tan leather, like my own. As he nods a greeting, the silver and turquoise around his neck jangle.

Ganzorig says Painted Horse has discovered two species of dinosaurs and I should trust his professionalism. I should embrace his burrowing microbot scanners and his ground-penetrating radar. Yet, both visitors know I have disappointed previous Western treasure-seekers, sending them home when they failed to revere the land after making a first finding, removing spirit without replacing soul.

"Why would this Navajo American working for Germans be different from the French, from the Brazilians? Does he believe in the sanctity of the soil?" I ask my ex-president.

"This is your ground and it is your decision," Ganzorig says, squinting and tucking into the pocket of his khaki shirt his sunglasses, their rims tiny halos of golden fire. "Hear his tale and consider."

As the visitors follow me clockwise to the east side of my *ger,* summer flies stop their buzzing to eavesdrop as we sit in folding lawn chairs in the shade facing the rounded, russet hills while the sage and shrubs of the *gobi* shimmer in the heat. I may have my daughter and her friends offer the travelers tea when it is cooler, if I feel hospitable.

While my ex-president interprets, the scientist says, "Dragons, dinosaurs of many varieties, once lived here and their stone skeletons tell stories. Your village rests above their bones, the previous academics must have told you. If you allow us to dig, we will look inside the Earth to learn the origins of all her creatures."

The Native American, whose ancestors came from this part of the world in one tradition's telling, waits for Ganzorig to translate. "I would tell you a story from my country, a tale of looking outward to find answers. May it reveal what is inside my heart."

I see a remarkable ring, carved of fire opal, on his pinkie, as I observe his fingers spread across his chest. With a chill, I notice the outstretched fingers of my left hand cover my ribs.

"His face is round like the moon when it waxes full," I tell Ganzorig as I drop my hand to my lap, "round like my daughter's, Sarantsatsral, who tells folk stories."

Sarantsatsral goes by "Clair de Lune" and she'll be "Moonlight" in French, not *mongol,* until the young women in my village wear through the names the Parisians draped upon them.

The paleontologist's brown eyes are bright, yet his moon-face shows no track nor trace of grasping my vexation. My hand clenches and I ask, "Will he take or will he give?"

Before Ganzorig can translate my question, Painted Horse bows his head and removes a silver-and-turquoise treasure, leans over and places around my neck a heavy necklace.

He says, *"Yá'át'ééh."* His round face, not flat, but not hilly, his complexion the red-brown of our land, his eyes tell me, it is Navajo for "it is good."

In *mongol,* I tell Painted Horse, "I will listen to your fable."

I caress his treasure-token, letting its weight settle around my neck, feeling its heft and coolness upon my chest and noting it complements the fiery opal ring he wears. The breeze offers the scent of Painted Horse to me, sweat and sage, sage that grows on our *gobi*, and also on his soil?

As I nod my readiness, the Navajo says, "Men from my country six times visited a wise sky woman, flying on fiery wings into the heavens to listen to her. In her voice, I will tell you the story she told. This is the *Moon's Tale*.

"'Like any children, you want to know your father for he seems remote,' the Moon said to her space-suited visitors as they collected regolith and stones. 'When you ask your mother, the Earth, she replies your father was a great drake, a Celestial Dragon who came from beyond the Sun's flaming corona. But you wonder if she quotes a fairy tale to quiet you.

"'You love your mother. She has provided all you have ever needed, save one thing. She withholds answers to life's mysteries, and you cannot stand naïveté. In darkness, you cannot abide. Your darting eyes ever dash and dart, and you hope to solve your riddles with a glimpse into night skies.

"'Eons ago, the Earth, your mother, was lonely,' said the Moon. 'The Earth revolved around the Sun with her sister and brothers, though they were not close kin. Mercury doted on his father and rarely ventured forth from behind the Sun. Venus was too vain, too cloaked in self-indulgence to be a kind sibling. Mars, Jupiter and Saturn had no time for their sisters, for they tended harems of moons, while Uranus, Neptune and Pluto remained distant cousins.

"'Yearning for fulfillment, your lonesome mother cast her desire on the Celestial Wind and an ethereal traveler, a lonely sphere known as Theia, heard her plea. She sped to your mother's side, buoyed across the cosmos, to unite with the Earth.

"'But Theia's aim faltered. She struck your mother a glancing blow, continuing on her heavenly path until the Sun drew her in and swallowed her whole.

"'Great, rocky pieces of your mother sped into space, shards of the failed friendship. Did you think I was always a sphere, round and feminine? In those early days, I formed a hoop of heated dust, a band of burning rocks, a ring of fire. In time, the inferno cooled and coalesced and made me who I am. While I am not so vain I would center this story on myself, I speak of my birth.

"'Your mother and I grew close. I became her confidante, playing the sister Venus could have been to the Earth, learning her secrets and her desires. For uncountable revolutions around the Sun, we danced as soul mates in the heavens, bound by gravity, tethered by affinity.

"'The Earth yearned for a different companion. She was sufficient for me, although I could not be the male consort she sought. A second time, she cast her desire on the Celestial Wind.'"

The Navajo-American looks into my eyes for a sign I believe the Moon's fable. From him, I seek a sign of sincerity. As his right eyebrow arches, my left eyebrow surprises me and rises.

Painted Horse continues through his translator and his voice brightens. "The Moon asked her astronaut-visitors, 'Of your father, what has your mother told you? He was a magnificent creature, a great, flaming dragon of amber and golden flames, tangerine and persimmon fire, burning crimson iridescence. He sped to your mother, heaven-sent, a hunter's arrow penetrating her to the core, heating her hotter than a cold spinster-stone like me into a glowing, scarlet ball more scorching than her conceited sister, Venus.

"'Your father was most virile, a potent dragon, I assure you. He swam inside your mother, heating her, creating quakes, causing eruptions. Your father's steamy breath sheathed your mother in an atmosphere of clouds and wistfulness and she wept from happiness, great tears forming oceans and salty seas.

"'The Earth feared I would be jealous of the children she bore by your Celestial-Dragon father and she preempted my envy with a gift, one I still hold dear. I would move her tides, would stir the oceans filled with her tears of joy. She hid her brood in the seas where I was blind to them. I rocked their very cradle, not knowing I held such influence.

"'And your mother's children evolved. As they matured, they became proud. They crawled forth onto the dry places where she could not shelter them, could not restrain them. They grew lungs and, with lungs, they grew voices and, with voices, they grew defiance. This second brood bore their father's features, for they were reptiles, fierce, terrible, thunderous lizards. They deigned to rule.

"'Had you not come to visit me, I would not have told this tale. Still, I cherish this chance to confess my guilt. The Earth tended two clutches of children, but I was barren. I had been ignored so long, forgotten by your mother with her fire-drake consort swimming eternally inside her, that I sent forth my own desires on the Celestial Wind. Other dragons answered my call.

"'They were stealthy, swift and selfish. Many streaked into her, one most unlovingly. With his unwelcome touch, this dragon's coarse caress caused a great ripple in your mother and hurled pieces of her into the heavens. A second ring of fire encircled the Earth while she reeled from the impact. For years, stony flames rained down upon your mother and, in shame, she shrouded herself in dark clouds. The darker dragon nearly destroyed the second generation from your mother's first lover. The thunderous lizards were nearly no more.'"

The American Navajo waits for his translator and scuffs the sacred soil at his feet. Is he already digging? I find myself fingering the silver necklace as he looks into my eyes and resumes his tale.

"'I must say, because you have come to see me, my jealousy has waned,' said the Moon to her visitors. 'Because I felt guilty calling deadly dragons down upon the Earth, I intercepted their paths, as you can see from my cratered form.

"'Let me cast off my disgrace by favoring you with the plain truth. Your father is that very first dragon, the father of all life on the Earth. While your troubled, second-litter brothers ran rampant, you, the third generation, huddled in the shadows, small, meek creatures with warm blood and fuzzy fur, waiting until your day would dawn.

"'Of the cruel dragons I summoned, please beware, for their ilk lurk in the dark sky and may pay a visit some fiery night. I have come to know you, Children of Earth and Celestial Dragon. Your curiosity will cause you to quest upward and outward to learn about your father. Atop distant aeries, you will seek knowledge of him and his kind, your kind. You will fly the Celestial Winds as you have flown here. You cannot deny your questing nature.

"'It was most gracious of you to come and sit at my cold hearth. This story is my boon to you, since you must go home where the air can give your lungs breath to repeat the tale.'

"This is how the Moon concluded," Painted Horse finishes his story, "but it is only part of Man's exploration. The direction in which we search reflects our inner values, be they wonder, faith or desire."

A cloud shrouds the Sun and his rays make a ring of orange fire behind my white felt *ger,* casting us in indigo shade. In this light, the Navajo American tells me, if we let his expedition excavate, his German university will engage my village, unlike the previous teams. This will be a Mongolian dig and it will respect our reverence. With programmable microbes let loose in the soil, we will paint underground pictures and we will shape and sculpt long-wave sonar signals. My ex-president says our village could catalyze a technological revolution in Mongolia, while Painted Horse expects to unearth unknown dragons. He promises to name the first *Drachesaurus tengrii,* from German and Latin for "dragon-lizard" and incorporating *Tengri,* Mongolia's Sky Father.

I must take time to consider his tale. My daughter, "Clair de Lune," and her friends Narantsetseg and Bayarmaa, bring us tea they've brewed and *airag,* the fermented mare's milk non-Mongolians rarely can drink. We men talk about the new Japanese snowmobiles and flyfishing in Montana until the light turns lavender.

Later, in the rays of the setting sun, I watch my daughter and her two friends, the three would-be-French girls, flit between tents, following the former president and his companion as they weave through my village's *gers* to lift off at lilac dusk in their olive-green helicopter. The flying machine's blades churn the air in a swirling current of ocher dust, soil that could stir up valuable knowledge.

The Moon crests the horizon, full and shining silver in the sunset, and Painted Horse is not the only one whose ears can hear her tales. As my fingers trace the textures of the Navajo's gift, treasure the cold color of the quicksilver orb, I listen as she tells me to trust the paleontologist. She says he will give as much as he takes and our village, here in the *gobi,* will provide answers to mankind's questing curiosity, and will spark a scientific evolution.

"*Yá'át'ééh.*" I say in Navajo. It is good.

~ * ~ * ~

Living in Morrison, Colorado, working in aerospace, driving a vintage Volkswagen, making landscape photos of Colorado, **Sean Jones** writes speculative fiction, often swords & sorcery.

FIRE BREATHER

Thomas Canfield

No sign of seismic activity was evident. The monitoring instruments had detected nothing unusual or out of the ordinary. But a thin wisp of black smoke curled up from the summit of the volcano, had been doing so for ten days now, and it had to mean something. Van Doren decided to investigate and see for himself what was going on.

This was a part of the Indonesian archipelago, after all, set on the notorious Ring of Fire where tectonic plates collided. The eruption of Krakatoa, though it had happened over a century before, remained a vivid memory in these parts. No one wanted to see such a cataclysmic event take place again.

Van Doren corralled a visiting scholar from Leyden University to accompany him, enlisting a local youth from the village to act as guide. They set out early in the morning to trek up the mountain on a warm, overcast day. Five hundred feet from the summit Van Doren began to discover fragments of pyroclastic rock, which had melted and rapidly cooled to a glass-like finish. He examined these specimens, perplexed. The last eruption of Mt. Galungung had occurred, according to the records, back in 1709. Yet these samples showed no signs of weathering. In fact, they appeared very recent.

"It is curious." Dr. Karl Barends, Van Doren's colleague from the Netherlands, turned one of the rocks over in his hands. "You would need seismic activity to spew forth rocks of this sort. Yet it could hardly have been so faint as to escape detection. The monitors are calibrated to a much finer degree than that."

"Let's hope that they are. If the volcano starts acting up now, things could get very ugly, very fast."

The guide, a supple-limbed youth of twenty named Rafi, also examined one of the stones. He stared into it intently, as if seeking to discover his own reflection in the glass-like surface. He ran his fingers over the stone then, suddenly, gave a short bark of laughter. "Kadal," he said. He slipped the stone into his pocket.

"Kadal?" Barends inquired.

Van Doren shrugged. "A creature of local legend and folklore. They seem confined to this set of islands and haven't gained a foothold elsewhere—at least not to my knowledge. Think of a Komodo dragon, only bigger and more formidable, and you'll have some idea what it is alleged to resemble. They are said to bathe and to reproduce in molten magma. I have, alas, yet to encounter one, and so cannot testify as to their existence. The locals hold them in high regard, however, so it is considered impolitic to speak ill of them or of those who credit their existence."

"Speak ill of them?" Barends grinned. "Heavens, man, the thought would never have crossed my mind. An organism that can reproduce in molten magma is surely worthy of the highest regard."

Rafi, who before had set a leisurely pace, now seemed eager to push ahead to the summit. His whole person, in fact, seemed animated by excitement. He spoke rapidly, employing a pidgin dialect which Van Doren could scarcely understand. "He wishes for us to hurry," was Van Doren's only attempt at translating.

Rafi led the way up the rubble-strewn slope, pushing ahead at a punishing pace. The two scientists struggled to keep up. Overhead, the sky was an unbroken mass of cloud stretching from horizon to horizon. Beneath them lay the lush canopy of the forest and, beyond, a broad expanse of open water, the Straits of Makassar.

Nearing the rim of the caldera, Van Doren detected, or *thought* he detected, the scent of sulfur in the air. Fumes seemed to be seeping up out of the earth, refuting the assumption the volcano was dormant.

Rafi reached the summit and stopped. Something in the set of his shoulders, the intent, expectant look on his face, warned Van Doren he should be prepared for pretty much anything. He stumbled up to the lip of the caldera, gasping for breath.

Beneath, lay a pool of liquid magma. It seemed to have collected there as rainwater might after a tropical downpour.

"What the hell is going on?" Barends might have lifted the question from Van Doren's own mind, so nearly did their thoughts coincide.

"God alone knows." The expression, as Van Doren employed it, could well have been interpreted literally, that only God could account for what they were looking at. Van Doren certainly could not.

"Wait," Rafi addressed Van Doren in broken English. "Remain still. Watch." The magma cast a red/orange glow upon the walls of the caldera, lending the scene a surreal aspect. "Kadal!" Rafi repeated the name of the mythical creature and bobbed his head with conviction.

A ripple rolled across the surface of the magma. Van Doren watched in horror as gas bubbled up from the depths, fearing they had arrived just in time to witness an eruption. Little spurts of molten rock jetted into the air. Something breached the surface, sounded, then came up for air once again. Van Doren's jaw dropped. A dark form paddled through the magma, as though enjoying a dip in a pool of fresh spring water.

"Kadal!" Rafi clapped his hands and pointed. He began to chant in a singsong tone, using words Van Doren did not recognize. The Kadal swam across the caldera, head lifted, giving it the appearance of an enormous serpent. It clambered up onto a jutting shelf of rock, tongue flicking at the air. The creature did, indeed, resemble a Komodo Dragon. It possessed the same reptilian cast to its features, the same profile, but was at least twice the size; perhaps twenty feet in length. The beast would have fit in admirably well in the Pleistocene era. Here, in the present day, it was a singular spectacle.

"Bloody hell!" Van Doren ran a hand through his hair. "Somebody tell me this isn't happening. Tell me I'm seeing things." The Kadal snorted air through its nostrils, glanced up at the rim of the caldera with sleepy malice.

"Did you see it?!" Barends was rushing back and forth in excitement, flinging his hands about with abandon. He appeared to have lost his head completely. "Swimming through liquid magma! That's the most extraordinary thing ever! Its hide must be as thick as armor plating. I must get closer. Damn me, why didn't I think to bring a camera? I shall have to make do with my cell phone. Here, hold this." Barends thrust his rucksack into Van Doren's hands.

"Don't do anything to antagonize it!" Van Doren was alarmed. "Better to stay as far away as possible. You have no idea how it might react or what it might do." Van Doren paused, added, "It's not a pet iguana, you know." But Barends wasn't listening. The scientist had taken over, blotting out any possible concern over his own safety. All Barends had a thought for was to collect evidence that would establish the existence of such a monster.

"See here, Barends—come to your senses. It's as plain as day that…" Barends walked away as Van Doren was still talking. He picked his way around the rim of the caldera, searching out the best vantage point from which to capture a picture. Van Doren would have started after Barends but Rafi rested a hand upon his forearm, gave a cautionary shake of his head.

The Kadal had stretched itself out on the ledge. It seemed aware of what was going on above, but not in any way concerned. It kept snorting air through its nostrils. Gradually, Van Doren became aware of little puffs of smoke accompanying this action.

Barends managed to position himself almost directly opposite the Kadal, eager to achieve the best possible angle to photograph his subject. He was standing precariously near the edge of the caldera. One false step and that would be the last anyone would ever see of him.

"The damn fool is going to get himself killed," Van Doren remarked.

"Killed, yes!" Rafi bobbed his head with enthusiasm. "Very much. How do you say—human sacrifice? You understand 'human sacrifice'?"

Van Doren turned toward Rafi, thinking he must have misunderstood "What exactly are you saying? Tell me again, so I get it right."

Rafi seemed surprised. "Sacrifice," he repeated. "Did I misspeak? The volcano demands a sacrifice. So it wasn't—doesn't? —erupt." Rafi peered at Van Doren. A small measure of concern, of doubt, had appeared in his face. "Isn't that why you brought your friend along?"

The sudden recognition he and Rafi had been talking at cross purposes overwhelmed Van Doren. He staggered backwards. What must Rafi think of him to believe him capable of such a thing? What could Van Doren have said to create such an impression—and how did he now undo it?

"Let me make one thing clear," Van Doren spoke with icy authority. "There isn't going to be any sacrifice, human or otherwise. The very idea I could entertain such a notion… "Van Doren sought for some way to convey the horror and repugnance such an act aroused in him, in *any* civilized person, for that matter. "It isn't going to happen," he concluded, recognizing it was futile to attempt to explain his reasoning.

"No?"

Van Doren could not make out whether Rafi's reply was an honest question, or a sort of taunt, a negation of what Van Doren had just asserted. But the next moment, it all became academic. The Kadal had at last succeeded in clearing its bronchial passages.

Without warning, an enormous jet of flame erupted from its throat. The flame washed over the walls of the caldera. The Kadal lifted its head, appraised the situation of the three spectators above. It might—had it been capable of such a gesture—have smiled. Why Barends didn't turn and run at that point Van Doren had no idea. His peril could not have been any more plain. Perhaps he was still searching out the perfect photo opportunity.

The Kadal emitted a tentative flicker of flame, gauging the range. Barends recorded this with his phone, seemingly lost to everything else. The next instant a torrent of fire washed over him. He swayed back and forth as the flesh seemed to melt from his frame. He tottered on the brink, pitched forward and plummeted headfirst into the pool of magma. A brief sound, as of oil splashed on a hot skillet, resounded across the summit. What remained of Barends, a carbonized mass of gristle, teeth and bone, sank into the depths. Rafi did a little shuffle of celebration.

The Kadal was more brazen. It slid into the magma and performed a victory lap, rolling over onto its back like an otter and snorting little jets of fire into the air. This display outraged Van Doren. It seemed to demonstrate a singular incapacity for compassion and fellow feeling on the part of the giant lizard.

Van Doren turned away in disgust and headed back down the mountain. A nagging feeling of guilt pursued him. Had he, in fact, done his utmost to caution and protect Barends? Or had he instead allowed events to follow their own course? Hadn't Van Doren suspected there might be something behind the legend of the Kadal? Wasn't he eager to verify the truth about the fabled creature? His motives seemed mixed, to say the very least. But then, Barends' death, while inconvenient, had certainly served a worthy purpose.

Van Doren cast a last look over his shoulder. A thin coil of smoke issued from the summit of the volcano. The Kadal, the fire breather, was in his glory, defusing yet another volcano before it could erupt. Van Doren could only hope one victim was sufficient and that another would not be required.

Only so many university scholars came to visit, after all.

~ * ~ * ~

Thomas Canfield's phobias run to politicians, lawyers and TV pitchmen. He likes dogs and beer.

GRAVEWATCHER

Thomas Nicholson

Gavin thought he'd been very clever, choosing his spot. A public place to sit and eat lunch, where no one forced him to buy anything. The neatly trimmed trees offered decent shade. Parents usually kept their kids quiet on their brief visits. And if he felt like a little cry, no one gave him any funny looks. It took a while to settle on one, but eventually he had made his choice. A single plot far out of the way, near the rear wall. A spot with few visitors. Where anyone could rest without fear of disturbance.

The inscriptions on Lenny Fry's headstone were barely visible. A layer of dark green moss had crept over the rock, hiding any memory of the man lying beneath the earth. To assuage the guilt he felt about their arrangement, Gavin worked on making the gravesite a touch more respectable. He weeded the grass. He wiped away the bird droppings smeared on top of the stone. He made his accomplice as comfortable as could be. It was the least he could do, given what Lenny provided. A symbiotic relationship, if you could call it that with one half dead and buried.

Once he had cleared the stone face, Gavin learned all there was to learn about the man in a few lines.

"Here Lies Lenny Fry,
Born 14 August 1985,
Died 5 January 2021."

The only other carving was wedged between the two dates. A scrawling, looping thing, full of jagged lines and bumps that rose, then twisted back on themselves. Unlike any Christian imagery he'd ever seen. Not a book or movie reference he could recall either. A secret Lenny had taken to the grave.

Words wrapped around the carving, encircling it like a manacle.

"To any who wonder, we are whole again."

~ * ~

Gavin was chewing his cheese sandwich one Thursday afternoon, when the crack of a twig behind him made him jump. He choked and leaned forward, dusting a coating of frost that had grown over Lenny's death date. Snowflakes rained down over the carving, filling in the cracks.

"Hi. Excuse me," said a voice. "Sorry, I didn't mean to disturb. I was just wondering if you had a spare cloth."

He turned to see a young woman standing in the adjoining row of headstones. She had a shawl clutched in her hand. A tear ran down one side, like it had caught against a sharp rock.

"I forgot to bring one today," continued the woman. "They just get so dirty so quickly, don't they? I thought… You look after yours so much better than me."

Gavin fumbled with his lunchbox, tugging a wad of paper napkins from under the remains of his sandwich. He held them out, and the woman sidled between two graves, tucking the shawl back around her neck as she went.

"Thank you so much." Her eyes flicked to the headstone in front of him, stopping for a moment on the odd symbol. "Who was he to you?"

"Old school friend," Gavin made up on the spot. No need for the truth. He could already envisage the worried look on the woman's face if he mentioned his preference for the company of dead strangers over live colleagues.

The woman raised an eyebrow. "Were you close?"

Gavin shrugged, stared down at the grass. Less was more in these situations, he found.

"Sorry. I'm intruding. Ignore me. I don't get to speak to people much. It's just, I see you here a lot. I remember the service. Not a lot of people came."

"You were at the service?" Gavin asked, against his better judgement.

"Well, kind of. I work here." She pointed to the reception hall by the main gate. Smoke from the chimney next door twisted in the air, drifting towards them. "I was on the desk that day. I see a lot of small funerals, but his…" She drew in a breath, and Gavin was sure he heard a catch in her throat. "His I remember."

~ * ~

The woman grabbed two coffees from the vending machine by her desk. Snow fell gently against the windows, and rather than head back to work early, Gavin waited to hear more about his underground acquaintance. Maybe he'd learn Lenny had a fondness for a certain type of flower. If he could lay the occasional bouquet of daffodils by his grave, he might look more like a regular mourner.

"I'm Rachel, by the way," supplied the woman in the shawl. "Sorry, I didn't ask your name."

"L—Lawrence," Gavin fumbled, unaccustomed to giving his name so freely.

"Pleasure to meet you." She shoved the styrofoam coffee cup towards him. "So, how come you weren't at the funeral?"

"Oh, erm, I…"

Rachel winced. "Sorry, sorry. Shouldn't have asked. Too personal. Mum always said I was too nosy. Kept saying someone would chop my nose off one day if I wasn't careful."

"No, no. It's fine. I guess I'm just not a big fan of funerals, you know?"

"I get that. When mum went, I was in bits for days. Couldn't get out of bed. I don't even remember much of it, to be honest with you. It's all a bit of a blur."

She took a sip from her cup. Gavin tried to copy her, then recoiled as the liquid scalded his lips.

"I thought," said Rachel, lowering her voice. "Maybe you'd heard how he went. I thought that might be why no one came."

Gavin's hand stilled around the cup, the heat forgotten. Whose grave had he chosen to visit, exactly? He could lie. Say he knew. No. Too much risk. Best to say as little as possible.

"What did you hear?" he asked.

"I really shouldn't say," she said, looking around them as if checking for eavesdroppers. "Although, according to Seb, our embalmer, he was into some weird stuff. When he came in he had these marks on his body."

She ran a hand over her stomach, then up to her ribs, fingers splaying outwards. Gavin was just beginning to feel uncomfortable. Neither of them knew this man. Rachel certainly shouldn't be giving out these details. Didn't they have a confidentiality clause? Or did that stuff stop mattering when you died?

"Seb did his best to get them off, but they wouldn't come away.

In the end, he had to seal the lid shut. Said he didn't want anyone to think he was bad at his job. It wasn't easy, mind, since Mr. Fry got the cheapest coffin we offer. Those things come apart near as soon as they're in the ground."

The snow settling outside was looking more and more inviting by the minute, yet Gavin couldn't deny his curiosity. He'd spent so long with Lenny, yet knew nothing more than his age.

"You think someone might have done it to him?"

"No. The police were sure of that."

"Police?"

"Well, yeah. They were the ones who found him. A neighbour called them. Said they were worried Mr. Fry had done something. When they broke down the door, he was lying on his living room carpet. He'd got his wife's ashes, smeared them everywhere. On him, up the walls. That's what the marks were. They were pretty sure he'd lost his mind." She glanced at the front doors as a gust of wind sent a flurry of snow thudding into the glass. "There were rumours, though."

Gavin said nothing. If he stayed silent, a court might see it as wanting to remain in respectful ignorance. No judge could say he was fishing for gory details.

"Course, everyone who works here loves a spooky story. There was something different about this one, though. Seb told me," She leaned closer, her voice barely above a whisper now. "Seb told me he'd heard Mr. Fry had ideas about contacting the other side. The poor man's wife died last year. Story goes he wanted to bring her back for one last chat, and he'd found a way to do it. You've seen that picture on his headstone? His will had specific instructions on how to engrave it. Guess that's why he couldn't afford a decent coffin. They're not cheap, stonemasons. Especially for something so intricate. Anyway, Seb reckons it was some sort of enchantment. Like a spell. Apparently, he'd drawn the same thing around himself before, well…"

Gavin twisted the coffee cup on its coaster. Strange how quickly rumours spread. Rachel sounded so confident in herself, he almost believed her. Still, it was good to know that Lenny had been a bit of an outcast. He could be sure none of his estate were going to turn up and ruin another lunchtime.

"How did you say you knew each other, again?" asked Rachel.

"From school."

"Right." Her face seemed to brighten. "Maybe we're the same age, then. When did you graduate?"

Gavin tried to do some quick maths in his head. Lenny had been born two years before him. August, though, so would he have made the cut off? He'd have graduated in... When exactly?

"Oh, err. That would be...2002?"

He thought he'd been quick, but Rachel seemed to note the hesitation. Her eyebrow twitched, and she smiled down at the table.

"Long time to stay friends. Don't think I know anyone from back then anymore. I suppose you just drift away, don't you? It happens everywhere. No one stays in my job for more than a few years. I've been here a while though. You see grieving families taper off their visits over the years. Husbands and wives who come down with their new partners. Everyone comes and goes." She looked up, straight into Gavin's eyes. "Not you, though. Never known someone with so many friends buried in different places."

He knew it. Someone had been keeping an eye. He'd got too comfortable. He should never have kept coming to the same place. He should have just gone home at lunch, closed his curtains, sat in the dark, alone, like he deserved to.

"Most of them you got bored with fairly quickly, by the looks of things. Not him, though. Maybe you heard the rumours, too. Maybe there's someone you wanted to speak to as well."

Enough of this. He should get going, before this got even weirder. Before this woman said or did something that he didn't want to hear or see.

"Look, I just wanted somewhere to eat my sandwich."

Rachel sat back. The steam from her cup had evaporated. The coffee long gone. "I get it," she said. "You're curious. Nothing wrong with that. I don't have a problem where you sit. My bosses, though. I don't know. And what about your friends? If they found out, don't you think you'd look a little odd?"

Gavin imagined going back to the office, walking through the doors and hearing conversations cut off as his colleagues caught sight of him. He saw the smirks they gave each other before heading back to their work. They already thought he was a waste of space. This, on top of everything else...

"Don't worry," Rachel said, the smile returning. "I'm not

gonna tell anyone. If you help me."

Don't ask. Nothing good can come of asking.

"Help you with what?"

"I want to speak to my mum again."

Gavin tried to picture the doors behind him. How quickly could he get there and push down the handle? How quickly could he run to the bus stop? How quickly could he get back to the desk and the judgemental looks? How long until his boss called him into her office? Would she already have heard about his habit by then? If this woman had video of him visiting the graves, it could be on the internet before he'd reached the cemetery gates. How many had he even been to? How long would the footage go on?

"I know it sounds stupid. I know it's probably not going to work. I just want to try. That symbol, I think Seb was right. If I can recreate it," The words were pouring out, uncontrolled and messy. Rachel took a breath, steadying herself. "She's been gone five months now and every day I think about her. I know it's selfish. I know she was ready to go see dad again, but I miss her. One more chat. It's not much, is it?"

The muscles in his legs tightened, ready to spring from the chair. He felt for the edge of the table. Push it away and run, go— where?

Rachel's eyes were shimmering as she spoke.

"I sometimes wonder if I've already met all the best people I'm going to meet. When you start thinking like that, losing even one is so hard. If I could just speak to her again and get my head sorted." She sniffed, and the flicker of a smile creased the corners of her eyes. "It's so much easier talking to the dead, isn't it? No one to answer back."

She had a point. No dead boss had ever shouted at him for calling in sick. No dead wife had ever cheated on him on their dining room table. The living had done those things. The living had caused all his problems. And it was the living who didn't understand. There were so many times he'd rather have chatted to people who weren't here anymore, rather than those who were left.

"How?"

"I've been researching. I think Mr. Fry was close. He only messed up on one thing." She reached forward and touched the rims of their cups together. "He didn't have a friend to help."

~ * ~

For the final time, Gavin walked through the cemetery gates, wondering what he was doing. He passed the car park and the reception and the crematorium, shut up and silent as night descended. He pulled his coat close as the snow blistering down the path stuck to his hair and his hands. This would be over soon, and he wouldn't have to worry anymore.

Rachel waited two rows back from his usual spot, carrying a large vase in her arms. On the ground around her she had drawn a dark circle, lines crisscrossing and overlapping within. A headstone clawed out of the ground at its center. Gavin knew the shapes, the bumps, the indents. He'd stared at them long enough.

"Don't worry," she said, as she noticed him eyeing the vase warily. "They're not ashes. I got this from the smoking area out back. It doesn't need to be from the person. That was a flourish on Mr. Fry's part."

"What do you need me to do?" asked Gavin.

"Just stay there. If you see me start to fall, make sure I stay on my feet." She placed the vase on the ground beside her, then from her pocket she pulled a length of fiber webbing. It looked like it belonged wrapped around a coffin being lowered into the earth. "I don't think it will, but if anything goes wrong, I need you to pull me out. Don't cross the edge, though. That's very important. It's hard enough with two."

Rachel wrapped one end of the webbing around herself, tying it at her waist. The other end she tossed to Gavin, who caught it lamely.

"Are you sure you want to do this?" he asked.

She tugged at the webbing, checking it was secure without looking back at him. "Positive."

Gavin shuffled back towards Lenny's grave, putting a row of headstones between them. Somehow it made him feel safer, like he had a friend nearby. He watched as Rachel took a deep breath and stepped into the circle. She moved slowly, taking care not to disturb the lines she had drawn. The webbing tugged in his hands, and he held on tighter. He considered wrapping it around his wrist to make sure it didn't slide out of his grip, then thought better of it. He wasn't going to get dragged any further into this weirdness.

Rachel opened her mouth. For a moment, Gavin heard nothing, her voice drowned out by the snow pelting his ears. Then, the words reached him. Not English. Not Latin, or some other dead language she had convinced herself held otherworldly power. Guttural, instinctive sounds, like they were being dredged up with chains and pulleys. Sounds he'd never heard from a human mouth. Closer to oceans crashing and thunderstorms crackling than fully formed sentences. They struck the headstone, spit from her lips swirling like snowflakes. The real snow had stopped falling around them. It continued to settle on the gates and the path he had walked down. Where they stood, the world was still. If anything, it felt warmer. Puddles of sweat were forming under his armpits. He unbuttoned his coat, and the webbing fell from his hands.

By the time the first breeze rushed over his ribs, the circle had changed.

The ash was alive, glowing white. Whiter than the fresh snow around their feet. Gavin looked away, then back again, untrusting of his own eyes. The glow remained. With each second it grew hotter, brighter, until it hurt to look at. Rachel's face strained, like she was struggling to hold herself together. He moved towards her, but she held out a shaking palm and he stayed where he was.

A sound from behind made Gavin turn. Among the snow-capped trees and dusted headstones, one plot was free of any pale blanket. The symbol under Lenny Fry's name was glowing, too, and the grass Gavin had worked so hard to keep neat began to shake.

Rachel's voice picked up speed. The noises became harsher, tidal waves hitting rock, whirlpools sucking in great ships. Gavin looked for the gates. What if someone came now? How would he explain this? Among the snowfall, he found the reception hall. Were the lights on when he'd walked past? Was someone coming to get them? To stop them? To save them?

Grass loosened from dirt, and a rumble shook Gavin's shoes. Sweat glistened on Rachel's forehead, her eyes wide and alert. Her circle had transformed into a patch of pure light emanating upwards, rays bursting forth past her tortured form. The symbol on Lenny's grave had changed likewise, the heat pouring out of it so strong that Gavin felt it scorching his hands as if he'd plunged them into boiling water. Leaves shook on the trees, casting more snow down and burning it before it hit the ground. Not that there was anywhere for it to settle. The ground churned, and something was coming through.

A corner first. A rotten, wooden corner. Then another, and another, until the earth ejected Lenny Fry's coffin like a whale carcass washed up on a beach. Despite Seb the embalmer's best efforts, the coffin had not fared well in its time underground. The lid had disintegrated, and as Gavin watched, the splintered remains fell away entirely. The shadow of the moon peeked through the newly barren trees, and what was left of Lenny's face—the face Gavin had been imagining for months—stared back at him.

All ideas of why he was there disappeared from his mind. Gavin made towards the coffin—to do what? Push it back down? Hide it? He had no plan, but he needed to do something, and in that moment, running towards the corpse of his friend felt preferable to approaching Rachel's infernal circle. As he got closer, he almost fell on his face as the inside of the box became clear.

Neck bones were shifting, turning, like Lenny was searching for something. A voice spoke through the box, and Gavin couldn't tell if it was coming from the body itself, or being carried on the wind.

"Ella? Ella, where are you?"

Lenny's empty eye sockets swivelled up to the sky. He sniffed through lungs turned to dust and a nose reduced to an empty hole in his skull, producing a sound like dirt gurgling down a sinkhole. The voice came again, and Gavin's legs gave way.

"No. Please, no. Let me go back. Not here. Not here. This is not our world. This is not our place. Please! We were happy there. We were happy there. We were together in the air and the trees. It took so long, but we did it! Don't take me back! Don't leave me again!"

The voice came strained, buffeted and pulled apart by the air. Despite the desperation in the pleas, they reached no further than Gavin sprawled on the ruined earth, frozen in place. He had never believed there was anything beyond this life, but faced with the firewarmed box in front of him, his notions melted in an instant. He was wrong. This was wrong. What they were doing was wrong. Whatever other worlds existed, they were best left alone. Those who had moved on had earned their places. He and Rachel had not. Who were they to disturb anyone's rest? There was somewhere else, and from Lenny's reaction to being dragged away from it, it was somewhere beautiful. Somewhere he was whole again, where his wife had gone already. How could you take someone away from that, bring them back to this muddy field in the cold and the wet and the deep, deep loneliness?

Muffled whimpers came from the box, and Gavin knew Rachel's plan would not work. The rumours she'd heard were misguided. Lenny had not been trying to bring his wife back. He had been trying to join her, to bring them together, forever. Wherever she went, whenever she went, he was not willing to risk death separating them over years. He had made the decision to find them a new home, on their terms. His body had stayed here, leaving his mind free to move on, until they'd interfered.

A crack brought Gavin back to the cemetery. One of Rachel's legs had flailed, knocking over the vase. She was being pulled to and fro in the circle, jerked about with her shoes barely holding on to the ground. More groans sang from the earth, but her mum's coffin had been better made than Lenny's. Heavier. Still struggling to break through.

Gavin dragged himself to his feet, heat rushing to his head and purple spots flashing. This was not what Rachel wanted, to be dragged down before her time. Sweat dripped into his eyes as he cast around for the other end of the webbing. A flash of fabric, flopping like a stranded fish. With each twitch it inched closer to the edge of the glowing circle.

Rachel stumbled, grunting like she'd been punched in the stomach. Behind her, the light in the reception hall had changed. No longer a yellow gleam. Flashes of blue passed over the glass every few seconds, along with the distant echo of sirens.

Gavin leaped around a headstone, and his fingers caught the line. He felt Rachel's weight pulling it away, but he held on, hands burning. She fell to one side, and as her legs twisted under her, he gave a great tug. Her feet left the ground and she landed, smashing spine first into another forgotten headstone. Outside the circle.

~ * ~

The news of Lenny Fry's disinterment made far greater headlines than his death. Gavin read the story on his lunch break. He sat at his desk, ignoring the whispered jokes and sly jabs from his colleagues about him and his ex-wife. They didn't matter. There was more to life than they knew. And if he tried hard enough, there was something wonderful waiting for him when he was done with this place. If he was very lucky, he might even find someone to share it with.

He did not risk returning to the cemetery. He had been lucky to get away the first time. When the police car had trundled through the gates, he'd jumped over the rear wall and ran for the nearest alley. He'd waited, trying to still his thudding heart and prayed the wisps of cold breath belching from his mouth would not give him away. When he hadn't heard any more sirens nor flashing blue lights, he'd risked emerging from his hiding place before beginning the long walk home.

He closed the article on his phone and threw the last of his sandwich in the bin. Probably the media spinning things as usual, but he couldn't help feeling a little more upbeat as the tabloid rumours cycled through his head. According to some rag journalist, when Lenny Fry's body was reinterred the following day, he had been smiling from sunken cheek to sunken cheek.

Thomas Nicholson is a teacher and designer from the UK. His short stories have appeared in anthologies around the world, including recent publications from Madhouse Books, Thuggish Itch, and Scare Street.

BY FIRE SHE WAS CROWNED

Frank Sawielijew

The ring of fire on Cassinda's head was an unwelcome companion. It appeared out of nowhere almost a year ago and burned away the trappings of her old life. Losing her hair to its ravenous hunger had been painful, but worse her inability to sleep in beds. Anything the fire touched, it burned.

The ring of fire began at her nape and moved upwards from there, crawling up behind her ears and coming together where her hairline used to be. Like the laurel wreath worn by Vitulia's Eternal Empress, it rested on her head as a crown.

While its licking flames heaved a dozen inconveniences upon her, the fiery crown was not malevolent. Her skin bore not a single blister, for the fire did not harm her. It had chosen her as its bearer, not for punishment, but for a greater purpose.

Even though it could not speak, she knew it was sentient. It sent her visions when she slept, flickering images she could barely comprehend, and nudged her onward with a strange tingle that crept down her spine all the way into her fingers and toes.

It sent her east. Far east, away from her home city of Uscula on the western coast, far past the territories of the Allyran city states, beyond the borders of the Vitulean Empire and the many chiefdoms of barbaric Gallthya.

She followed its nudges willingly, eager for answers. The journey led her along major trade routes, but she was denied the comforts enjoyed by regular travelers. Thinking her a sorceress, people treated her with either adoration or suspicion, nothing between. Some gave her free food and drink in exchange for a blessing, while others had only suspicious glances to spare and kept their hands on their weapons when she was near. Even the friendliest of hosts did not grant her lodging.

The only beds she had known since the fire's appearance were barren earth and hard stone. She dared not even make herself a bed of grass or leaves, afraid to start a forest fire. And while her legs were clad in a long silken skirt, knee-high socks and sturdy leather boots, the only garment covering her torso was a strip of cloth wrapped around her breasts to cover their nudity. Shirts and cloaks caught fire when she tried them, and her attempt to hide the flames beneath a cowl was doomed to failure from the start.

The people of Gallthya considered her a witch, even though she knew nothing about sorcery. She marched through their lands quickly, hoping to find a more tolerant people beyond. Even this far from her home, the fire kept driving her onward. Its destination lay far beyond her knowledge of geography.

"Why did you choose me, little fire?" she mused. "Because of you, I have to keep my head shaved. Because of you, I cannot sleep in beds. But deep down I feel that you are friend, not foe. Yet still I know nothing about you."

It did not answer. It could not answer. But when she made her bed in soft soil that night, the fire sent visions into her dreams, much clearer than usual. She sat in a building of stone, red-clothed women kneeling around her with arms raised over their heads. They were chanting, singing. Some whispered words whose sound was almost familiar to her ears, while others spoke in tongues primordial. Each wore a robe of a different cut, and each had different hair: some had clean-shaven heads like herself, while others wore short curls or long braids. Different as they were, they all sang the same song. Each had her own tongue, yet still they sang as one.

When she awoke from the dream, she still knew little about the fiery companion on her head, yet she felt as if she had been granted a glimpse into its very soul.

"It's not much further, is it?" she asked her fiery crown. "I'll have my answers soon. And I hope they were worth the journey."

She marched on into unknown lands, much further from her home than she had ever expected to be. The fire offered reassurance, filling her heart with warmth. Its goal was within reach, and it was getting excited.

~ * ~

"Tarva, look!" shouted a man, pointing his finger at the passing Cassinda. He was young, but looked older than his years. His face was covered by a thick black beard, and a large hat shielded his eyes from the sun as he worked in the fields.

His wife looked up from her fieldwork and dropped her hoe

when she beheld Cassinda. She looked a little younger than the man, and her muscles were thick from years of labor. Her dark hair was cropped short, little curls sticking to her sweat-stained forehead. "Sacred fire!" Her hand made a circular motion across her chest.

"Firebearer! Over here!" the man called out. "Quick, before you're spotted by the god-king's men. The road isn't safe."

She wasn't sure if she could trust the man, but the fire was. Trusting its judgment, she approached. He led her through fields of grain towards his house, far from the road. His wife stole glances at her as they walked, eyes staring in disbelief. She kept repeating the circular gesture above her chest.

Cassinda ducked down when she entered the man's home, careful not to let the flames touch the doorframe. The house was built entirely of wood, as were most of the household items she saw inside. Being there made her nervous. She didn't want to incinerate their livelihood by accident.

"I always knew you would come, firebearer," said the man. He took off his hat and bowed low.

His wife fell to her knees and caressed Cassinda's foot, placing a dozen kisses on her boot. "The sacred fire has returned! Oh, thank you! May your searing justice deliver us from the god-king's tyranny."

Cassinda stepped back, withdrawing her booted foot from the woman's embrace.

"Please, calm down. I am no savior. The fire appeared on my head one day and told me to go east. I don't know why. It tries to communicate with me, but I only understand snippets." She closed her eyes and focused on the fire's wordless voice. It spoke in feelings, vague notions, faint images. This close to its destination, she finally understood. "Its home is not far from here. It wants to go home."

"It is the sacred fire." The man performed the same circular gesture as his wife. "For thousands of years, it burned in Jalata's great temple. But then came the warlord who claims himself a god. He defeated our armies and made us subject to his dominion."

"The god-king forbids any worship not directed at him," the man's wife said. "He toppled the brazier of the sacred fire and turned the temple into his own. The priestesses were made slaves, forced into worshipping him. Those who refused were tortured into submission."

"When did he defile your temple?" asked Cassinda.

"A year ago, when his armies occupied our lands."

Cassinda's hand reached up to touch the flames. They caressed her fingers softly, their heat merely warmth to her skin. It had been almost a year since they appeared on her head. At first, she had tried to resume her regular life in spite of her fiery companion. It took her a long time to even understand what it wanted from her.

She finally had her answers.

"I still don't know why your sacred fire chose me of all people. It wants to return to its temple. And I shall bring it there."

The man shook his head. "If you enter Jalata like this, you will die. Anyone suspected of following a faith other than the god-king's is taken by his men and executed. You must cover your head before you go."

"Anything I cover my head with burns away." She ran a hand over her shaven head, the flames tickling her arm where they touched it. "I did not cut off my hair by choice, but to keep it from catching fire."

"Tarva," he nodded to his wife, "bring her the firemoth cloak."

The woman vanished into a smaller room, emerging soon after with a dull grey cloak in her hands. She offered it to Cassinda, who hesitantly ran a hand over its fabric. It was smooth and soft to the touch.

"It is made from the fur of firemoths," the man explained. "They are large insects drawn to the flame. Their fur does not burn."

The woman looked down, tears welling up in her eyes. "Their numbers are so few these days. The god-king's men have been hunting them like vermin."

Cassinda took the cloak and tossed it over her shoulders. Its large hood concealed her fiery wreath and lack of hair, making her pass as a regular traveler. The wondrous cloth did not catch on fire, even when she rubbed it against the flame.

"Thank you for giving me answers," she said.

"May the sacred fire guide you well, traveler," the man responded.

With the hood pulled tightly over her head, she returned to the road and walked toward the city of Jalata.

She did not need to follow the road signs. The sacred fire knew the way.

~ * ~

The bricks of Jalata's walls were adorned with a bright red glaze, shining like fire in the sunlight. But the bricks on the gate were glazed with purple, and Cassinda spotted groups of workers hewing the red bricks off the wall, replacing them with purple one by one.

Soldiers patrolled the road, clad in purple cloaks over hauberks of iron scales. She felt her heart pounding in her chest, blood rushing to her face as she approached the heavily guarded gate. But the god-king's men just waved her through, too busy rummaging through a merchant's cart to bother with a simple traveler.

She pulled the hood more tightly over her head. Jalata's streets swarmed with guards. It was a beautiful city, its buildings decorated with elegant arches, its colorful cobblestones forming vast mosaics underfoot. But a bloodstained scaffold dominated the central plaza, and the iron grip of the god-king's tyranny could be felt in the atmosphere.

The temple lay beyond the marketplace, a majestic building flanked by two narrow towers reaching for the sky. Their domes were shaped like flames and painted in bright yellows, reds and oranges. The central building was a massive block of granite, imposing in its fortress like strength. Above the huge arch of its entrance, Cassinda could still discern the faded outline of a flaming symbol now replaced by the god-king's effigy.

A wave of melancholy washed over her as she walked into the temple. The sacred fire had returned to its home, yet it was occupied by the enemy. Even within these sacred halls, the god-king's soldiers stood watch. Two of them stood flanking the altar, observing the priestesses to ensure their loyalty. An ancient brazier lay toppled on the ground, and the god-king's statue had its bronze foot upon it. He was an imposing man, a long mustache framing his angular face, his lapis lazuli eyes radiating malevolence. Whenever they passed by, the priestesses placed a kiss upon the statue, displaying their loyalty under the watchful eyes of his soldiers.

Cassinda decided to explore the temple's interior. As a foreign visitor, the guards paid her little heed. The walls were inlaid with mosaics, many of which had been damaged by the destructive hands of the god-king's men. They relayed the faith's history, beginning with a group of naked savages sitting around a fire, and leading to the temple's foundation and the establishment of a priesthood. Many of the little stones had been torn away, leaving the story fragmented.

Only the central scene behind the altar was left pristine. It depicted a group of young priestesses casting offerings into the sacred fire. Some sheared off their hair and gave it to the flames in what seemed like a ritual of initiation. Many of the priestesses were shown with bald heads, and those with long hair wore it in elaborate braids adorned with bands of red cloth. All wore red robes with yellow trims and went barefoot.

The priestesses walking through the temple's halls looked nothing like those in the mosaics. Their robes were a dark purple, their long hair pinned up atop their heads, and their feet stuck in black leather shoes. They wore a new lord's habit now, their old dress discarded.

Cassinda approached one whose robe bore embroideries of gold and silver, figuring her the high priestess. "Priestess! Can we talk?"

The priestess turned to face her, a warm smile on her lips. She looked a little older than the others, around her fortieth year. "Of course, young pilgrim. What troubles rest on your heart?"

"I heard much about the god-king's power and came from far away to give him praise. There is much I wish to know. But…" She swung her head around, looking at the other priestesses in an almost theatric motion. "Can we talk in a more private setting? I don't feel comfortable discussing my beliefs in such a crowd."

She moved a hand to her face, making as if to brush away a strand of hair, and lifted her cowl ever so slightly.

The priestess's eyes widened when they spotted the dancing flames above Cassinda's ear. "I will gladly teach you in my private chambers. Come."

She indicated for Cassinda to follow and walked towards a door to the right of the altar. When they passed the guard, he nodded approvingly and said, "Praise be to Alkor!"

"Alkor be praised," Cassinda replied before she quickly vanished behind the door, glad to be out of his scrutiny.

The priestess led her through a long hallway leading to the sleeping quarters of all the priestesses, until they finally reached hers at the end. It was a lavish bedroom with richly decorated furniture and the softest pillows Cassinda had ever seen. The walls were painted with scenes of conquest, dominated by the victorious figure of Alkor the god-king.

"Even in your private chambers you find no reprieve from this man," Cassinda said.

The priestess let out a sigh. "This self-proclaimed god-king has invaded every aspect of our lives. The day he conquered our city, he personally extinguished the sacred fire we kept burning for thousands of years. He allows no other worship but his own. His workers even erase our history from the walls, so our children grow up knowing no other lord than him."

Cassinda pulled back her cowl, revealing the fiery crown that danced upon her shaven head. "But the fire still burns. I bear it."

The priestess touched her hand to the flame and smiled. Her skin was not burned by its heat. "I wish I could celebrate its return. But three days from now Alkor will arrive in person to celebrate the anniversary of his conquest. If you reveal yourself now, your execution will be the highlight of his victory parade."

"Then we lay an ambush! When Alkor arrives, I unleash the flame upon him and you drive his men from your city."

The priestess shook her head wistfully. "We are not warriors. They would slaughter us."

"You once were!" Cassinda countered. "In the damaged mosaics I saw priestesses in armor defending their faith with their lives. The sacred fire did not give up when the warlord tried to snuff it out, so why should you? Did I come all this way only to learn my journey was in vain?"

The priestess looked her in the eyes and held the gaze for a long while. Finally, she nodded. "I can see why it chose you as its bearer. Very well. The guards will leave at nightfall. Return then, and we can prepare."

Cassinda pulled the cowl back over her head and smiled. "I carried the fire this far. I won't leave until it is returned to its rightful place on the altar."

The priestess led her back outside, and she offered praise to Alkor again when she passed the guard. Little did he know what secret she harbored underneath her hood.

She spent the rest of the day exploring the city as she waited for nightfall. When the sun downed, most guards left the streets and returned to their barracks.

Cassinda entered the temple, ready to reveal herself to the fire's devotees.

~ * ~

All the priestesses were gathered in the temple's main hall. The high priestess had informed them about the sacred fire's return, yet they still gasped in awe when Cassinda pulled back her cowl.

"The fire has returned," the high priestess informed the others. "Our secret prayers have been answered."

"Yet it does not wish to return to its altar yet," Cassinda explained. "I have spent almost a year with the sacred fire as my constant companion and learned to read its thoughts. It wants to reveal itself during the god-king's visit. He intends to celebrate his conquest. Let us make sure he gets the celebration he deserves."

"What do you want us to do, firebearer?" one of the young priestesses asked, her voice uncertain.

Cassinda pointed to the damaged mosaic depicting priestesses clad in armor, weapons of war in their hands. "Take up arms, like they did. Drive the enemy out of your city."

"The warrior-priestesses lived centuries ago," objected the young priestess. "We are not trained in the arts of war."

Another removed the pins from her hair, unbound locks flowing freely down her shoulders. She stripped off her shoes and socks and asked a fellow priestess to braid her hair in the pattern of flame. "We still have our old robes. The fire never stopped burning in our hearts. Once you give the command, Flamebearer—"

The high priestess raised her hand, and the others fell silent. "If the sacred fire commands it, we shall fight. But not today. Vallaya, pin up your hair and cover your feet. We must wear the conqueror's robes a little while longer. Come. I will show you a place his men never found."

The high priestess went ahead, and the others followed. From their expressions, Cassinda could tell they didn't know about the place, either. It had to be some kind of inner sanctum known only to the high priestess.

The high priestess led them into a storage chamber stacked with crates and barrels. Most of them held food and drink. Grains of rice, dried meat and fruit, legumes and nuts, beer, wine, and water. She asked two other priestesses to help her move some crates aside, revealing the faint outline of a door against the wall. Her hand pushed a brick that depressed into the wall upon her touch, and the door swung open.

The priestesses exchanged excited whispers. Every day, they went into this chamber to retrieve their food, yet none had known about this hidden passage.

They descended down a flight of stairs into the unknown darkness below. The sacred fire on Cassinda's head was their only source of light, but it was more than enough to illuminate the narrow subterranean corridor. At the bottom of the stairs, they emerged into a large chamber whose walls were lined with stone slabs upon which rested the remains of long-dead priestesses clad in armor of bronze. Their thick breastplates were stained green with patina.

Despite their age, the flesh of their bodies and the cloth of their garments did not rot. Cassinda recognized their faces, the style of their robes, and the short crop of their hair from the vision the fire had sent her only a night ago.

"Today, we give our dead to the sacred fire," the high priestess explained, "but long ago, we buried them here. These women built our temple and defended the sacred fire against its enemies when Jalata was young and without walls."

Cassinda went from slab to slab, examining the long-dead priestesses. Hundreds were buried here, their bodies preserved by a sweet-smelling salve. The oldest generation was clad in thick breastplates, their hair cut short, their weapons simple wooden clubs studded with spikes of bronze. The younger generations had longer hair and shorter robes. While their armor became lighter, their weapons became deadlier. Heavy breastplates gave way to bronze scales sewn onto leather shirts, while wooden clubs turned into deadly maces, axes, and picks.

The same voices she heard chant in her vision now spoke to Cassinda again, the words as ancient as the mouths that voiced them. Only she seemed to hear them, for none of the priestesses reacted. They spoke through the sacred fire, their souls alive within its dancing flames.

"They want you to use their weapons," she announced. "They want you to fight and defend your faith like they once did."

The high priestess nodded. "Thank you for returning our spirit, Flamebearer. The god-king's men broke us into submission. Now we know what we must do."

She embraced Cassinda and placed a kiss upon her brow, lips brushing against the flames.

The other priestesses followed suit, kissing the fiery crown in reverence.

"Please," Cassinda begged, overwhelmed by the gesture, "don't worship me as your savior. I only followed the road the sacred fire led me to."

"You're the one who brought it here," replied the high priestess, gracing her with the warmest smile. "It chose you as its bearer, because it knew your inner strength. Don't deny the weight of your own deeds."

Cassinda closed her eyes and breathed in deeply. She had only wanted answers.

Now, she bore responsibility for an entire city's destiny.

"I hope you did not misjudge me, little fire," she whispered.

If her little rebellion failed, all Jalata would suffer Alkor's rage.

The fire's warmth spread reassurance through her veins. For thousands of years, it had burned in the sacred brazier. It had watched its people survive countless wars, famines, plagues.

And even a god-king's ambitions could not extinguish it.

~ * ~

During the day, the priestesses kept pretending to venerate Alkor, the self-proclaimed god-king. On the instruction of his men, they prepared his upcoming victory parade, decorating Jalata's streets with festive banners.

At night, they trained with weapons in the crypts below the temple. They only had three days until Alkor's arrival, and Cassinda did her best to prepare their hands for battle. She had studied swordsmanship under the tutelage of Allyran fencing masters. The ancient weapons of the warrior-priestesses were much heavier than the elegant blades she knew.

On the last night before his arrival, Cassinda realized they would never match the god-king's professional soldiers in skill. Still their will to fight was strong. She decided to skip the lesson that night, sending them to bed early so they would be well rested.

Cassinda stayed in the crypt and slept among the bodies of the ancient warriors. She rolled up her firemoth cloak and used it as a makeshift pillow.

The night's dreams were vivid with the memories of the dead. She saw the triumphs and defeats of the ancient warrior-priestesses, their tactics and their strategies. They taught her much about war.

The next morning, she awoke with a battle plan fully formed in her mind.

~ * ~

Cassinda mingled with the crowd around the central plaza, just another foreign visitor excited to watch the god-king's arrival. Purple flags and pennants billowed above the streets, dyeing Jalata in Alkor's royal hue. His soldiers were clad in golden ceremonial armor and long cloaks that trailed behind them as they walked.

The priestesses were assembled in front of the temple, ready to welcome the god-king they were forced to serve. Beneath the purple robes of his cult, they wore the panoplies of their warlike ancestors.

The wait was torturous. The sacred fire itched to be unleashed, and Cassinda felt it on her scalp. She didn't dare to scratch for the risk of revealing her secret.

Alkor arrived with great fanfare. He walked alone through Jalata's wide streets, two trumpeters following behind. He had no guards with him. Endowed with sorcerous powers, he believed himself divine and immune to danger. Wizard and warrior alike, his tall frame struck an imposing figure. The scales of his iron shirt were colored with purple enamel, and all his clothes bore that royal color, from the heavy cloak draped around his shoulders to the long socks sticking out of his black leather boots.

The crowd was still, watching him in silence. An arrogant fire burned in his eyes, the covetous gaze of a jealous god. None dared to move, fearing the consequences if they caught his attention. Even those who had come to cheer him kept silent. His presence enveloped the city in a shroud of dread.

He walked into the center of Jalata's grand plaza and raised his hand, pointing a black-nailed finger at the priestesses gathered before the temple.

"High priestess. Approach."

Cassinda watched nervously as the high priestess approached the tyrant. If he noticed the deception, if he gained the initiative…

The high priestess grasped his outstretched hand and kissed the golden ring on his finger.

"I see my banners flying across every street. You prepared a worthy welcome, priestess. An acceptable display of loyalty."

"Thank you, oh king of kings, greatest of men who stands above all gods, whose mighty hand reigns supreme over the world. We live only to praise your glory."

He put a hand on her head and twirled a loose strand of hair between his fingers. "But your attention to proper attire has lapsed. Your hair is not tied the way I taught you."

"I apologize, my lord. Allow me to fix it."

She removed her hairpin. Instead of loose locks tumbling over her shoulders, it was a long braid in the pattern of flame worn by the priestesses of the sacred fire.

She rammed the hairpin into Alkor's throat. He reeled back, gasping for air.

The other priestesses followed her lead and rid themselves of the hated god-king's habit. They tore off their purple robes, revealing robes of fiery red and breastplates of ancient bronze underneath. They freed their flame-shaped braids from their tight updos. They stripped off their shoes and socks and, now barefoot, marched forward to fall upon the god-king's men. The soldiers' ceremonial armor of soft gold offered little protection from the priestesses' fierce blows, and many tripped over their overly long cloaks as they scrambled to assume formation.

Alkor pulled the hairpin out of his throat. The wound closed within seconds.

"Betrayer!" His voice was hoarse, his throat still sore from the rapidly healing wound. "Your sacred fire is gone, yet you still wear its colors?"

As the soldiers threw off their cumbersome cloaks and formed a defensive line, the priestesses retreated towards the temple.

Cassinda stepped out of the crowd and pulled back her cowl. The fire on her head was blazing, a mighty crown of roaring flames burning with rage against the tyrant king.

"The fire has returned! All your powers were not enough to extinguish it. Leave Jalata and go back from whence you came!"

She stepped into the pile of discarded clothes and allowed the fire to have them. The raging flames engulfed the cloth, and the crowd started to disperse. They smelled the danger in the air and ran for shelter. Utter chaos engulfed Jalata's streets as bodies pressed against each other and hundreds of voices screamed in terror.

"You dare mock me, mortal?" Alkor's voice trembled with cold anger, the rage of a god-king scorned. "Your little tricks are nothing compared to my might. Prepare to die."

He chanted words of magic and moved his fingers in intricate patterns. Cassinda dodged the sorcerous projectile just in time. It hit the burning pile of clothes and left a massive crater in the pavement. A deadly shrapnel of cobblestones and flaming cloth showered the crowds, escalating their panic.

A barrage of arcane forces bore down upon her, tearing through the streets beneath her feet. Alkor grasped her firemoth cloak with an ethereal hand and dragged her towards him. She threw off the cloak and headed for the temple.

"There's no use in running! You can't escape my wrath!"

A shockwave behind her pushed Cassinda to the ground. Alkor's hand reached for her again, grabbing her by the foot. She struggled against his arcane grip as he dragged her towards him, bare arms scraping against the broken road's jagged stone.

"I will cut off your head and blow out that fire like a candle's tiny flame," he proclaimed. "But first I'll have you watch as my men tear down your temple and flay the treacherous priestesses alive. Their wails shall remind all of treason's consequences."

Cassinda loosened the laces on her boot and pulled it off. Freed from his grip, she plucked a loose cobble from the pavement and launched it at Alkor. It flew against his forehead, dazing him.

She got back to her feet and ran towards the temple. She burst through the entrance and collapsed to the ground, heaving for breaths. The priestesses lowered their weapons when they realized it was her.

"Flamebearer! We are ready to defend the sacred fire until our last breath," the high priestess pledged.

Cassinda gathered her strength and got back to her feet. She walked over to the altar where Alkor's triumphant statue stood and pushed against it with all the strength her arms could muster. It fell over, hitting the floor with a loud clang.

"If he sends in his soldiers, hold them at the entrance. If he comes in himself, retreat." She took a deep breath and stared out through the narrow entrance. Alkor stood in the center of the plaza, shouting orders to his men. "I will face him on my own. His magic is powerful, yet he is merely a man. And all men have their weakness."

The soldiers formed up and marched towards the temple. While their iron swords were sharp and deadly, their ceremonial armor of gold offered little protection against the priestesses' vicious picks and axes.

The entrance was so narrow, only two men could march abreast. As soon as they stepped inside, they were assaulted from all sides. Though the first ranks fell to the priestesses' bronze arms, they soon established a foothold and slowly pushed the priestesses back. It was a grueling assault, a slow grind of blade against armor, iron against bronze, and bronze against gold.

The priestesses' arms grew tired, and some suffered wounds. Alkor's men had greater numbers and better training. Despite the advantageous position, the priestesses were slowly losing ground, and the longer the battle lasted, the more it changed to Alkor's favor.

The soldiers were veterans of many wars, their souls steeled against the terror of battle. Weapons did not scare them. Like all men, they feared what they could not fight.

Cassinda charged into the fray and threw herself at a soldier. She grasped his arms and grappled with him. The sacred fire's flames jumped onto his sleeves and ate their way up to his shoulders and down underneath his armor, crawling across his tunic, his undershirt, down to his trousers, up into his beard.

He dropped his sword and pulled away from Cassinda, wildly flailing his arms to extinguish the flames on his body. As he backed away, he bumped into the man behind him, and the fire spread. It jumped from soldier to soldier, and soon they were all in a panic. They tried to retreat while reinforcements still poured in from behind, clogging the narrow entrance and crushing the men caught in the middle. The panic turned into a rout as more and more men dropped their weapons and attempted to escape, and soon even those outside lost heart and retreated.

The priestesses put down their weapons and went to nursing their wounded. Most had survived the battle, but none remained unscathed. Their armor was battered, their robes torn, and their arms weary.

"We cannot survive another assault like this," the high priestess sighed. "They already pushed us to the limits of our strength."

"There won't be another," Cassinda promised. She stepped through the entrance to confront Alkor. He may have been a powerful sorcerer-king, but she had the sacred fire on her side.

The warlord stood tall and proud, his arm stretched out towards the temple. A group of soldiers surrounded him, their swords raised. Cassinda struck a much less imposing figure. Her arms were covered in scratches, her clothes torn, and she was missing a boot. Only the fire atop her brow blazed with undiminished ardor.

"Your resistance is futile," Alkor called out to her. "If you do not yield to the sword, you will yield to hunger and despair. My men shall lay siege to your temple and starve you out. Surrender, and I shall grant you merciful deaths."

"You cannot extinguish the fire in our hearts, tyrant," she shouted back. "Just like you couldn't extinguish the sacred flame itself."

He laughed at her words of defiance; a laugh filled with mocking derision. "Persist in your folly, then. In time, you will come to know the extent of my power. Many tried to revolt against me. Their cities are now rubble, while my empire remains. Your fate will be no different."

Protected by his soldiers, Cassinda could not get close enough to unleash the sacred fire upon him. She did not have to.

Cassinda pulled off her sock and filled it with rubble from the broken streets. She touched the cloth against the flames and set it alight. Like a sling she swung the burning sock and launched it at the god-king.

It sailed over the heads of his men and hit him in the chest, glancing off his armor.

The flames caught his cloak and spread. He laughed at Cassinda's folly and muttered an incantation.

Nothing happened.

Irritated, he chanted it again. He held his palm over the spreading flames and whispered words of arcane power. The flames did not extinguish. Again, he repeated the spell, his gestures much angrier this time.

"You are no god," Cassinda shouted, "yet the sacred fire burns with true divinity! Your powers are not enough to extinguish it. Jalata shall be free of your tyranny!"

The fire kept spreading across his clothes, and his frustration turned to panic. The licking flames jumped over to his soldiers, who dropped to the ground and desperately tried to put them out, rolling to and fro while they screamed in panic.

From the fields outside the city, flocks of firemoths rose into the sky. Dozens of the large furry insects sailed over the walls and into Jalata. They swarmed around Alkor and tore strips of cloth from his burning cloak, carrying them to the purple pennants streaming above the streets. Soon, every single symbol of Alkor's reign was consumed by the sacred fire.

The crowd stood transfixed. Jalata's streets were still filled with people trying to flee the scene of battle. The flight of the majestic moths stopped them in their tracks. They looked up in awe and watched as they carried the flames from flag to flag.

"The sacred fire has returned!" someone shouted, and a cheer went through the crowd.

Desperate to rid himself of the flames, Alkor ripped off his cloak, his armor, his tunic, until he stood half naked in the city's central square, a god-king stripped of his royal garments. He stared at Cassinda in anger, and their eyes locked. She saw utter, unbridled rage in them, and expected him to unleash spells of death upon her.

Instead, he pulled a long strip of parchment from a pouch on his smoldering belt and tossed it into the air, shouting an arcane phrase as it was caught by the wind and carried away. The spell gave him the power of flight, and he soared into the sky like a bird of prey.

Majestic as his figure appeared in the sky, he did not swoop down to attack his enemies from above. He flew over Jalata's rooftops, passed over the city walls, and fled back to the lands he came from. A few firemoths harassed him on his way. Once he left the limits of Jalata's outskirts, they returned to the city to perform a celebratory dance in the air.

His remaining soldiers dropped their weapon and followed their leader, heading towards the city gates while the cheering population pelted them with stones and rotten fruit.

While the people celebrated the fire's return, Cassinda went back into the temple.

"It is done," she announced to the weary priestesses.

"Flamebearer!" The high priestess fell to her knees, touching her forehead against the floor. "You brought us liberty."

Cassinda walked over to the toppled brazier and raised it up. She ran a hand over her head to feel the flames tickling her fingers one last time before they left her. As much as it had impacted her life when it appeared, she had grown fond of her fiery companion during her journey to Jalata.

The circlet of fire turned into a ribbon as it crawled onto her shoulder, down her arm, and jumped off her fingers into the brazier.

"I returned your sacred fire to its ancient home. My quest is complete, and I gained all the answers I sought. May you always persevere, little fire." She watched it dance within the brazier, a bright red flame that could never be extinguished. A symbol of hope and defiance.

She had learned much from it.

"What now, Flamebearer?" asked the high priestess. "Will you stay and help us rebuild?"

Cassinda shook her head. "I came here to bring the fire home. Now it's time for me to return to my own. I only have one request before I go."

"Anything, Flamebearer."

"A soft bed, and a pillow under my head for tonight. I haven't known this comfort in a long while."

The high priestess led her into her own bedroom, and Cassinda thanked her from the bottom of her heart. Her bed was softer than any she had ever laid on before, and its pillows felt like ethereal clouds caressing her weary head. It was still early in the day, but she fell asleep within minutes.

After a year of sleeping on the ground, this was the greatest reward she could ever have wished for.

~ * ~

The priestesses had arranged a great celebration for tonight. Cassinda snuck out of the temple before they came to fetch her. She said her final goodbye to the sacred fire when she passed by its brazier and marched out into the city streets.

The sun had already gone down, and Jalata's streets were

shrouded in darkness. Without the fire on her head, she moved unseen from shadow to shadow. The people were gathered in the central plaza where they kept a large bonfire burning at the spot where Alkor had dropped his cloak. They drank and sang and the grey-furred firemoths danced above the spectacle, diving into the fire and out again.

One of the moths approached Cassinda and sat down on her bald head, nuzzling her face with its long proboscis. She shooed it away. If the crowd noticed her, they would drag her into the central plaza and celebrate her as a hero.

Cassinda had no desire for that kind of attention. She was only a simple woman who had returned the sacred fire to its people because it was the right thing to do. Anyone would have done as she did. At least she liked to think so.

With Alkor's men gone, the city gate was left unguarded. She left Jalata under the cover of darkness and set out on her homeward journey. The firemoth returned, settling on her head again even as she walked away from Jalata's gates.

"Shoo! I'm going home. Go back and celebrate with your people," she told the moth.

It jumped off her head and circled around her, a bright gleam in its big black eyes. There was something familiar about it.

She grinned and stretched out her arm, allowing the moth to settle on it. With her other hand, she stroked its soft grey fur.

"So, you've grown fond of me as a companion, too, haven't you, little fire? I like you much better in this shape. You're less of a fire hazard this way."

And so she left Jalata behind, but a part of the sacred fire went with her.

After what they went through together, their souls were united forever.

~ * ~ * ~

Frank Sawielijew is a Russo-German author with Bulgarian roots whose stories are heavily inspired by the pulp classics and often mix elements of fantasy and science fiction into a flavorful blend. He writes in both English and German and had a handful of short stories appear in various anthologies since 2015. With a background in ancient and medieval history, he regularly draws inspiration from mankind's most ancient tales and cultures, from bronze age Mesopotamia to high medieval Europe. He has also contributed his writing and level design to computer games developed by small independent companies.

A STORY OF INYODO

or

How the Kappa stole the Tidal Jewels from the Dragon King

Carol Hightshoe

Late one night one of the troublesome kappa looked down on the island of Japan and smiled in that mischievous and somewhat scary manner only those who are up to no good can smile in.

"It has been many turnings of the seasons since these people have seen a change in their fortunes. For too long has Fuku Riu favored them and now they no longer understand the blessing they are receiving."

The kappa spoke to his kindred and together they developed a plan to change the fortunes of the people of Japan. The kappa would steal the Tidal Jewels belonging to Ryujin, the Dragon King, and use them to cause a tidal wave to strike the island of Japan. It would not be enough to completely destroy the island, but it would remind the people to give thanks for the blessings the gods had bestowed on them. Being only a minor demon, the kappa only saw things in absolute terms. The gods had blessed the people of Japan after the devastation they had suffered during their last war. They had rebuilt and were now a wealthy and powerful people. Wealth and power many of them seemed to take for granted, forgetting that Fuku Riu, the luck dragon, had blessed them and luck could change on a whim.

The kappa and four of his kin descended to the Evergreen Land beneath the sea and came to Ryugu—the palace of the Dragon King Ryujin. The crystal and coral palace was immense, but they were determined to find the Tidal Jewels. Of the five kappa, one went directly to the throne room of the Dragon King while each of the others went to the cardinal wings of the palace: North, South, East and West as none of them knew where the Tidal Jewels were kept.

The first kappa came to the Winter Hall and paused at the beauty of the falling snow. Forgetting why he was there, he began playing and cavorting in the winter playground—throwing snow-balls at imaginary enemies.

The second kappa came to the Hall of Spring and wandered among the cherry trees with their pink blossoms, entranced by the music of the nightingale which filled the hall.

The third kappa came to the Hall of Summer. There the warm night breeze and the songs of the crickets lulled him into slumber.

The fourth kappa came to the Autumn Hall and was soon dancing among the beautiful multi-colored leaves of the towering maple trees.

The fifth kappa came to the great hall of the Dragon King and stopped at the entrance. Ryujin was sitting on his crystal throne and there on the arms of the chairs were the Tidal Jewels. He watched as the Dragon King glanced up at the image of the moon that was on the ceiling of the palace and carefully stroked one of the jewels. The kappa closed his eyes for a moment and let his senses feel the magic. It had been the high tide jewel Ryujin used. This was the one the kappa wanted, but he did not know how to get it away from the Dragon King.

The kappa glanced around the room, which, as expected for a dragon, was cluttered with treasures and trinkets collected over the millennia. He had heard a rumor Huchi had given Ryujin her ring made of fire to guard his palace. With that ring, the kappa knew he could distract Ryujin and then steal the Tidal Jewels.

Ryujin looked toward the entrance to his hall and the kappa darted into the stacks of treasures. Where to find the ring made of fire he wondered. The Dragon King had been collecting treasure for millennia—most of it from ships lost beneath the waters of his ocean. However some of it had been offered as tribute or gifts by fishermen and sailors and others had been given as gifts of friend-ship or alliance such as with Huchi's ring.

The kappa knew the ring gave protections to the palace, so he doubted it was thrown haphazardly in with the rest of the items. It was fire contained by powerful magic; he should be able to sense it. There, no wait, there. The kappa found himself spinning around as the magic seemed to surround him. A ring made of fire. The Ring of Fire—now the kappa understood.

He wished his kin were with him as the five of them would be able to more easily accomplish what he was about to do. He concentrated, focusing his magic on the Ring of Fire. Just a nudge should be enough to cause a minor quake. Just enough to distract the Dragon King and draw him away from the Tidal Jewels.

The palace shook and the kappa heard Ryujin roar. He ran as objects began falling around him, the shaking growing in power. He ducked behind a large chest as the dragon king flew past him and out of the palace.

The jewels were unguarded, and the kappa knew this was his chance. He paused in front of the throne as the shaking continued to grow in strength. Perhaps the quake would be enough to accomplish his goal. There came another rumbling of power, unbalancing the kappa who grabbed for the arm of the throne to steady himself. His hand dropped on top of the high tide jewel, and it glowed brightly.

"What have you done?"

The kappa spun around to see Ryujin standing in the doorway. The dragon had adopted his guise as an elderly human male; a disapproving smile was on his lips.

"I am reminding these humans to be thankful for the blessings they were given."

Ryujin shifted back into his dragon form, steam seeping from between his lips. "You thought you would take it upon yourself to interfere in the lives of the mortals we are supposed to protect?" The dragon lowered his head until his gaze was level with the kappa's. "You would tell Fuku Riu he should withdraw his blessing? Only he can decide when it is time for their luck to change—not you!"

The kappa cringed as he was surrounded by steam and fire.

"Go—see what you have done." Ryujin's voice echoed throughout the palace.

~ * ~

The kappa looked down on the island of Japan and for the first time in his long life he cried. The force of the tsunami he had created had devastated the area it had hit. Instead of reminding the people of Japan to give thanks for the blessings their gods had given them, he had given them reason to curse their gods.

He saw Fuko Riu also crying. The grief and despair of the

mortals was taking a heavy toll on the luck dragon as he circled the island trying to restore the balance that had been destroyed by the kappa's actions.

The kappa flew to Hachiman's palace; he was the protector of the Japanese people. Surely he would be able to do something about this disaster the kappa had created. Many of the other gods were there, also demanding Hachiman do something to stop the disaster that had befallen their people.

The kappa was disappointed as Hachiman turned him and the others away, saying because the kappa was a deity, however minor he might be, the other gods could not reverse what he had done. They could assist the Japanese people as their powers allowed, but they could not change what had been done.

The kappa looked down at the island. His simple idea of sending a tsunami to remind the Japanese people to give thanks to the gods for the blessings they had been given had brought extreme disaster. Now the full consequences of his impetuous actions were becoming clear as another, even greater disaster loomed. The mortals were fighting valiantly to prevent that disaster, but he could see their strength and faith were failing. What could he do to help them? The other gods were blessing the island as their powers allowed, but would it be enough? He was a minor deity with no strong powers, except to cause mischief. What could he bless them with that would help?

The kappa smiled again, not the devious smile of one who wishes to cause mischief, but a sincere smile. He remembered the stories the gods told of an ancient power that was reborn several years ago, during another disaster—perhaps he could persuade that power to visit Japan and bless these people as he had blessed others throughout the ages.

The kappa concentrated on calling that power, a gift to all mortals from another group of gods. The kirin that appeared before the kappa shimmered with a silver light. "We are the bringers of justice and luck to those who are just," the kirin said lowering his horn. "Now you have given us a new purpose in times like this. We will bring hope."

The kappa found himself staring into the sun-flecked eyes of the kirin just as the horn found his heart.

"You have been judged guilty of your crime against the mortals," the kirin said. "Justice has been dealt, now hope can prevail."

"A Story of Inyodo or *How the Kappa stole the Tidal Jewels from the Dragon King*" was originally published in Healing Waves
from Sky Warrior Books

~ * ~ * ~

A native Texan, **Carol Hightshoe** found her way to her current home in Colorado by way of a five-year detour in The Nederlands —courtesy of her husband Tim and the US Air Force.

An avid reader at a young age, her strong desire to write came from her love of (her husband calls it her obsession with) Star Trek. It was this early love of Star Trek that led her to the Science Fiction and Fantasy genres.

In addition to her writing she has worked as a receptionist/office manager for two veterinary clinics, a deputy sheriff in El Paso County Colorado, Assistant Fan Club Manager for the Professional Bull Riders, and as a Rodeo Keyer for the Professional Rodeo Cowboys Association. Now retired—she hopes to be able to devote more time to her writing.

She has been published in various anthologies and magazines including "Creature Fantastic", PanGaia Magazine, "Stories of Strength", Baen's Universe, Tales of the Talisman and "Kepler's Dozen". Her books include: *Call of Chaos, Chaos Embraced, The Road into Chaos,* and *Chaos Challenged.*

In addition to her own writing, she is the editor and publisher of the online e-zine: **The Lorelei Signal** as well as running her own micro-press: **WolfSinger Publications.**

DRAGON'S FIRE

Bronwyn Dauth

The stories of dragons had always been etched in rich fantasy that rarely ever seemed as though they could be real. I know these to be true as my grandmother was the last dragon rider of her age. I recalled the days I would sit beside her, the old wicker chair creaking beneath our weight. Nan would look out at the courtyard, to the beautiful blossoms, which floated down to the cobblestones below. The tree created an illusion of everlasting snowfall with the courtyard, all except for the circle around the tree itself. Nan explained it to me one summer's afternoon.

"You must understand this, my love," she had said, her fingers gently caressing my hair, softly scratching my scalp and lulling me into a peace only she could bring. "The dragons were beings of magnificent power. Their gifts were extraordinary and one could never fully understand where they came from. To ride on a dragon, my little love, it is a freedom I cannot explain. But, as with all things, the dragon's time had to come to an end. And what a truly sad end it was.

At the start I recall the last time I ever felt that power. It was the battle of our lifetime and everything came down to the important moment before us. All our training and adventures led to battle. I had seen friends fall to the blades of our enemies, their dragon's breath dying to the cooling air. There would be time later to cry, to mourn their loss and wonder what life would be like now, since they were gone." She had said, looking off into the distance and it was as though she could see the memory within her mind's eye.

The academy I had trained in was under siege, and I knew the walls would not hold for long. My eyes wandered to the walls, where the head Mage stood, proud and tall. My breath caught in my throat at the fear that I saw there. It was a look I had never seen before, and it was one I never wished to see again." Nan had always looked pained in the moments of describing the Mage's fear. It had always felt as though it was her very own fear.

"My dragon, a beautiful black beast, breathed deeply beneath me. Her scales brushed against my pants and I felt her muscles move beneath mine. She always felt so warm, an eternal fire roaring within her. Her fire was what kept me alive on flights meant to chill me to my bones. It was her fire which gave me the strength we needed to make the decision we did. With a snort to the riderless dragons beside us, we sprang into the air. We had soared once over the wall of the academy, flying close to the Mage who stood guard. I had reached out to her, my fingertips brushing against hers as she had whispered our mantra into the air." I had always interrupted here, wanting to be a part of the tale Nan wove expertly.

"Till the dawn's first sweet caress." I loved the mantra, as it had kept me going through many of my own trials. Nan had merely smiled down at me, her fingers brushing aside my hair and she had kissed my forehead.

"Yes, little love. We spoke the words to one another, a promise to always find our way back to one another. Together, my dragon and I soared over the battlefield and the advancing enemies. I recall her whispering into our connected mind as we drew closer to the enemies below, *'breathe, little one, you aren't to die.'* Her voice was ancient, more ancient than even the mountains we flew around. The deep timbre of her voice allowed the strength to seep back into my bones. I touched my palm to the warm scales beneath me, feeling the gentle hum of her fire thrumming beneath her hide.

'One last time, my friend.' I had said, the only words we ever needed, and she flew higher into the sky. Soaring around our quarry, I looked down to see that the army below us had stopped to look up at us. Their archers had taken aim, but their weapons were useless against the ancient beasts who filled the sky along with us. The heat below me began to boil further and my dragon opened her maw. A familiar flame blew down to the earth below, setting the dried grass alight.

The horses had reared, attempting to throw their riders off in futile attempts to escape, but it was too late. The dragons had created the perfect ring of searing fire. As the dragons kept rising higher into the sky, so did the wall of flames.

There would be no escape, for you see little one, the fire wall would soon become a dome and all those stuck inside would be lost to this world. But, my darling, my dragon would not let me be lost to the world and she roared once at the Mage. A strong wind lifted me from my saddle and carried me gently to the ground.

I had knelt there, watching as my dragon…my friend disappeared behind the circle of fire. The flames rose, curving into the perfect dome. I had watched as the flames grew hotter, until they died completely. Within the circle, the earth was tainted black and dusted with ash."

Nan had always stopped at that point, the pain evident in her eyes, and I knew she missed them. The dragons had sacrificed themselves for my Nan. They had chosen to die, so my Nan could live, and could keep her promise to her best friend.

I now stood on the wooden patio which bordered the courtyard, looking out at the circle no longer covered with falling blossoms. Nan always told me the blossoms fell around the circle because they would never fall where a dragon's scale lay. I thought of all these things, memories of what Nan had once told me.

And so the legend goes, the weeping blossom tree will never break the circle of fire in which the dragons had sacrificed their lives. It is said, if you walk within the circle, you can still feel the heat of their flames. And if you were to touch the bark of the tree, you would feel the hum of the dragon's breath. I could never bring myself to walk in the circle, a circle where Nan had been reunited with her dragon once more, and her Mage friend. Together they would lay for an eternity, within the Ring of Fire.

~ * ~ * ~

Bronwyn Dauth is an aspiring author, spending most of her time envisioning new worlds of fantasy. She loves the finer art of mixing a dystopian future with fantasy worlds unexplored. Having studied Professional Photography, Bronwyn hopes to capture loving moments through her lens. A South African native, Bronwyn spends her days writing about the worlds she wants to get lost in and her weekends playing with her niece and her nephew.

Bronwyn spends a lot of her time reading fanfiction, when she isn't reading the books she's managed to get her hands on. She also enjoys fanfiction as a way to get out of her writing block slumps. When she isn't writing or reading, she is painting or journaling. Bronwyn spends her quiet days cuddling with her two cats, before being interrupted by the pup. She will deny it if you ask, but the puppy girl is growing on her.

Bronwyn hopes to have her books published one day, bringing joy to readers as books have always brought to her.

HEART PROOF

Holly Schofield

Kamik heaved the iron box onto the cart, her muscles aided by anger as well as decades of blacksmithing. Her next push centered its weight on the polished boards.

As she threw a rope over the box with more force than necessary, Techan appeared by her shoulder. "Let me give you a hand, old woman."

Behind him, the market square blazed unnaturally bright, silhouetting the bonfire dancers. Smoke drifted to the dark sky above where the god Welmit nibbled away the moon. The dancers would tire soon and the moon would return, allowing the villagers a few hours of sleep before the craftspeople's pilgrimage would begin.

"No need, old man." She ran rope through the cart's worn side slats.

Techan brushed a strip of birch bark off his shoulder and stretched out his gnarled, chisel-scarred fingers for the other end of the rope. "You could have affixed iron loops to the sides of the chest. Easier to tie it down." The iron chest was not designed to be transported but, among her completed pieces, the priest had deemed it her only sufficiently complex craftwork. The beaten iron side panels, the thick fire-proofing layer of fluffrock, and the heavy lid were almost more than Kamik's wooden cart could support. Loading it into the cart just so she could watch it burn in Welmit's Maw, the lava-filled mountain to the east, made it feel all the heavier.

"I could have done a lot of things," she said, yanking her knot tight.

As Kamik and Techan started to load the gear piled by the cottage doorway, their neighbor strode by, strips of birch bark wound tight in her hair. Markith's teeth gleamed in the firelight and she shouted well wishes across the darkness, making the cart horse stir in her traces. Kamik paused in her work only long enough to wave a hand.

Close on Markith's heels, the village priest trotted past, solemn as always. He glanced at the chest and gave the sign of blessing, crossing one wrist over the other, palms inward, then thumping his fists against his shoulders.

Kamik fiddled with a knot and pretended not to see.

Techan, of course, returned the blessing, holding the gesture until the priest was nothing but a narrow black shape against the bonfire. As a cough took him, his fists dropped and he clutched his stomach. The low hacking sounds carried over the reveling dancers' shouts. Like beetles consuming the heartwood of an ancient tree, Techan's cancers were eating him from the inside out.

Finally, he slowed and spit noisily. Kamik heaved a tool bag into the cart, barely glancing at the glossy black mass of blood spattered across the iron band of the cart wheel and the toe of her boot. She kept her tone even. "I see I'll be taking your blood along the overroad, even if your stubborn self will be fighting marsh bugs."

Techan wiped his lips then snorted. "The overroad! You're really going to go that route, like a common merchant? Just to save two days of devout contemplation? Pah!"

"Welmit shouldn't care how a person gets there, as long as they throw away their life's work when they do," Kamik said, thumping a barrel of fresh water down beside the iron chest. "The overroad is perfectly all right to use, you old fool. The priest and his most devout followers."

"The priest is an upstart, promoted beyond his abilities. And as for Welmit's devout followers having built it, *I* wasn't asked to help, was I?" Techan thumped a fist on the cart's sideboard, making the mare startle.

Despite her simmering anger, Kamik managed not to point out that only the young and healthy had been asked to cut down trees, move rocks, and apply the clever slurry which hardened to coat the new overroad. Techan didn't need a reminder of his age; just getting out of his cot in the morning was reminder enough.

"Just be glad I'm coming, old man." She moved away from him and slung her kit bag aboard. Unable to hold in her thoughts, she muttered below her breath. "Welmit's doctrines, senseless, destructive. Making us burn up treasures in his maw, doing no good for anyone. Might as well throw in the village and all the people too."

Techan drew in his breath with a loud sniff. His ears must be better than she had thought. She could feel her face redden.

His voice was dangerously low. "You presume to say what Welmit should and shouldn't care about?" He uttered a short apologetic prayer to Welmit—as if it had been he who had blasphemed—and crossed his arms with hard shoulder thumps. "You presume too much, old woman."

Kamik gripped a sideboard. "Just be glad I'm willing to throw the fireproof chest into the only forge hotter than my own! It took me three years to perfect, as you well know! I'll be left with nothing but a drawing of my proudest creation and for what? A sacrifice to a god I no longer believe in!"

Techan stepped into the shadow of the cottage as two giggling pottery apprentices stumbled past, oblivious to their argument. "Hush, woman! The neighbors have big ears."

"And hard hearts," she said loudly, not caring who heard. She placed a foot on the running board and threw her bedding onto the seat. Lack of a sacrifice to Welmit required a person to leave the village, to travel "until the nuts and fruits themselves are unfamiliar" and to never return. The penalty was so severe, she had never known anyone to go against the doctrine.

She stepped down, turning toward him. The dangling birch bark entwined in his hair did nothing to soften the planes of his face. She touched his shoulder. "I'll do what I'm supposed to do, like I always have. Not for the priest, nor for you, old man. For Garva's sake, and the babe's. A child should have a grandmother." Their daughter's stomach had barely started to swell, but Kamik had stayed up all last night making her a supply of herbal tonics for the days Kamik would be journeying. She had taken great pains to follow the exact recipe copied from the priest's scrolls, cooking the herbs in the small metal stove box she had installed after the chimney fire.

Two steps took her to their cottage doorway where she grabbed a small crate from a stack of three. "This is my traveling food. I've packed you twelve days' worth," she said, her voice gruff, nodding at the remaining boxes. "Bring your cart around and we'll load it." Kamik had forbade herself to assist him that morning in loading his own sacrifice into his battered and ancient cart. The graceful wooden chair, which rocked at the touch of a finger, was light enough. Offering to help pack it would have only wounded his pride.

"I don't need twelve days of food. Just six." Techan's voice was flat.

It took her a moment to manage the sharp tone he'd be expecting. "Not planning on coming back, is that what you're saying? Trying to shock me, are you, old man? Forty years together in this cottage, I know what you're thinking. And, you're wrong, you *will* come back and you'll be around long enough to see Garva birth her child."

She could not see his face in the dying light of the distant bonfire. It was a moment before he spoke. "I have already said the nine moon prayers for her babe."

Kamik set down the crate before it fell from her fingers. Saying the moon prayers in advance of the birth was against doctrine, against all tradition unless death was clearly inevitable. Techan really did believe his cancers would send him upward to the endless sun. Had he been hiding his stomach pain more than she knew? Or was he just disheartened at the way growing older ground a person down like spices in a pestle?

For a long moment she busied herself placing the food crate in the storage area below the cart's seat before swinging back down onto the rutted road. One foot slipped and she landed on her bad knee. She stayed in the welcome shadow of the cart for a moment before rising, crouching in the bitter-smelling mud that had grown slick with strips of birch bark.

~ * ~

There was nothing Kamik wanted more than to have this pilgrimage over and done, and both of them back safe. However, despite an early start each morning of the four-day journey, despite not stopping at any villages along the way, she was not the first to arrive at Welmit's Maw.

Markith had forced her horse and cart past Kamik on the last stretch of the overroad, where the forests gave way to open grassland followed by bare rock. The fierce eagerness on Markith's face as she had passed, eagerness to toss her river raft with the clever deerhide floatbags into the inferno, made her normally pleasant face look insane.

Kamik had long since stopped looking back over her shoulder. Behind her, a long line of carts stretched, full of all the other mad and driven folk.

Techan was not among them.

Of all the village craftspeople, only Techan had chosen the more traditional route along the underroad. It would be two more days before Kamik could expect him to arrive at the Maw. Kamik's heart, which Techan once described as clad in the strongest iron, ached more than her swollen knee. She should have gone on the underroad, foolish as it might be.

"Give me a hand, neighbor?" The shout from ahead demanded a response. Markith had already reined in at the largest of the open, smoking lava pits and unstrapped her raft. Her voice rasped like Techan's after long hours in a smoky workshop. Kamik should have crafted her an iron stove too, but in the past few years she had not found the time, spending every spare moment on the fireproof chest.

There was scarcely room to squeeze between Markith's raft and cart bench. The woman must have slept uncomfortably on the narrow bench the whole journey.

A push from them both and the raft slid on its wobbly leather underbags through the cart's open gate. Kamik scarcely had time to notice the tiny careful stitching on the bags before the raft sunk into the fuming depths of the pit. The molten rock seethed, mirroring the colors of the late afternoon sun.

Kamik reluctantly echoed Markith's crossed-arm blessing before clambering down off the woman's cart onto the shiny black rock that ringed the smoking crater.

"Welmit renews all!" Markith's wrinkles creased in a smile as she climbed back onto her cart bench and slapped the reins. Her horse pulled the cart forward on the path between the open pits. Words drifted back over her shoulder: "Your turn, Kamik."

Her turn. Her turn to throw years of work into the fires of one of Welmit's many maws. It had hurt three summers ago, the last time Welmit had eaten the moon, when she had tossed in a wrought iron lantern and it would hurt more now.

"Hurry up, then!" A young apprentice, one of old Perga the weaver's boys, held his horse's reins and gestured impatiently at the pit. Behind, others climbed down from their carts.

"Give me a minute. I'm in contemplation. Have you no respect for doctrine?" Kamik frowned at the boy.

Doctrine.

She slowly loosened one rope that held the chest fast.

Doctrine had made her take this pilgrimage.

Doctrine said the fireproof chest she had worked on so long should be consumed by Welmit's greed.

Anger filled her.

Why should an ancient destructive tradition, probably developed by a priest who had never lifted a brush nor carved a stick in his life, dictate what she should do?

When would she become old enough to outgrow this childish custom?

Why did Techan willingly undergo such needless suffering?

Her horse shifted uneasily in its harness. The shouts behind her grew louder as the queue of villagers grew more impatient. Welmit would bring bad fortune to the entire village if anyone failed to burn their offerings before sunset of the day of their arrival.

"Kamik, elder. Why do you delay? Do you not want to feel the ecstasy that comes from sacrifice?" She had not seen the priest approach. He spoke mildly but with narrowed eyes.

"I'm sorry, Priest, forgive me."

"Only Welmit can forgive, elder. And he will be grateful for this sacrifice. If this chest can protect our written doctrines from fire, then the improved chests you build in ensuing years will please him as well. Your offering is both clever and worshipful."

"Thank you, priest."

"However, I'm sure you don't want to deny the others their turn. It will be evening soon." The priest's face grew sly. "And you don't want to miss seeing the tiny face of your new grandchild, I assume?"

Kamik clenched a fist behind her back. She cast around for excuses. "I must wait, Priest. I must wait for Techan to arrive so we can experience the ecstasy together. It will be his last chance to do so."

She almost bared her teeth in grim pleasure when the priest hesitated. She had finally shut the man up.

He raised a finger. "I...I would have to pray on it, but I do believe it may not satisfy our living god, our sacred god, Welmit. Such an action, however kind it may seem, is not necessary according to the doctrines."

"It is necessary to *me*. In fact, I must go find him." She climbed into her cart. A slap of the reins and her mare broke into a brisk trot.

The priest's shouted prayer for her soul and for the village fortunes grew faint behind her. She kept up the harsh commands until the mare was almost at a gallop and the cart was swaying, until the fork in the road was in sight.

She pulled the reins. "Whoa."

If she turned left, this path would loop back to the overroad with its fast dry track, and she could be warm in her cottage in just four days. She might never see Techan again, but that was Welmit's way, creating people who lived solitary lives, even those who shared a cottage. She had heard there were lands where it was different, where people led their lives as a couple, compromising at every turn, but such a practice seemed hard to fathom. There were no reasons, no doctrine, no promises which required her to turn to the right, down the unkempt underroad toward Techan. He would not expect her to do so. The pitted underroad, treacherous in the growing darkness, threaded between open lava pits, pits no longer used for sacrifices due to their propensity to cave in at the edges.

She glanced back at the smoke-filled landscape behind her. Beside the queue, the priest was looking her way, one hand on his brow to shield the setting sun. She crossed her arms as if in prayer and mumbled a short apology to Garva and the unborn babe before ostentatiously thumping her shoulders. The mare whinnied in surprise when she yanked the reins, forcing the cart to the right, to the underroad.

As the moon rose, the mare picked her way, slowly, steadily. Kamik's head began to nod. Sleep had been scarce the last four days.

A jerk broke Kamik's gentle doze. The mare avoided some brambles, leading the cart over a particularly stony stretch. A faint glow from the ground ahead decided the matter and Kamik called a soft "whoa". A quick exploration revealed a bubbling, steaming spring next to a small lava pit. It would give her hot water for her dirty face, maybe even a bath.

She pushed aside some stunted birches exposing the pit further, a concave opening agleam with hot red coals. Molten lava, crimson and black, flowed down one side, disappearing into a crack.

The pit was old, abandoned. The lava must have resurged out this vent just today, a sign of Welmit's wrath with her. No, she shook her head, still half-asleep. This was simple good fortune. Perhaps she could heat up her supper too.

An idea occurred to her and she sketched it idly in her mind. If she could make the chest smaller, the size of a flask, she could keep her dinner hot for hours. A fine idea that would take some tinkering to work. A wave of homesickness swept over her. Oh, to be in her workshop, pumping the bellows at her forge, pounding iron on her anvil until sparks flew. The things she could invent!

The fireproof chest was only the beginning. She pictured the drawings she had left behind. All the details of how she had beaten the side panels to the perfect thickness, tough enough to withstand most cottage fires. How she had found the right combination of coal and size of forge to make the fluffrock expand and pop like corn kernels. She had drawn the diagrams on fine deerskin and left them on the hearth at home, as if challenging Welmit to burn them while she was gone. It had only been a few years since her careless housekeeping had caused the fire which had consumed all of her and Techan's lifetime of records. Now, it seemed almost as if another person had lived that life. Another person had built that chest.

A new thought struck her: here at this tiny pit, she could give the iron chest the ultimate fireproofing test. The cart held a small shovel, useful for wheels stuck in the mud. That and the water bucket should do.

She approached the smoking pit, shifted her feet to a firmer footing, paused as yet another thought struck her, and began to scoop the almost molten rock.

~ * ~

It was not until late in the third day along the underroad that she found him, where a widening marsh had softened the road. Techan's cart lay tipped at the road edge, the broken wooden axle raw and white against a large moss-covered boulder.

She rushed forward. Why had she not crafted him an iron axle? Why hadn't she strengthened the iron bands that wrapped the wheels?

Techan's horse raised its head from where it was hobbled in a drier patch that was more reeds than grass. Where was the old fool?

"I'm over here, woman." The voice was weak but—Kamik was relieved to hear—sounded irritated.

He lay at the edge of the marsh on a pile of wet leaves. He had apparently gathered wood some time ago but not managed to light a fire.

"Techan. Are you hurt, my one?"

He looked startled and she realized she had not used that particular endearment for several years. She touched his weathered hand.

He began to answer but coughing wracked his thin cheeks. The food crates she had packed for him all those days ago lay nearby, looking almost untouched.

"There was no point in you coming," he finally managed to say. "I will not complete the pilgrimage."

"Shush," she answered, as if he was a child. She began to gather fir boughs, chopping off the springy green branches with her hand axe.

By sundown, she had made him a comfortable bed and cobbled together a broth from dried deer meat and herbs.

The fire crackled, sending sparks up into the darkness. Techan managed to swallow a few spoonfuls of broth before he set the bowl aside.

"Are you well enough to sit up, old man?"

"There is no point in tending to me, I keep telling you. I will not make it to Welmit's Maw. I may as well close my eyes here and not open them. To have promised that chair to Welmit," —he gestured at his tipped cart— "and not sacrificed it, it's blasphemy. I will die a blasphemer." He closed his eyes to drive the point home.

"Silly old fool."

Kamik re-hitched her mare and backed her cart across the sodden uneven ground until the rear end was steps from where Techan lay. She snuck a look and was pleased to see the firelight reflecting in his watching eyes.

She walked over to Techan's ruined cart and rescued the rocking chair. The seat back, carved into an image of Welmit's many fiery mouths, caught the firelight.

Techan had closed his eyes again.

"It's fine, not even a crack," she said flatly. "You can stop pretending you're not looking."

"Taking the chair yourself to Welmit's Maw does not cease to make me a blasphemer. I must witness the sacrifice. Did you forget that, old woman?"

"Fortune favors you, old man." Kamik set the chair carefully on a clump of marsh grass next to her cart.

Techan cracked open an eye.

She used a stout branch to pry open the fireproof chest. The lid lifted then crumbled. Smoke and heat surrounded her and she fell back, coughing hard. After a moment, eyes streaming, she was able to see the coals she had shoveled in were still fiery hot. A river of lava cut a channel as she watched, oozing like scarlet mud. Sure enough, the chest had held the temperature steady.

She could not hide the pride in her voice. "There is nothing in the priest's doctrines which prevents Welmit's Maw, or a few buckets of it, coming to you, old man, is there? That should be just as worshipful as you visiting the Maw."

Techan tilted his head to one side, as he considered her words.

Kamik sat on the fallen log she had pulled close. Side by side, they watched the lava cool, swirling into patterns of red and black, much as they had watched the fire in their hearth every evening all those years.

"Woman?"

"Yes, dear one?"

"Do you know why Welmit wants the sacrifices? Why he designed such a practice?"

Kamik threw a twig on the fire in disgust. "Your last few words, and you want to waste it by explaining doctrine to me? Do you know me at all?"

Techan continued as if she hadn't spoken, "Why did you make the chest?"

"Because I wanted to protect all of our diagrams, since I can't protect the craftwork itself from Welmit's greed, his complete and total avarice." It felt good to have somewhere to direct her anger.

"Why did you want to protect the diagrams?" His voice was as patient as the stars overhead.

Kamik practically sputtered. "The waste, you old fool, the waste, burning all the good craftwork we create!"

"If you could have kept the chest, would you have made the diagrams? If there were no sacrifices to Welmit, would your mother have been as diligent in teaching you the blacksmithing arts? Would you have been as diligent in teaching Garva? Would Markith have taught her sons to make those clever boats?" His voice was thin but sure.

Kamik sat straighter.

"Perhaps not," she conceded after a moment, rubbing her knee. Could Techan be right? Would every minute detail of the village's craft knowledge and artistry be completely communicated to other generations if not for Welmit's demands? Would the younger villagers have created such a clean fast road surface if the trip to the Maw had not been necessary?

Techan rose up on one elbow. "Don't believe in Welmit's powers, old woman. But do believe in Welmit's results. They work." Coughing wracked him. "Take an apprentice, pass on the knowledge, record what you can and keep it in many marvelous chests like this one. Maybe even burn an offering or two." More coughing. "No matter where you end up."

Techan lay back, his energy spent.

A crooked glowing line appeared along the left seam of the chest. It, too, was at the end of its natural lifespan.

He was right. Without sacrifices to Welmit, the village would not have so many marvelous things. They would live in mud and squalor, dying young, like people did in other lands. The offerings were an essential part of a complex, deliberately repetitive system that passed on knowledge from one villager to the next, from one generation to the next.

Kamik rose and held the rocking chair in her strong blacksmith's hands. With snapping sounds like splintering bones, she broke it into several pieces, destroying the chair Techan had shortened his life for, the chair Garva would never use to rock her babe to sleep.

Piece by piece, she fed the bits of chair into the smoking contents of the fireproof chest. Techan watched closely until the last piece was consumed, his face slack but his eyes bright.

Later, much later, as she held Techan's body in her lap waiting for the dawn, she realized a new village, a new start so far away the trees themselves were unfamiliar, meant the chest's design would now travel much further than the nearby villages—banishment was yet another way to keep the new knowledge secure.

Welmit, or whoever had designed the doctrines, had thought of everything. She slowly raised one fist and thumped it against her shoulder.

"Heart Proof" was originally published in Lightships & Sabers
anthology in 2016 from Wolf Singer Publications.
It has been reprinted in Luna Station Quarterly in 2018,
and won the Remastered Words audio contest in 2019.

~ * ~ * ~

Holly Schofield travels through time at the rate of one second per second, oscillating between the alternate realities of city and country life. Over 100 of her short stories have appeared in *Analog*, *Lightspeed*, *Escape Pod*, and many other publications throughout the world. Her works are used in university curricula and have been translated into multiple languages.

Find her at hollyschofield.wordpress.com.

FIRE WALL

Kat Heckenbach

I clawed past the crowd. Day after day they gathered, clustering to watch the fire as it encroached. It moved impossibly slow, like a wall of advancing soldiers surrounding the city. Heat singed the air, and the acrid smell of burning grass filled my nostrils. Smoke lifted above the fire and dispersed, but somehow never entered the interior of the circle.

As I cleared the crowd, I turned and looked above the milling bodies. Flames licked the sky in an uneven march. Step by step, millimeter by millimeter, closing in on its final meal.

How could everyone just stand there, staring? Didn't they understand it was coming to consume us as it had every other city?

"Joshua, where are you going?" Ryan stood at the edge of the crowd, gazing at the tower of flames. Orange tendrils reflected in his vacant eyes. "You can at least watch. It can't hurt you from here!"

I shook my head and started running.

No heat or odor reached past the crowd. The air felt warm and comforting. I held my gaze low and kept running, determined to get home. The brick walls of my house would be no protection once the fire reached them, but maybe someone would figure out how to stop it before then. Before more people ended up on the other side of the flames.

~ * ~

The next morning I could see the fire clearly from my bedroom window. It pulsed as if alive, devouring its prey as it passed. Why did they not move out of the way?

One woman reached out and touched the fire, and immediately withdrew her hand. Her scream pierced through the dawn as she dropped to her knees. I mimicked her movement and gripped the edge of my bedroom window, unable to draw my eyes away from her.

The woman's hand shone in the early sunlight, glinting like…

yes, like gold.

It couldn't be.

She gazed at her hand, turning it, examining it from every angle. Then she reached out again, touched the fire, and stepped through.

My head dropped forward into my hands. Why would she do that? And what had happened to her hand? Did the same thing happen to the rest of her?

Curiosity gripped tighter. I stood and raced down the stairs and out the front door. I had to see for myself.

I rounded the corner of a building, only yards from the fire. Ryan was there, staring into the flames. I grabbed his shoulder. He didn't look at me.

"I'm going in," he said. "I want what they have."

"They? Who?" I shook his shoulder, trying to force his face toward me. "Those people are dead! They've been burned! Is that how you want to die?"

Ryan finally turned and looked me in the eye. The emptiness I'd seen in his eyes the day before had been replaced by hunger. "Better now, this way, than later."

"What are you talking about? Of course you'll die later, Ryan. We all will. But you don't have to volunteer! Someone could find a way to stop this and we won't have to die for years and years."

He shook his head, and his eyes held something strange. Pity? I couldn't tell.

"Nothing can stop it, Joshua. The only way is through the flames."

"But they'll kill you, Ryan."

"Yes, but only once. And then I can never die again."

He grabbed me in a bear hug that nearly knocked the breath out of me, and then released me and dived through the fire.

Stunned, I stared after him. The fire danced happily where he'd stepped through, and I had to fight back the urge to reach out and grab it. I wanted to pound the flames, but instead I dropped down and slammed my fist into the ground, angry tears dripping into the soil.

Someone tapped me on the shoulder, and I looked up, tears still streaming down my cheeks. A man stood over me—tall, thin, dressed in an elegant black suit. The shirt beneath the jacket was blood red. A smile barely curled his lips and the fire reflected in his black eyes.

"I know how to stop it," he said. His voice snaked through the air, smooth and deep, and settled around me. I watched the flames play in his eyes, knowing they surrounded us completely. He had to be crazy. But I allowed myself to gaze into the dark eyes in search of hope.

"It's simple, son," he said, and tilted his head, smiling brightly. "We build a wall of ice. But I need your help."

I laughed then, through sticky tears. "Ice? You're insane, mister."

He shook his head, ever so slightly—admonishing—and raised one black eyebrow. "It's not just *any* old ice, Joshua."

I felt a prickle at the back of my spine. "How did you know my name?"

"Oh, I heard you and your friend talking." He gazed over at the fire, the muscles in his face tightening, hardening the line of his jaw. He looked as angry as I felt. I sat back on my heels as I considered him. *We're on the same side here, I think.*

I stood, and he turned back to face me.

"Okay, mister. Where's this special ice you have?"

One corner of his mouth lifted. "Let's go build a wall."

~ * ~

We started the wall as close to the flames as we could. The ice blocks were enormous, but not nearly as heavy as they looked. They felt oddly cold, not like ice at all, but rather frozen metal. I moved them as quickly as I could for fear my fingers would stick, soon breaking into a sweat despite my freezing hands.

Block by block the wall rose. Each one fit perfectly on top of the others, sliding into place with a strange slunking sound that made me think they'd fused together.

"What kind of ice are these made of, mister?" I hadn't asked the man's name, and he hadn't offered. For some reason I couldn't quite pinpoint, I was glad.

He moved swiftly, adding blocks to the wall with an ease that implied years of physical labor. Yet, his body was long and sinewy, all graceful arms and legs, reminding me of a giant spider. His hands looked as if they should be flowing across a piano keyboard, and as

I watched him move I could almost hear music in my head. Ghostly wisps of music, like the sound of souls swirling through darkness.

I was beginning to think he hadn't heard me when he finally spoke. "Bricks are made of chaff and mud, are they not?"

"But you said this is ice."

"Yes, indeed I did, didn't I?" He stopped moving, and looked around at the steadily rising walls. Not so much as a bead of sweat showed on his forehead. He'd removed his jacket, and his crisp, blood red shirt bore not a single crease. A smile tipped his face, and he nodded toward the outer side of the wall. I followed his gaze.

The fire had stalled where we'd laid the bricks. It continued to lick at the air and dance. Only this time it didn't have the gleeful movement it had when Ryan stepped through. Seemed more like angry.

I shook my head. *It's fire, Josh. Just fire. It can't be happy* or *angry...*

But then again, ice can't be made of mud and chaff either.

No matter. Let this guy be secretive about his building materials. Whatever they were, they worked. That's all that mattered. The fire couldn't—*wouldn't?* —pass through them.

We resumed our work. I focused on my movement, trying to match the smooth lift/stack rhythm of my mentor, and the walls quickly grew.

I shifted to another section, and my line of vision swooped past a group of people standing outside the wall. The fire moved toward them. I recognized one of the men. He locked his eyes on me for a moment, then began glancing furtively back at the encroaching fire before staring at me once again.

He spoke, and his words seemed to diffuse as they crossed over the low section of wall. "You needn't do that!" he said. He held his hands out to me. "Come, please. We'll leave together."

The fire behind him swelled, and I stepped back, shaking my head. I could envision nothing but fire, consuming me.

"No! Leave me alone!"

His eyes lowered and he turned slowly, and for a moment all I saw was his back surrounded by flame. Then he stepped forward and was gone.

I watched as others followed him through the flames. Some hesitated while some plunged in, but none stayed behind. I wondered why they hadn't asked about the wall I was building.

We laid the last brick together. It *slunked* into place, the sound echoing through our windowless building. I spun slowly, taking in the walls surrounding me. The area had seemed so much larger when we began. I glanced down at the pitiful collection of food and clothing I'd brought. In my panic to escape it felt like so much.

My throat and chest tightened. What had I done? I was trapped, with not nearly enough food to survive.

And no one outside to fight the fire.

My mentor's voice slithered around me, caressing my shoulders and neck before registering in my brain. "What's wrong, Joshua? You're safe now. You've gotten exactly what you asked for, have you not?"

I lifted my eyes to meet his. The black reflected nothing now. I raised my head—where there had been flame hovering beyond the top of our walls, I saw only darkness.

"The fire's gone!"

"In a manner of speaking."

My heart leaped in my chest and I ran toward the wall. I tried digging my fingers into the tiny groove between the ice bricks. They were too tightly fitted. I felt around the edges of brick after brick, my fingers scrambling, panic slamming my heart.

"Help me! Let's get out of here!"

There was no answer, except a chill swept across my back, a hollow whisper spoke of solitude. I turned.

He was gone.

A scream scratched through my throat as I spun, fist aimed at the wall behind me. But the sight of the wall snagged my hand mid-air, and I stumbled back.

No longer the frosty-white of ice, the bricks sparkled like crystal, glass-smooth and perfectly transparent.

The ground upon which I sat seemed to have risen. I was high above the city now, my view spanning for miles in every direction.

I slumped to the ground, staring at the scene surrounding me. Sobs choked down the scream pounding inside my chest. People were everywhere, unharmed by the flames. If anything they seemed healthier, brighter. Smiles adorned every face as people greeted each other, hugging, crying joyful tears…

I watched as a mother lifted her son to her hip, kissing his shining face. Not a trace of fire was evident. The grass was a piercing green, broken only by the speckling of colorful foliage.

I dug my hands into the dry, crumbling grass underneath me, my lungs burning from the wilting air.

Something in the distance grabbed my attention—a glinting of sunlight reflecting from…a wall of glass. I crawled as close as I could to my own wall and strained to see.

Yes, it was another icy prison just like my own, atop a hill. Inside, a woman clawed at the walls, her mouth open wide, face contorted, frantic. I couldn't hear her, but her scream scraped at my bones. The only sound penetrating my brain was the music of souls swirling through darkness.

"Fire Wall" was originally published in
The Absent Willow Review (2010).

~ * ~ * ~

Kat Heckenbach graduated from the University of Tampa with a bachelor's degree in biology, went on to teach math, and then homeschooled her son and daughter while writing and making sci-fi/fantasy art. Now that both kids have graduated, her writing and art time is constantly interrupted by her 96 lb. boxer mix. She is the author of YA fantasy series *Toch Island Chronicles* and urban fantasy *Relent*, as well as dozens of fantasy, science fiction, and horror short stories in magazines and anthologies.

Enter her world at katheckenbach.com.

More Great Anthologies from WolfSinger Publications

Out of the Darkness – edited by Carol Hightshoe

Mental Health issues have long been stigmatized, with those facing them pushed into the shadows, often unable to deal with the darkness they find themselves trapped in.

In this collection, stories explore many types of darkness—Suicidal Ideation, Death from Suicide, Survivor's Guilt, PTSD, Chronic Pain, Chronic Illness, Depression, Death of a Loved One, Secrets, Bullying, and other forms of darkness are explored. Some related to mental health issues and some not, but all of them offer very human perspectives. As in real life, some stories have happy endings and sadly others don't.

We offer these stories of darkness without judgement, but with hope and compassion. Some roads should never have to be traveled—but we understand that for many they are being traveled alone.

Proceeds from sales of Out of the Darkness will be donated to the American Foundation for Suicide Prevention—for more information on AFSP please visit their website at: afsp.org.

For those who may be in crisis—PLEASE call or text 988 to connect directly to the 988 Suicide and Crisis Lifeline. For those outside the US please connect with your local lifeline

Never Cheat a Witch – edited by Carol Hightshoe

Magical curses. Arcane revenge. Being transformed into a frog. Things evil witches do to mere mortals who cross their path. But, what if there is more to the story...

Deals made with a witch are magically binding and can bring dire consequences to those who even think about breaking them.

Whether they are seeking revenge for wrongs done to them, helping others or simply trying to live their lives—it is NEVER wise to try and cheat a witch.

Open your spell book and join our authors as they relate tales of witches and mortals. From classic fantasy witches to modern day witches and even the legendary Baba Yaga. Good and Evil as well as every shade of gray in between. And, yes—there is a prince who is turned into a frog.

Time Capsules – edited by Carol Hightshoe

Time Capsules—history and mystery—a gift or a message from the past to the future. Messages that can easily be misunderstood.

What were the reasons for passing along a pair of pink, fuzzy handcuffs?

A glass vial containing a perfect dandelion puff?

A Japanese Katana?

A red and blue scarf?

A wooden spoon?

What magic do these items contain? What stories do they tell?

From the past to the future. Mysteries and meanings abound within these pages, as well as reminders of the things people find precious. What will you find?

US/THEM – edited by Carol Hightshoe

Fear of the *Other* breeds hatred of the *Other*

They aren't like us—so they must be bad...inferior... dangerous...

Humans are by nature social animals, but we tend to bond with other humans with whom we have something in common: beliefs, experiences, likes and dislikes, etc.

With the expansion of humans across the planet, it seems that, even as our numbers grow, we find ways to whittle our groups into ever narrower, specialized, and exclusive blocks. We target the *Other* for the most minor differences and interpret everything from *THEM* as an insult or an attack.

Within these pages you will witness hatred, intolerance and fanaticism as well as love, understanding and acceptance. Most of all, I, and the authors, hope you discover stories that will cause you to pause and think before condemning someone as being *THEM* and not *US*.

Crunchy with Ketchup – edited by Carol Hightshoe

It has been said that one should never meddle in the affairs of dragons—for you are crunchy and taste good with ketchup.

Come enter the dragon's lair.

Take your chances with other would-be heroes and heroines who decide to face off against one of the biggest, baddest predators ever.

Witness a dragon civil war.

Hear the true story of the Battle of New Orleans.

Find out what it's like in the belly of a dragon.

Discover why cats can spell disaster when stealing a dragon's egg.

Meet a group of dragon riders who protect us from nuclear devastation.

Follow legends of modern dragons, only to find something very unexpected.

And more…

Crunchy with Chocolate – edited by Carol Hightshoe

It has been said that one should never meddle in the affairs of dragons—for you are crunchy and taste good with chocolate.

Come enter the dragon's lair and roll the dice. Within these pages you will still meet some of the biggest, baddest predators ever—but if you are lucky, you will also discover some that have a sweeter side.

Meet a dragon with a soft spot for hard luck cases and another who is a hopeless romantic.

Enjoy a musical battle between a dragon and the specter of one of the greatest guitarists to ever play.

Meet a dragon in trouble with other magical creatures because he enjoys hanging out with human children.

Join a mother and daughter and their teams of dragons on a dangerous cross-country race.

Reconnect with an imaginary friend—who is not so imaginary and escape the isolation of the pandemic.

And more…

So enter in BUT tread carefully—remember you are crunchy and taste good with chocolate.

Visit us at **wolfsingerpubs.com**

www.ingramcontent.com/pod-product-compliance
Lightning Source LLC
Chambersburg PA
CBHW060642260626
47161CB00008B/2969